DISTANCE HAZE

JAMIL NASIR

An Authors Guild Backinprint.com
Edition

iUniverse, Inc.
New York   Bloomington

Distance Haze

*Cover Illustration: Detail from "Discovery of the
Hidden Pathway" © 2009 John Grazier*

iUniverse books may be ordered through booksellers or by contacting:

*iUniverse
1663 Liberty Drive
Bloomington, IN 47403
www.iuniverse.com
1-800-Authors (1-800-288-4677)*

ISBN: 978-1-4401-8740-7 (sc)

Printed in the United States of America

iUniverse rev. date: 11/19/2009

For Jack, Pat, and Bob

1

Wayne Dolan had attended a great University in the Mid-Atlantic Region, and while his classmates enjoyed beer parties, girlfriends, and football games, he had gravitated toward his own company. In the summers he had lived in the near-deserted residence halls to earn tuition money cleaning and refurbishing the giant university kitchens, and on blue weekend evenings, warm and still except for the hum of air-conditioning systems on the dark, vacant buildings, he had wandered the empty sidewalks of North Campus brooding on his loneliness and exaltation, imagining sometimes in the dusk that She walked toward him through a doorway in the air from Her distant realm.

Now that he was older he sometimes dreamed about the university town, but in his dreams it was enchanted, the great buildings of Central Campus rising like towers and battlements above an ancient forest, and on its outskirts great old houses overlooking a wooded shore.

Downtown he had met an overcoated woman who he realized was a goddess; he had followed a girl with a long, blonde braid who he knew was an angel, and slept with her in an old house hung with handmade quilts; he had swum from the wooded shore across a vast ocean until on a watery horizon he sighted in the mist a far green continent. On the night before Tom Del Mar called, he dreamed he was on Liberty Street near the old Liberty Theater; it was autumn, chilly and drizzling, and on the cracked sidewalk he met Her, ancient yet young, like spring, with her long silver-gold braid and luminous skin, and from her an intoxication radiated, so that the world became paradise, and he knew that he would never die.

He woke up looking at a wall.

It was that way every morning: a blank white wall and a faint sigh from the registers blowing stale apartment-building air. A sinking feeling came over him then, which he tried to resist at first, telling himself that this was the beginning of a new life, that today he would rise up and seize it. But there seemed to be a kind of sorcery in the silence and stale air and blank white wall, a numbness bespeaking apartment complexes with plush sales offices and gay flower beds in front, but disconcerting hints of depression in the "garden apartments" in back among their carelessly mown lawns, cheap trees, and access roads: the sink disposal that didn't work; the cigarette-butt smell of the carpet; the tiny, dirty balcony overlooking parking lots; a sullen smudge on the wall of the miniature living room; the faint sounds of other listless lives in other apartments: a brief hiss of water, the boom of a door closing, a hint of voices, of colorless music, the slow-moving, monotonous sunlight through venetian blinds.

Wayne rolled over, the bliss of his dream draining out

of him. His cramped bedroom was a shambles. After eight months his clothes were still jumbled in cardboard boxes, a pile of dirty laundry reeking in the open closet. No bustle, no crying or fighting or crowing of children, no clatter of dishes (his dishes lay unwashed in the sink), no vacuuming, no female voice, or even his own male voice, because there was no one to talk to.

He had wanted Ann and the children to get the house, of course, and at first it had soothed him to visit there, as if it were an anchor to some kind of home life. But then he and Ann had had the terrible fight, and she had gotten a restraining order against him, and since then his older girl Alice was always too busy to talk on the phone; only the baby would get on and start to babble in his baby's voice, saying things Wayne couldn't understand.

Wayne had imagined something quite different during the months—years, even—that he had dreamed of divorce. His bachelor apartment would be small, certainly, but full of books, quiet and overlooking trees and the fall of a hill, so that in the evenings he would gaze out the window and think vast thoughts (in these daydreams, oddly, he smoked a pipe); and there would be women: young, educated, silky daughters of upper-class families. He had known these were fantasies, of course, but he had reasoned that out there somewhere must be a girl beautiful and young and educated that would love him, blonde with silken skin who unclothed was all catlike languor and fire, sighing, gasping, and sobbing in her light, bell-like voice when she reached orgasm. They sat in a quaint café and talked about Emily Brontë and Shakespeare, Doyne Farmer and God, complexity and love and the structure of the universe, their eyes locked together, until he could feel the earth turning about him, the blood rushing in his veins, time bringing the sun to light the flowers in the window boxes, the rain to water them. In her eyes were meadows and forests, sunset on the ocean, dusk on a dock where they walked in the evening hand in hand. They were married in a dazzling church wedding, and he could beat all her clean-cut, handsome brothers at arm-wrestling; he had met them when she took him home to her parents at their big house on Martha's Vineyard. They went on a honeymoon in Aruba and she taught him scuba diving, and they spent every day in the crystalline blue waters, eating fresh crab, making love, and lying in the breezy shade of palm trees.

It wasn't impossible, was it? It could still happen to a good-looking, six-foot-tall man with thoughtful greyish eyes, a shock of unruly dark hair, thick arms and chest, even though he was 43 and getting creases in his fore-head and at the corners of his mouth. And he was a novelist. Women loved novelists. Didn't they?

Yet so far something had prevented any part of this fantasy from coming true. It was a subject of speculation what that something was. For one thing, he had gotten into a bad habit of sleeping late, so that by the time he had taken a shower and eaten breakfast it was already afternoon, almost too late to do anything. Then he would usually either sit in near-catatonic depression over his laptop or pace his apartment in a strange restlessness, trying to make up his mind where to go, how to break out of his slump finally.

Sometimes he actually did go out in the evenings, the cooling air washing over him with its excitement; sometimes he actually did drive out of the parking lot onto the long, new parkway where light-poles were stacked by the road, and where the hillsides were brown and tracked over with the digging for new town-house complexes and shopping centers. But where to go? A singles bar? The idea both repelled and tantalized him. He holding a drink and sliding through air-conditioned dimness toward a half-seen hairdo in the smoke, which would probably conceal a drunk dental hygienist or secretary who, smelling his fear and uncertainty, would sneer him away in her stupid vocabulary and bad grammar. He didn't know where any singles bars were, and anyway even if he managed to pick someone up he would have nowhere to take her but his smelly, disheveled apartment. He should turn the car around, go back and tidy the place up first.

But it would take days to tidy up, unpack, wash the dishes, vacuum. He would put off the singles bar until he could get his life a little more in order.

And so he would drive around, livid glare of the streetlights making the pavement, sidewalks, grass, and trees a uniform greyish-green, looking for—he wasn't sure what. Even if a carful of careless, vapid, laughing blonde college girls careened to a stop next to him at a light, stereo booming, to them he would be just some grim, frowzy, middle-aged mommy-hubby who ought to go home to his bulging, gravity-defeated wife or rubber love-doll.

And so he would go home, not to a wife or even a love-doll, but to his TV, which he would watch in stupefaction until a prickling in his eyes and a sagging in his body told him it was too late to be awake, and then he would weakly brush his teeth and roll into bed. But in an hour he would start awake, heart pounding, hands sweating, the panic and sorrow of the divorce shaking him, as if revealed in all its horrible mistaken stupidity, the throwing away of his family, his whole life. Then he would lie, body stiff and hurting with rage and grief like chemical substances injected into him, and sleep would be impossible for hours.

The phone rang, a vigorous electric trill. The sound sent vague tendrils of anxiety and hope through Wayne. This was the beginning of a new life. He propped himself on an elbow in his bed and fumbled for the handset balanced on a cardboard box. "Hello?"

"Is this Wayne Dolan, novelist extraordinaire?" asked a deep, humorous New York/Mississippi drawl.

"No."

The drawl chuckled. "Well, is this Wayne Dolan, who has thus far deprived his avid public of any hint as to the substance of his sixth and finest book?"

"How are you, Tom?"

"How are you yourself? You don't sound like your normal sparky self."

"Just woke up."

"Aw, come on now. It's almost one o'clock. I guess you were up late last night working on the outline for book number six?"

"No," Wayne admitted.

"Well, now, we've got to talk about this."

"I'm still kind of getting moved into the new apartment."

"I hear you. And I'm awfully sorry about you and Ann, I've told you that. I hate to bother you about it, you know I do. But Irv is getting worried, and when Irv gets worried, I get worried." Irv Feingold was Astrid Books' Executive Editor.

"Fuck Irv."

"I don't go that way. And if I did, I wouldn't try it on Irv." There was an apologetic pause. "You got writer's block, huh?"

"No."

"Leave all to father," Tom said broadly, as if he hadn't heard Wayne's denial. "I got an idea for you's going to make you scream with ecstasy."

Wayne's bowels drew into themselves. He listened stonily.

"You've heard of Tracy Kidder, right, and James Glieck, Mitchell Waldrop, Kitty Ferguson? All those best-selling *auteurs* who make millions not thinking up their own ideas—uh-uh, that's too hard. What they do is go find some far-out, hard-to-believe, real-world science and describe it with some vivid analogies and colorful characters, and then they go to the bank and take their satisfied editors and executive editors along with them. Am I right?"

"Tom, I'm a *science fiction* writer," said Wayne tightly. "*Fiction.* I don't do science journalism."

"Now just wait a little minute until you let the fullness of my genius flow over you," said Tom. "Have you ever heard of the Deriwelle Institute for the Technological Study of Religion?"

"The what?"

"That's just what *I* said. Turns out this screwy schmillionaire from the Bible Belt died a while back and left an *x-hundred-million-dollar* trust to fund an institute for the study of religion using electronic technology."

"Jesus."

"Only in America. It's been up and running a few years now, and nobody's paid any attention outside a couple little magazine articles. Can you believe that? They have the latest equipment, pay outrageous salaries, even have a couple Nobel laureates on staff—it's a piece of postmodern, millennial, apocalyptico-fundamentalist techno-Americana, and nobody has thought to go down there and write the thing up."

The Deriwelle Institute for the Technological Study of Religion was in an out-of-the-way part of an obscure region called Southwestern Michigan, far from any cities or other landmarks, where Wayne's AAA Road Atlas showed no thick red or blue lines, nor even any thin white lines, but only some thin black lines representing county routes. It was a two-day drive from the Mid-Atlantic Region, and on the second day, turning his old Honda north off the thick blue line of Interstate 90 at South Bend, Indiana, he followed County Route 31 past strip malls and car dealerships until these petered out into sooty warehouses with broken windows, barbed-wired tractor-trailer lots, and deserted gas stations, and then small frame houses with dirt yards and car seats on their porches. After that the land opened into gently rolling cornfields green and shoulder-high in the cloudless July afternoon, orchards with fruit stands displaying melons and tomatoes, far-off woods dark green and still in the sunlight. At intervals the highway slowed to 25 mph and passed through miniature towns built 150 years ago along the St. Clair River, with historic red brick firehouses, antique homes shaded by huge oaks, and tiny shopping centers. Sometimes the road ran close to the St. Clair, giving him glimpses through the trees of its murky green and shaded waters, like some river out of Middle-Earth or *Huckleberry Finn*. The map said it ran into Lake Michigan at the town of St. Clair, which in its heyday had been a port for the shipping of iron ore and a summer resort for rich people from Chicago.

The air through Wayne's wide-open car windows smelled alternately of plowed earth, woods, and hot blacktop. He was driving between rolling fields where a slow distant tractor moved patiently against a far backdrop of trees when he felt the air change. It was subtle but unmistakable, the far-off sense of a large body of water, perhaps a front of the healthful negative ions that blow off lakes and oceans. It entered him as an emotion more than a smell or sensation, bringing back for the first time in years, with sudden clarity—like a memory that had been packed carefully for frequent inspection, but then forgotten—his childhood summers at the ocean, relaxed, lazy, yet underlain by a vague excitement, as if anything might happen.

Soon the speed limit subsided once more to 25 and the county highway became a main street through quiet Victorian neighborhoods with great old trees nearly motionless in the crystalline sunlight. On a high front porch with an American flag an old pear-shaped man in suspenders rocked and watched the few passing cars. Now Wayne could actually smell the lake in snatches, like a layer of nearly unconscious excitement, subtly keen and cool even in the hot air, subliminally damp and fresh and grey-green, as though the hot, still afternoon were charged with a hint of fresh sea gales and the dangerous cries of mermaids.

—

St. Clair's small downtown had elderly storefronts canopied and ornamented with stone- or ironwork, old-fashioned groceries in red brick buildings with parking lots around back. The Holiday Inn stood across from a small park at the corner of a hundred-foot bluff above the mouth of the St. Clair River. Wayne put his suitcases in his room and went out there. A corny Civil War statue looked out over five blocks of summer-house neighborhoods on the lowland at the bottom of the bluff, and beyond them was the Lake, vast, sparkling restlessly chill pale blue, stretching beyond sight into bluish-grey haze like an ocean, a half-world of water overwhelming the land with its vast, vertiginous atmosphere, which made the temperature under the park's old leaning trees tropical-paradise cool and gave the town a smell and feel as if it did not exist anywhere on this earth, but rather in some story. Wayne stood and stared for a long time, feeling somehow that this great body of water, 60 miles wide and 150 miles long, knew him and had been waiting for him. Finally, he broke away and gazed up the St. Clair River. A hundred yards inland a soot-blackened railway bridge crossed it, and farther inland a road bridge. Gulls wheeled in the vast air above the river mouth, mewling. An old lady walked along the sidewalk across the street, slowly pulling a folding shopping cart.

He had had to admit in the end that he liked Tom Del Mar's idea—after he had soothed his ego by getting angry at being treated like some work-for-hire media-spinoff franchise hack. But Tom had figured out exactly what he needed, both spiritually and logistically, and had arranged everything. Wayne was to meet with the Deriwelle Institute administrators next morning, Tom having apparently persuaded them that nothing but enlarged public understanding could flow from Wayne's project.

So at 8:00 A.M. Wayne threaded his Honda through the narrow, waking streets of St. Clair, quiet at this hour, as if it had the luxury of sleeping late, the still air full of the dampness and smell of the Lake. He crossed the breathtaking span of the river bridge, and on the other side smelled woods and new-mown fields, rays of sunlight cutting across the county highway. Seven miles north he took a right on Institute Drive. There was half a mile of woods, and then he emerged into the Institute's grounds.

Institute Drive's brand-new, lamppost-flanked asphalt climbed in a graceful curve between vast lawns where a few ancient oaks and cedars arched gnarled branches nearly to the ground. Several sprawling three-story buildings were surrounded by shrubs and flower beds. Away to his right two pillared, domed structures like Classical-style observatories sat on hills landscaped like English Romantic wild gardens. Sunlight made green brilliance of

the forest treetops, and was just beginning to fire the
flower beds and dewy grass. The whole place exuded af-
fluence, like a particularly businesslike country club.

The Administration Building entrance was a heavy
plate-glass door of watery green. Within was a high
atrium with trees in huge pots, walled and ceilinged with
the same glass; morning sunlight made a bright shaft on
expensive-looking Oriental carpets in faded red motifs. A
reception booth contained a confection of long brown
fingernails, auburn hair, and green eyes, as if she had been
picked to match the decor. Wayne was acutely aware of
his own jeans, T-shirt, and slightly sweaty sports jacket.
He mumbled that he had an appointment with Dr. Rilfsbane, and she spoke into a headset.

Dr. Alan Rilfsbane, when he came down the open
staircase at the back of the atrium in a dark double-
breasted suit, shiny black loafers, and silver cuff links,
looked more like a symphony conductor or the maître d'
of an exclusive restaurant than the administrator of a scientific foundation. He was big and handsome, with a
high, aristocratic forehead and intelligent, beautifully
formed hands. His black hair was carelessly ducktailed in
back like a college professor's or a sporting British lord's.
He came forward heartily to give Wayne a firm handshake, but there was also something lithe and watchful
about him.

"Mr. Dolan," he said in a soft, deep voice. "How nice
to meet you."

He gestured gracefully toward the stairs.

"We are naturally flattered to have attracted the interest of so accomplished a writer," he said as they climbed.
"Mr. Del Mar tells me you're the author of some half
dozen critically acclaimed books."

"Five," said Wayne reflexively. "And critically acclaimed and a dollar'll get you a cup of coffee."

Rilfsbane laughed, rearing back his head in approval. "I thought we would go directly up to the office of Dr. Florisbund, the Institute's Director. I assume you have heard of him? The pioneering neurobiology researcher?" He held another heavy glass door on the mezzanine between elaborate, glass-walled conference rooms, led Wayne down a pearl-white hallway with doors on either side. Through those that were open Wayne saw spacious, well-appointed offices, some neat, some messy, occupied by persons in various stages of reading, writing, or staring out the window. At the top of another flight was an even more silent hallway, flooded with sun from skylights, with precious-looking vases on wooden stands and a rusty Oriental runner. Rilfsbane ushered Wayne through a door at the end. An ancient secretary whose brocade dress and golden hairdo sat on her like armor gestured toward an inner door. Wayne followed Rilfsbane in.

An old, sunken man sat behind a desk in a big, sunny office with windows that looked out over the Institute grounds as over Paradise. As Rilfsbane and Wayne came in he was holding a paper in a quavering hand, as if trying to remember which of the piles in front of him it belonged to. He looked up at them with dazed, intelligent, rheumy eyes. Wattles of flesh hung at his neck, and the grey hair on his narrow head stood up stiffly.

"Ah, Dr. Rilfsbane," he said in a wavering voice. He looked politely at Wayne.

"Dr. Florisbund," said Rilfsbane cordially. "May I introduce Mr. Wayne Dolan."

Dr. Florisbund now rose slowly and shakily, helping himself with a hand on the top of the desk and another on the arm of his chair. Once he was all the way erect he held a Parkinsonian hand behind a large, veined ear and looked at Wayne again. There was a hearing aid in the ear.

"Mr. Wayne Dolan," Rilfsbane said again loudly.

"Ah, Mr. Boyland, welcome," said Florisbund. Wayne shook a cool, bony, trembling hand.

"Please, sit," said Dr. Florisbund, lowering himself slowly and painfully into his chair again, until he dropped the last few inches with a deep sigh. Wayne and Rilfsbane took two comfortable armchairs. Rilfsbane's cordial, smiling expression had been on his face long enough to look slightly phony by the time Dr. Florisbund had settled himself. He said, loudly: "Mr. Dolan is a well-known writer who is working on a book about the Institute."

The rheumy, intelligent eyes surveyed Wayne. Then his slow, wavering voice said: "Mr. Boyland, welcome. I suppose Dr. Rilfsbane has explained the philosophy and mission of the Institute?"

"We haven't had time," Rilfsbane said loudly. "I brought him directly to you."

"Ah," said the old man. He tremblingly opened a drawer and scrabbled in it, came up with a three-color brochure, which he unfolded clumsily. He put on a pair of thick reading glasses. Wayne could feel the muscles of his own face strained from keeping a look of earnest attention. He wondered if his edginess was a result of 21st-century short attention span, or whether it had always been this tedious listening to the wisdom of elders.

"Mr. Deriwelle observed in his bequest to the Institute—" Dr. Florisbund read slowly and waveringly from the brochure "—that 'the wonderful potentialities of Electricity, which have accomplished so many marvels in the areas of Commerce, Science, and Domestic Life, have inexplicably never been put to service in the study of Religion. It is my fervent belief that the Electrical Study of Religion could illuminate many of the dark recesses of this most important Matter, throwing light upon questions heretofore the subjects only of Dry Speculation and Fruitless Metaphysical Debate. I therefore devise my entire estate [with the exception of reservations mentioned elsewhere in the will for the support of certain distant relatives of Mr. Deriwelle's] to the exclusive and perpetual establishment of an Institute for the Electrical Study of Religion.' "

"The Electrical Study of Religion," said Wayne.

"The Institute's Board of Directors has interpreted the phrase in the sense in which Mr. Deriwelle obviously meant it," Rilfsbane said, glancing at Florisbund. "As 'the use of modern technology in the study of religion.' "

"So you're using modern technology to try to prove the existence of God?"

"Our forty Senior Research Fellows come from every shade of the spectrum of religious belief. Some are dedicated atheists, others devout believers, with every gradation in between."

"Where do the two Nobel winners come out?"

Rilfsbane smiled urbanely. "I believe they 'come out,' as you put it, in different ways. But I hope you will avail yourself of the opportunity to speak with them personally, and to observe their experimental and theoretical methods."

Dr. Florisbund nodded approvingly, though Wayne wasn't sure how much of this he had heard, and went on in his courtly, old-world way. "My point is, in a culture where we study everything to death scientifically, even the smallest item, nowhere in our intellectual landscape until the establishment of the Deriwelle Institute for the Technological Study of Religion has there been a single institution dedicated to studying what is after all the thing that concerns us most closely."

Both Rilfsbane and Florisbund were smiling at him now, as if they had gotten him on their team and were just awaiting the flood of questions he would certainly have.

"So, how did you decide to set up in this part of the country?" he asked obligingly.

"That was part of Mr. Deriwelle's will as well," said Rilfsbane. "In addition to the groundbreaking research undertaken here, Mr. Deriwelle's bequest has also accomplished a significant work of historical preservation. The Institute campus and the surrounding areas owned by the Institute are part of sacred medicine land used until early in the last century by the Blue Water tribe of Native Americans, a people now completely extinct."

Florisbund scrabbled in his drawer and held waveringly across the desk a blurry three-color brochure titled "The Blue Water State Historical Preserve," which looked like it had been published by some local society.

Wayne put it in his jacket pocket, and then as he paused to formulate his next question his eyes went to the pearl-white wall above Dr. Florisbund's head. A portrait hung there in an ornate frame with a brass plaque that said "Percival Deriwelle." It was a photograph, actually—a black-and-white full-bust close-up, as if to show Percival Deriwelle in the same light as the railroad and banking barons of the 19th century. At first glance he certainly seemed of a piece with them, with his old, hard face, white hair, and wire-rimmed glasses, but on longer inspection there was something slightly wrong with the face—the eyes seemed cocked off in different directions, the jaw clenched unevenly so that one side bulged out; there was a hint of dishevelment in the hair, even a hint of uncleanliness about the skin.

Staring at the photograph, Wayne could feel the Deriwelle Institute for the Technological Study of Religion falling to pieces around him, the Oriental carpets and dolly receptionist, the plate glass and manicured flower beds, the mission statements and scientific credentials all crashing into a heap, the spell he now realized the place had begun to cast over him broken. All of it had simply been bought, with lots of money supplied by the lunatic in the picture, a cross between Andrew Carnegie, Scrooge McDuck, and Charles Manson. Wayne wondered whether Deriwelle had mandated that this particular picture be hung in the Institute, or whether it was just the best picture of him they had.

"Of course there are those who believe that Mr. Deriwelle was an eccentric," Rilfsbane said.

Wayne looked down at him, feeling slightly sick.

Florisbund still wore an oblivious, courtly politeness, but Rilfsbane was watching Wayne with a complicated look, part smooth assurance, part caution, part an almost haunted crestfallenness; it occurred to Wayne that this wasn't the first time he had seen the picture of the Institute's obviously bug-fuck founder throw someone who had just been buoyed by the sheer moneyed beauty of the place into half-believing there must be something to it. He guessed that the Institute must have to put up with a lot of ridicule, even beyond the few articles he had read.

"Yet the Institute's particular brand of open-minded and free-spirited research has attracted some of the finest scientists of our generation," Rilfsbane was saying. "Frankly, we are hoping that an objective, unbiased examination of our work will help dispel mischaracterizations by persons unfamiliar with the Institute."

Wayne was getting over the shock of Deriwelle's picture, steeled by the cynicism that protects modern people against disappointment in spiritual things. After all, the crazier the better, right? A posh pseudo-science institute built on sacred Indian land by a multimillionaire fruitcake? Great, if you were writing a book about it. "Well, I have to admit that what I've heard so far is fascinating," he said, and it was his turn to be urbane. "We science fiction people pride ourselves on our refusal to blindly accept prevailing orthodoxies. Needless to say, I hope I'll be able to do you justice."

On the way downstairs, Wayne said to Rilfsbane: "I was hoping to find a sublet or summer cottage or something like that, not too expensive and not too far from the Institute. Can you make any suggestions about where I might look?"

2

Senior Research Fellow Dr. Alphonse Bolling—who inquiries from Rilfsbane had disclosed was letting out his house for the summer—had a slight British accent and looked like a clever gnome. His hair seemed particularly appropriate for someone engaged in the Electrical Study of Religion: it was white, and stood up on his head in a thin imitation of Einstein's. His face was smiling and curious, with a long, bulbous nose and many wrinkles. He was short and stocky, and the hand Wayne shook was thick and strong. He nodded patiently as Rilfsbane made flattering introductions, then closed the door behind him, as if politely glad to be rid of him.

Bolling's second-floor office had a balcony overlooking a narrow rock gorge though which a stream rushed and gurgled under the branches of forest trees. The office itself was cluttered with books, papers, and exotic religious paraphernalia: carved wood and ivory totems, tasseled and feathered smoking pipes, a small, cast-iron shrine of some Eastern deity. Amid the clutter wires ran from a console behind the desk to small, complicated devices like electronic broccoli in each corner of the ceiling. Waving Wayne into the one visitor's chair not piled with books, Bolling began flicking switches and moving dials on this console.

"A science fiction writer," he said as he did this.

"Yes sir."

"Why do you call me 'sir'?" Bolling turned around, not challengingly but curious, twinkling eyes under untidy white eyebrows fixed on Wayne. "Are you from the South? Or are you compensating for some negative feelings or thoughts? About the Institute perhaps?"

He and Wayne grinned at each other, an understanding passing between them.

"What's the place like?"

"It depends where you look. Just to put your mind at ease, Rilfsbane *is* an idiot, Florisbund *is* a geriatric, and Deriwelle *was* a lunatic. Now you needn't call me 'sir' anymore."

Wayne laughed, delighted. "But what about the scientists?"

"Some are doing groundbreaking work they couldn't do anywhere else. Some are out-and-out quacks. The Institute has had to, shall we say, cast its net widely to find research that falls under the requirements of the trust."

"Can you tell me about yours?"

"Is this for your book? How are you going to describe me?"

"The Tom Cruise of electro-religious research."

It was Bolling's turn to laugh. "I build computer models of the way peoples' lives should have been."

"How's that?" asked Wayne with a little chill.

"Mr. Dolan. Sir." Bolling folded his hands on his desk and looked at Wayne with sudden gravity, almost melancholy. "Is there anything in your life you should have done differently? An old girlfriend you should have married? A job that drained your life force for years? A road you never took that you now wonder about? Or even better, do you have a vague feeling that something somewhere went wrong, but you've never been able to quite figure out what?"

A dull ache came into Wayne's chest. "Of course," he said evenly.

"Of course," echoed Bolling. "I was a psychiatrist at a university hospital, and it struck me one day. I had always treated this feeling as a symptom of mild depression. But the more I listened to my patients' stories, the more I began to realize that people *were* married to the wrong spouses, *had* stayed in the wrong job until it was too late, *had* made wrong decisions that permanently diminished their lives."

A tiny insect buzzed near Wayne's ear, and he flicked a hand at it.

Bolling watched him with a sharp, interested look. "Many of these people dreamed too. They dreamed over and over about the old lover they should have married, the town they should have moved to, the career they should have had. It seemed to me finally that psychologists and psychiatrists around the country were hearing day after day not disguised descriptions of people's internal psychological dynamics, but literal, existential descriptions of ideal lives, as if these existed in some dream-space, some Platonic realm, not as psychological facts but as the real, objective facts of unfulfilled destinies."

The silky girl. The far green continent. The tightness in Wayne's chest was interrupted by another buzzing, which he swiped at. He looked around, but the insect was nowhere to be seen.

"What if we postulate that there *is* a fated life," Bolling went on, "a destiny for each person, and that one suffers in direct proportion to how far he strays from it? I developed computer models of people's lives and re-played them to see what would have happened if they had taken different paths. My theories took me athwart the accepted wisdom in my field, of course. After being passed over for endowed chairs first at Oxford and then at Harvard, I said the hell with it and came here. You're a very sensitive man, Mr. Dolan."

The invisible insect was buzzing maddeningly now, and Wayne found himself waving his hands around his head. He even slapped himself on the neck. "What? Sorry, there's a bug driving me crazy. I'm following you, actually—"

"It isn't a bug; I was testing your sensitivity to very small aural stimuli." Bolling turned and flicked a switch on the console and waved at the broccoli things. "Your perceptual thresholds are set very fine. Rilfsbane, for ex-ample, sits where you are and babbles insensibly even when the machine is turned up so high that *I* can nearly hear the stimuli from here."

Wayne looked at the broccoli things in surprise. "Is that—part of your research?"

"Yes. My findings have led me to be a believer in the 'still, small voice,' the inner direction, which most people ignore, planning their lives instead according to rational principles, practicalities, goals. Dreams, vague urgings, mysterious portents guide you on the path to your des-tiny; but you have to pay attention carefully, very quietly to them. I've been testing the hypothesis that this subtle inner attention is correlated with the ability to pay atten-tion to subtle outer things."

Wayne thought about that. "How does it square with religion, though?"

Bolling took two keys out of his desk drawer. "If there *is* a fated life, that means there's such a thing as fate, and if there's such a thing as fate, that means that all the lives of all the beings on this planet are woven together in an impossibly fine and delicate and intelligent way, and how could that be? It's a nonscientific idea because one of the basic tenets of modern science is that the universe is a stupid place, except for us, our intelligence. And even our intelligence is supposed to have arisen just by stupid chance. The idea that intelligence is one of the fundamental characteristics of the universe is a religious idea by default."

He smiled gently and held the keys across the desk. "I think you will like the house," he said. "I've made sure it's very quiet, so one can hear the inner voice."

"You're going to let me stay in your house?"

"Yes. Providential that you should come by today. I have to leave for Europe in"—he checked his watch—"two hours, and I hadn't been able to find anyone satisfactory to stay in it. That kind of coincidence is one of the signs of the fated life, I believe. So maybe neither one of us is so very far off."

Wayne wanted to contradict him, at least as to himself; and Bolling sighed with thoughtful melancholy, abstracted eyes looking at the sunlight through the open balcony door.

⟞

North of Institute Drive there were no more farms, just forest on both sides of the two-lane county highway, arching over an occasional house or a road winding away inland to Wayne's right. Alternately warm and cool air came through the car windows as invisible fronts and tendrils of atmosphere from the Lake drove out the smells of hot asphalt, warm leaves and grass. Finally at the bottom of a long hill a road sign said West Road. Wayne turned left, and it was dirt.

Dust rose behind the car. The shade of big oak and beech trees was broken by shafts of sunlight shimmering with pollen and dust. The dark, mossy ruin of a shack stood off the road amid the crabgrass, bushes, and wildflowers, its damp boards scored and black with age, bright, baby-green vines growing up it like feathered snakes.

After a quarter mile the road ended in a circle around an enormous beech at the very edge of a wooded bluff covered with ivy and orange daylilies among the trees. As Wayne got out of the car the long, lazy, wash of surf came to him from the beach 60 feet below, and between the branches the Lake glittered green with small, sharply etched waves, its atmosphere—cool, serene, exciting—surrounding him as if he were on a ship. To his right an ornamental wall of staggered, whitewashed cinder block enclosed a brick patio with potted geraniums, and beyond that was a two-story white wooden house with a lawn that sloped to the edge of the bluff.

It was a good-sized, all-weather beach house of the kind built in the first half of the century. Bolling had renovated it simply but expensively. There was a library with a fireplace, a screen porch with a hammock. The big front room had hardwood floors with Indian rugs, leather furniture, and a giant picture window looking over the water. It was full of the smell of beach houses, the dampness and quietness, the freshness and laziness of atmosphere, the background hush of waves. Everything was calm and quiet and sparkling, as if he had entered a celestial dimension, one of the intermediate planes between this world and heaven.

He opened his suitcases in the upstairs bedroom

overlooking the Lake, put on cutoffs, and went back down to the flagstone walk at the side of the house, the sun hot in the cool breeze. Flagstone steps led down under the damp shade and smell of the bluff trees to the beach.

It was 40 feet of pale sand, deserted as far as the eye could see. The only sounds were the gentle surf, the breeze, and the occasional mew of a seagull. The bluff curved away majestically north and south, wooded green or pale sand and clay along its abrupt slopes, until it faded into an aquamarine-grey distance haze whose obscurity suggested a storm coming. But there was no storm: the sun shone blinding in the clear blue sky: it was just an unaccustomed vastness shading into the opacity of the atmosphere.

He waded into the surf. Then it was as though he were a sinner newly released from purgatory: he dived down into the cold grey water underneath and floated in the warm crystalline water on top, abandoning himself utterly, his body water and his eyes sunlight.

At last he got out, climbed out of the vast landscape tired and tingling, up the flagstone steps, washed sand off his feet in the warm water of a sunning hose.

There was a wall phone in the kitchen next to a window looking out through woods sunlit green and stirring in the breeze. He noticed through the trees another house 100 yards away along the bluff.

Alice answered at Ann's number. "Oh, Daddy!" she said breathlessly, surprised out of her usual reserve.

"I wanted to tell you about the place I'm staying. It's a beautiful house in the woods on the edge of a huge lake like an ocean."

"Is it your house?" she asked anxiously.

"No, it's the house of a man who's letting me use it."

"Can we come see you there?"

He was about to say no, but then he wondered why

not. "That would be wonderful," he said enthusiastically. "You and your brother would love this place. We could go swimming every day. Ask your mother if you can come in a week or two. I'll pay for the tickets—or I'll drive back and get you."

Then the baby got on, saying "Daddy? Daddy?" in anguish, as if calling into a dark place.

Then Ann, in a fury: "The answer is *no*. You know your visitation doesn't allow you to take the children out of state. And I won't have you calling and getting them excited and putting me in a position where I have to be the bad guy. You keep this up and you won't have any visitation at all." She hung up.

He stood in the kitchen of paradise holding the phone, hollowed out suddenly with rage and sorrow and shame. Paradise wasn't his, it was only a brief loan he couldn't afford.

Next morning the Deriwelle Institute's forest-shaded grounds were emerald-green shot with gold as Wayne pulled into the parking lot of Laboratory Building B, halfway across the campus from the Administration Building where Rilfsbane had first received him. In the middle distance, across an enormous expanse of lawn, one of the domed Roman temple/observatory buildings stood on its crag; on a rise in the farther distance stood the other. The quiet morning sunlight made them look mystical and Ionian.

Rilfsbane got out of a dark green Jaguar sedan, shook hands with Wayne, and flicked a key card into a slot next to a metal door. Inside was a counter behind which a guard watched security screens. Rilfsbane showed ID. Through another metal door was a plain, modern hallway with indirect lighting. Rilfsbane knocked at the first door, lights on behind its pebbled-glass window. A young woman in a lab coat opened it. Behind her was a large room with computers on metal desks against the walls, brightly lit by ceiling fluorescents.

"Dr. Allison," said Rilfsbane. "Good morning. We have an appointment with Dr. Burschevsky."

"Oh," she said, and made a wry face. "Isn't it the damndest thing? It's nothing personal, of course. He's—" She put a finger to her head and laughed. She was a slim, pretty woman of medium height, with shoulder-length honey-colored hair, restless, thin, intelligent hands, and a tired, abstracted look.

"Dr. Maureen Allison, Chief Research Associate to Dr. Adam Burschevsky, the renowned Eastern Mysticism researcher," Rilfsbane introduced them. "Mr. Dolan is an acclaimed science fiction author who is taking time off to write a nonfiction book about the Institute. I'm showing him around, and I thought he might be interested in your machine."

"Oh, fabulous! My husband is a huge science fiction reader. I can show it to you, if you don't mind being chaperoned by the number two man."

They protested politely. Dr. Allison led them into a big back room that smelled faintly of oil and power-sawn wood. A giant wooden box or crate in the middle of it was pulled into two halves, full of styrofoam baffles cut away to fit around a large plexiglas tank mounted on a wheeled frame. The tank was connected by wires and hoses to machines and electronic devices surrounding the crate.

"This is our Sensory Reorientation Chamber," said Dr. Allison. "Soundproofed outer containment." She pointed to the wooden box and baffles. "Pumps for maintaining the water in the tank at skin temperature and maintaining a mixture of salts rendering the subject's body weightless." Some of the surrounding machines. "The only difference so far from a normal sensory deprivation tank is that the subject floats upright, since the ancient Vedic texts specify that the yogin's spine be perpendicular to the ground during meditation.

"We've also added some other enhancements. In deep meditation yogic adepts achieve a particular pattern of alpha- and theta-wave flux, so we've added a biofeedback loop that rewards for the target brain-wave patterns, which we've averaged from EEG measurements of meditating yogins in India and Tibet, our requirement being that they had to exhibit some supernormal quality, such as imperviousness to cold, cessation of breathing, control over involuntary bodily functions, etc., so that we knew we were getting the real thing. In that face mask you see hanging inside the tank are electrodes to measure the subject's brain-wave patterns, as well as earphones and goggles to deliver the feedback."

"So," said Wayne, trying to follow her, "you're using biofeedback methods to get the person in the chamber to have the same type of brain waves as meditating yogis."

"Yes, while the sensory deprivation mimics the yogin's detachment from outer stimuli."

Rilfsbane was looking on with bland benignity, arms folded comfortably.

"See that tube hanging down below the face mask?" It was made of transparent soft plastic, rounded at the end. "That goes into the subject's trachea—the windpipe. The pump it's attached to effects a constant gas exchange, pressurizing the lungs with a high-oxygen mixture and removing carbon dioxide, causing a cessation of the respiratory reflex."

"So—"

"The person stops breathing. But stays awake and alert because we're feeding him oxygen."

"But what are you trying to prove? Or study?"

"We're trying to render religious experiences, experiences of God, reproducible. It takes yogic adepts decades of meditation to achieve the cessation of breathing, the imperviousness to external stimuli, and the brain-wave patterns I told you about, which in turn are supposed to give them their celestial perceptions. Our hypothesis is that we can reproduce the same physical and neurological state in a much shorter time—perhaps on demand—using this device. If that is so, and if this state leads to religious experiences, then we should be able to create bona fide religious experiences on demand, reproducibly, providing the basis for their scientific study."

"So religion—seeing God—is just a matter of having certain brain-waves."

"Yes. And your talking to me right now is also a matter of having certain brain-waves. Certain states of consciousness are necessary for religious experiences, and states of consciousness are mediated by brain states, and brain states can be produced with the help of machines. Not very romantic, but reproducibility is necessary for research."

There were more doors in the hall. Rilfsbane knocked on one of them. After a minute it opened and a face thrust out at them, grey and loose-jowled, with a monkish beard and bald head. It looked disturbed, distracted, and unpleasant. "Yes?"

"Dr. Drensler," said Rilfsbane, "I hope—"

"I'm sorry, you'll have to come back later," said the face, its bearded jowls quivering, and the door was shut decisively.

Rilfsbane reared back, embarrassed. "Ah, that's unfortunate," he said. "The intensity of top-level scientists working on the most important questions of our day—I'm sure, if we make another appointment—" He wiped his face with a monogrammed handkerchief.

He knocked nervously on another door down the hall. It was opened by a large, round-shouldered, lab-coated man with a round sincere face, a shock of neatly barbered brown hair, and earnest brown eyes behind glasses. He looked like a lab student at some religious college.

"Is Dr. Daniels in?" asked Rilfsbane. The big man stepped aside and gestured mock-dramatically into a big room like the one where they had seen the Sensory Reorientation thingy, but this one crowded with workbenches, desks with computer terminals and electronic equipment, and a group of unmatched easy chairs around a big television set. Someone was getting up awkwardly from a workbench stool, a man in black jeans and a black dress shirt with colored pens in a pocket protector.

"Ah, Dr. Daniels," said Rilfsbane, leading Wayne forward. "Here is the gentleman I spoke to you about yesterday. Mr. Wayne Dolan, Dr. Raymond Daniels."

"Ray," the man mumbled, shaking Wayne's hand with a strong grip and looking into his face apprehensively. He was of medium height, thin but sinewy, with a pimply face and the kind of pale, curly hair mothers love, large, soulful brown eyes behind thick glasses. He looked like a melancholy farm boy.

Rilfsbane was listing awards and prestigious institutions that Dr. Daniels had won and taught at. Daniels looked embarrassed and intimidated by these honors, but when Rilfsbane mentioned that Wayne was a science fiction writer a muddy light kindled in his eyes.

"Science fiction?" he said. He had a peculiar, quiet, clipped, breathy way of talking, and at the end of his sentences left his mouth open as if savoring what he had just said. The big man in the lab coat watched the proceedings with voracious curiosity, his eyes switching attentively to the face of each speaker in turn. "I love science fiction."

"Mr. Dolan is doing a nonfiction book on the Institute,"

said Rilfsbane. "And in connection with it he was interested in seeing some of our research. I thought perhaps that your work—"

From among the clutter of a workshop table Daniels picked up a baseball cap loyal to the Cincinnati Reds.

"We make these things," he said. The big, white-coated man was grinning widely with excitement.

Daniels turned the cap over. Inside Wayne saw that it was crisscrossed with wires.

"Electrodes," said Daniels.

He ran his hand down a wire that attached the hat to a box the size and shape of a Walkman. "This is a processor and recorder. We pay people to wear these things when they sleep. Not this one; a version that fits inside a weird kind of nightcap. Then we measure their brain-waves while they dream.

"Then after we've taken their brain-waves for a few nights, we take them while they're awake. We talk to them or let them watch TV. If they're religious we show them all kinds of religious programs. If they're Catholic we show them this Catholic channel where they say Mass all day long. Or we might let them read the Bible. Then we show them all kinds of sex movies. Then we give them the hats and let them go out and go to work, or whatever they do all day."

"Well, but—what's it all in aid of?"

"We're testing a hypothesis!" the lab-coated man burst out squeakily. His body language was all teenage excitement.

"Did you ever hear of this Swiss psychologist guy Carl Jung?" asked Daniels. His voice inflected downward at the end of questions like an Englishman's, though his accent was Pennsylvania backcountry.

"Yes."

"He has this theory that people dream all the time.

They don't stop dreaming when they're awake, but their dreaming gets tucked into the corners around their waking sensations, which are 'louder.' When they go to sleep, the sensory input is switched off, so the dreams are what they notice. But that doesn't mean dreams stop affecting you in the daytime. Jung's theory is that dreams make up most of your experience all the time.

"What we do, we try to follow people's dreams into their waking brains. We want to see if they're really dreaming during the day, and how, and how much they conflate their dream images with reality, and what effect it has on them."

"What's the connection with religion?"

"Well," Daniels' soulful eyes looked suddenly haunted. "Jung talks about these things called 'archetypes.' They're like primitive patterns of thought and feeling that are common to all people. They determine the shape of your dreams. There's an archetype for God. There's one for the soul. We want to know if people's religious experiences are dreams they're having. We want to know if God, the soul, the afterlife, things like that, are people and things from the dream world. 'The Kingdom of Heaven is within you.' Maybe that's what that means."

3

Wayne drove into St. Clair, looked around a little in the quiet neighborhoods and the tourist streets near the Lake bluff, got some groceries from one of the old-fashioned markets, and got back to Bolling's house in the early afternoon. The air was warm, humid, and very still, bringing the sounds of birds singing and the quiet surf with an almost unnatural clarity. He went swimming. The distance haze had taken on a golden tint, perhaps from the smudge of humidity that had accumulated around the sun. The Lake was all little choppy waves that gurgled and splashed around him with cool innocence, but their surfaces were opaque, mirrorlike, reflecting the grey-gold haze as if to hide something they were doing underneath. There was a sense of waiting, of temporary stasis, as if a storm, still unmanifest, were brewing somewhere, the atmosphere quietly gathering its moisture and energy. From where he floated 50 feet out in the water the bluff curved off, sand and clay, trees and boulders, bushes and flowers tiny in perspective, like an infinitely detailed model of the shores of paradise.

Back at the house he showered. Perhaps the restlessness of the mirrored waves had gotten under his skin, but he felt like doing something. He worked on notes of his morning's interviews for a while, but his mind kept wandering. The Blue Water Indians brochure Florisbund had given him caught his eye, and he glanced over it. One of the Points Of Interest listed was:

Shaman's Mound—Located on a rise overlooking Lake Michigan, a sacred Blue Water site where tribal shamans received visions and revelations. It was believed that the spot had been discovered through divination and dowsing by ancestral shamans. The Mound is a landmark of great scenic beauty, serenity, and historic importance. It was purchased by the Deriwelle Preservation Foundation in 1992, and is open to the public.

A map showed that Shaman's Mound was no more than five miles north of West Road.

Research for the book; local color. Wayne got in the Honda and headed up the county highway.

He almost missed the dirt clearing on the left-hand side, creosoted logs laid at the ends to mark parking spaces. A small brown sign said: "Shaman's Mound." There were no houses in sight, just tall forest on both sides of the road. Wayne parked in the clearing and turned off the engine. The sound of a car on the highway increased gradually until it shot by, raising a faint dust in the hot, hazy sunlight; after it had gone the afternoon was very quiet.

There was a dirt path. Wayne followed it.

The path was humped with tree roots; the remains of a

rusty barbed-wire fence ran alongside. In a gap between
the trees a bar of sunlight fell blinding across the dirt, illuminating an old dump: the brown, disintegrated remains
of a water tank, an ancient refrigerator, a defunct washer
and dryer leaning crazily in the rubbish, old tires, what
looked like ancient pieces of farm machinery, a frayed
tennis shoe, all overgrown and decayed, looking as much
part of the natural world now as the rocks and bushes.
There was a buzz of insects from the undergrowth.

The path started to climb steeply. Wayne's footsteps
and breathing were muffled under tree branches that
hung thick and low. Finally the light brightened, and he
stepped out onto a high bluff overlooking the Lake.

It was a dozen-foot-wide ledge, part grassy, part grey
boulders jutting from the side of the hill over thick forest
that fell steeply to the water 150 feet below. From up here
the distance haze was whitish-grey, the Lake sparkling
grey-gold; below him was the deep green of trees. A gentle breeze stirred his hair. The calls of bird and buzzing of
insects were serene, unhurried.

One of the boulders was shaped like a natural seat.
Wayne sat on it. The feel of the warm, massive, ancient
rock against his back was stilling, soothing. He leaned
back and studied the view. The Blue Water shamans had
known what they were doing making this their power
spot, he thought. The quietness of it entered his flesh and
bones; tension and anxiety flowed out of him. He could
feel himself relaxing, as if for the first time in years. How
had his life gotten so complicated? He listened to the distant, wide sound of surf, felt a stray breeze against his
face. And what were the answers to those questions that
had been in temporary storage in the back of his mind
for so long? The last time he had really thought about
them was when he was a teenager, he realized with surprise. He had been waiting to get his balance, make his

way back through the labyrinthine complexities of life to a place where he could consider them again, but it had taken so long that he had forgotten he was trying to get back, and then things had gotten more complicated instead of less, until—But now suddenly here he was, back at square one again, and all because he had come out to this beautiful part of the Earth, and right out to this warm stone seat above Lake Michigan where it was quiet enough to think, finally. A deep thankfulness came over him, as well as a shudder at the realization that he might never have come here at all. As he relaxed even more he felt sleepy, as if an old sleep deficit masked by artificial stimulants like worry and work and complexity had just now been uncovered. He closed his eyes.

—

"We can help you with that for $5,000," said the Indian across the counter.

He was in a small office or reception room. The walls were a pale bluish-green, almost pastel but also slightly industrial, and not too brightly lit by the two fluorescent bulbs in the drop-ceiling fixture. It looked new, but there was no trace of luxury: the pale blue carpeting was thin and utilitarian, the counter Wayne stood at—which divided the room in half, separating him from the Indian— was varnished wood with a formica top, and had a panel you could lift up to go through. It was a start-up company, Wayne realized, or at least it had just moved to this location: there were cardboard boxes stacked near the couple of plastic chairs and the formica table on Wayne's side of the counter, and more boxes on the other side.

The Indian had reddish-brown skin, a powerful, curved nose, high cheekbones, black eyes, a face rugged and self-contained as the Indians in early American portraits, but this one wore a Southwestern dude-ranch outfit: a pearl-grey cowboy hat, string tie with a silver-and-turquoise clasp, light suede jacket over a blue-green shirt.

He repeated: "We can help you with that for $5,000."

Wayne made no answer. It was a strange proposition, and the figure seemed high to him. He looked into the Indian's impassive face, trying to figure out if he was serious. He certainly *looked* serious; Wayne supposed his frank, impassive stare was a cultural way of exhibiting honesty.

The Indian said: "You deposit the money at the Farmers' & Merchants' Bank, account number 30162415. As soon as you do that we can start helping you. Guaranteed results. Fast service. Account number 30162415."

There was a loud boom, and something hit Wayne in the face.

—

His eyes flew open in confusion; it took him a second to focus. It was grey-green twilight. For a moment he thought he had slept the afternoon away; then he saw that behind him the sky was still sunlit pale. But a puffy, ponderous, slate-grey ceiling hung seemingly motionless above the Lake, and the distance haze was now close and grey and wet, as if made of falling rain. Through the still air the surf was louder, the rush of waves on the shore long and vigorous, and he could see big swells in the grey water like advance guards of the approaching storm. All at once a lightning bolt forked down on the horizon, and a few seconds later there was another loud boom. Another raindrop hit him on the face, and others spattered down on the rocks and grass.

Wayne got up hastily. In the green downhill tunnel the air was dim and damp, and raindrops pattered above him, none penetrating the dense leaves. His watch said it was only 4:30, but when he came out to the parking area a passing car had its headlights on. He didn't have to use his wipers on the short drive home, going with his windows open to feel the wet, exciting air, but when he got to the end of West Road there was a sudden rush of wind, and rain began to come down fast as he ran from the Honda. Inside, the house seemed still and stuffy. He went around shutting windows, then went up to his bedroom and stood in the open lakeward window feeling the living wind from high, celestial regions, the rain on his face and clothes. Thunder muttered in the clotted greyness, and the bluff trees hissed in the gusts.

The modernistic phone on the bed table glowed and emitted a mellow trill. It was Alan Rilfsbane. "Mr. Dolan, I hope I'm not disturbing you. Can you come out to the Institute right away? I've managed to set up a meeting with Dr. Edmund Carvery, one of our two Nobel laureates. I apologize for the lack of notice, but Dr. Carvery is very difficult to see, and works only at night. I believe that his agreeing to an interview may be a momentary impulse of which we should take advantage."

Dr. Edmund Carvery's office was at the end of a hushed hallway on the second floor of the Administration Building. Outside, the sky grumbled, and the smell of wet earth, rain, and ozone came in an open window as Wayne and Rilfsbane passed. Most of the offices were empty, but in one an old woman sat smoking a cigarette and reading. Dr. Carvery's door was closed. Rilfsbane tapped at it.

"Come," said a voice.

Rilfsbane opened the door gently. "Dr. Carvery," he said with almost apologetic softness.

Dr. Carvery's office was dim and stuffy, heavy blinds drawn across the windows and closed balcony door, a single small lamp casting yellow light over a desk awash in books and papers. Boxes were half-unpacked, and new-looking furniture was pushed haphazardly against the walls. It reminded Wayne of his Mid-Atlantic Region apartment.

There was a stirring at the desk. "Ah, yes," said a voice, and someone stood up. The contrast from the dark, brisk atmosphere outside was disorienting, or maybe it was a lack of oxygen in the overbreathed air.

"How do you do, Dr. Carvery," said Rilfsbane, leaning forward and extending his arm far out to shake hands, as if availing himself of the opportunity without presuming to get too close.

"How are you. Come in, come in," said Dr. Carvery with attempted heartiness, though it was obvious that his visitors made no particular impression on him.

He was a small, thin, soft man with a pale face, whose soft-looking skull, almost saddle-shaped on top, still had wisps of dark hair. His vague, dark eyes gleamed in the lamplight. He wore expensive dress pants, loafers, and a thin beige sweater. He looked more like a retired financial advisor than a Nobel prize winner. Wayne thought he saw the edge of a child's game board sticking out from under a disorderly pile of papers on the desk, but he couldn't tell for sure before he was shaking a small, soft hand.

"As I believe I mentioned," said Rilfsbane, "Mr. Dolan is working on a book about the Institute."

"Of course, of course," said Carvery. His voice, which tried to be hearty, was dry, quiet, somehow ashen. "Please, sit down." He ushered them awkwardly into the disarranged area beyond the desk and fumbled at a floor lamp, turning it on so that a circle of light fell half on the sofa.

Wayne sat on the sofa, Carvery and Rilfsbane in armchairs. Thunder mumbled heavily outside.

"We won't take much of your time," began Rilfsbane.

"Not at all, not at all," murmured Carvery. He seemed partly ill at ease, partly hospitable, partly completely abstracted.

"Did you have any particular questions for Dr. Carvery?" Rilfsbane asked Wayne uncomfortably.

He did have one. "As a Nobel prize winner, do you believe in God? And if so, why?"

As a conversation starter it was effective. Wayne felt for the first time that Carvery looked straight at him. His eyes seemed to tighten, focus.

"Well, let me ask you a question," he said. "Do you *dis*believe in God, and if so, why?"

Before Wayne could reply, he went on. "Some people assume that *dis*belief in God is the default position, from which any deviation must be justified. But it seems to me the opposite is true. The vast majority of mankind has believed in a God for millennia, with only a tiny fraction— the so-called intellectuals and their hangers-on—taking the contrary position." Carvery seemed almost ferocious suddenly in his cerebral, abstracted way, as if some of these so-called intellectuals and their hangers-on had come into his office and were spouting their nonsense. "In a way, the question is like asking: 'Do you believe in the beginning of the universe, and why?' Everything has a beginning in the common experience; therefore the burden is on those who claim that the universe is different to prove their point. It is the same with the existence of God."

Wayne felt himself stung by the man's disdain, and at the same time flattered by his attention. "Yet there's no actual scientific evidence for the existence of God, am I right?"

"There is more evidence for the existence of God than for the theories of modern particle physics, for example," said Carvery.

"How's that?"

"Millions of people, both in the past and today, have had religious experiences. Only a very few have had experiences consistent with the theories of particle physics. The only way to detect the particles that these theories predict is to construct giant machines, wait many years, and then get experts to interpret the meager, faint, ambiguous data which result. There are only a very few experts in the world qualified to interpret such data—a high priesthood of sorts. On the basis of the oracular words of these half dozen experts as to the meaning of the incredibly faint traces amplified by the enormous machines, the edifice of particle physics is built. Compared to such a few, delicate, highly esoteric experiences, the huge number of experiences of God by ordinary people seems overwhelming evidence by comparison."

"But—but the technology resulting from this edifice of particle physics has enabled us to—"

"Yes; and like every culture that has developed a powerful technology, we think it proves the superiority of our gods—that's been true for civilizations from the Babylonians through the British Empire; except that our modern gods are physicalism, reductionism, atheism."

"But—"

"I'll tell you what," said Carvery, leaning forward suddenly, his eyes hot. "Forget all this. Forget these questions." He waved his hand impatiently. "There's only one question that really means anything, that's ultimately important."

"And what is that?"

"What happens to us after we die? If we go on existing and our state is relatively decent, then who cares if there's a God or an absolute ethical standard or a soul, or any of the other things people are always jabbering about? On the other hand, the universe could be chockfull of beneficent gods, angels, and divine beauty, and if death snuffs us out, then it's all just a cruel joke, eighty years spent on Death Row."

"But it doesn't matter, does it?" Wayne said slowly. "I mean, if there's nothing after death, we'll never know. We'll just go into that nothingness believing whatever we believe about an afterlife, and if we're wrong, we'll never be corrected. Right?"

Carvery looked into Wayne's eyes with his hot dark ones. "Mr. Dolan, have you ever traveled on the British Rail train system? Third class?"

"No."

"Well, the accommodations are adequate, but not what you would call comfortable. The seats are hard and the carriages aren't very well heated in winter. Now. Suppose you find yourself riding in one of these railway carriages in winter; out the window is a dreary grey landscape. You're on your way home at Christmas break. Your family and friends will be there, some of them people you haven't seen for years, and there will be feasts and fires in the hearth, to-bogganing and carol-singing, a big Christmas tree. Can you imagine that?"

Wayne nodded, his heart sinking a little. He had no family anymore.

"Now. Let's suppose you're riding on exactly the same train, but this time, instead of going home to your family for Christmas, you're on your way to a state penal facility to be executed."

Wayne stared into the man's hot, dark eyes.

"Everything about the train ride is the same. Both rides are uncomfortable, chilly, dreary. You're hungry, and your back hurts from the hard seat. But the first ride, going home for Christmas, will be completely different from the second, even though the physical conditions are identical.

"But now suppose again. Suppose you wake up on this same train; you've been sleeping, and you wake up, and you find that *you can't remember where you're go-ing.* You know it's either home for Christmas or to the executioner, but you just can't remember which. Then what uncertainty, what torment, what agony you feel. That train ride is our life, Mr. Dolan. The only thing worth knowing is what happens after."

As he and Rilfsbane stood by the door and shook hands with Carvery, Wayne squinted and tilted his head to see the game board half-buried on the desk.

It was a Ouija board.

———

It wasn't until that night when he was in bed, nearly asleep in the drumming of rain, that he remembered his dream of the Indian and the bank account number. Strange, he thought as he drifted off. Of course, dreams were strange.

———

He was in a plain, anonymous room, like a motel room or a dorm room that no one had moved into, with white walls, beige carpet, a metal-frame bed with blue wool blankets. The silky girl was there. She was beautiful and small and golden, with eyes that changed as you looked at them like maps of a magical country, or like the Lake. It was dusk, and the light from the window was dim and blue. They lay on the bed next to each other on their stomachs like kids, chins on hands and feet kicking up, talking in the dusk. Then they were under the covers and he held her, and she whispered sweetly in his ear: *30162415.*

———

The rain blew away during the night, and when Wayne woke up the morning air was so crystalline that by com-

parison even the previous sunny days in Southwestern
Michigan seemed murky in his memory. The sun sparkled
diamond-white on geraniums and drying patio bricks,
the Lake jewel-blue and glittering with little waves. When
he put his first spoonful of cornflakes into his mouth he
remembered his dream. *30162415*. The account number
from the Shaman's Mound dream. How strange. Had it
made such an impression on his unconscious? For a split
second he considered making the $5,000 deposit at the
Farmers' & Merchants' Bank, which would represent a
fifth of his advance for the Deriwelle Institute book.

It was still tickling the back of his mind after his
morning's interviews, with an ex-Jesuit who was building a computer model of God's personality based on input from all known scriptures, and two members of the
Institute's Board of Directors, a couple of old, comfortable, rich men who seemed partly respectful, partly confused, and partly bemused at the Institute's mission. A
concept was forming in Wayne's mind, a new angle for
the book. Not just an Institute where scientists in plush
offices conducted religious research ranging from the
crackpot to the inspired, but an enchanted stretch of
land along the shores of Lake Michigan bewitched by
primeval Native American shamans. . . .

———

The dirt parking lot by the county highway was quiet
and deserted, a few puddles remaining from the rain. As
Wayne got out of the Honda the only sounds were birds
singing and the faint tick of engine heat under the hood.
The tunnel of leaves up the slope was damp and cool, almost chilly. Up on Shaman's Mound the air and sunlight
were Alp-clear, and the distance haze showing the vast
curve of the coast in majestic perspective was far and

pale grey, suggesting far villages and towns, countries and continents. The stone he had sat on last time was grey and massive, dominant in its very passivity, like the Indian in his dream. He sat on it again, trying to quiet his mind and let the atmosphere and local color of the place sink in.

He looked out over the Lake and sky and forest, a feeling of well-being coming to him, the thoughtful quietude he had felt here before. He sat at a remove and considered his life: the bright distraction of childhood on the hilly streets of an imaginary town under fairy-tale clouds, the intense nocturnal wondering and expectations of adolescence, the work at college and the work at the newspaper and the work at his books, and things going faster and faster, the critical triumph of his second novel and the breathless excitement of book tour and movie option, the buzzing strength in his body and mind as if he were superhuman, then all of it fading slowly, frustratingly, and his marriage falling apart while his children grew, all of it winding tighter and tighter around him. . . .

"We can help you for $5,000," said the Indian across the counter. "Farmers' & Merchants' Bank. Account number 30162415." His face was powerful, convex, impassive, as if the stone on the Shaman's Mound had come alive and was talking.

Wayne jerked out of his doze, heart pounding. The same dream again—the same Indian, same room, same account number. And the feeling, unaccountable but intense, that the Indian was the personification of the rock he was sitting on.

—

As he came in, in a hurry to get to his laptop, Bolling's telephone was ringing, and when he answered in the kitchen it was Ann, her voice defiantly cheerful.

"Since you've decided to take a vacation at the beach, we've decided to go to the beach too for a few weeks."

"Oh? Where? Around here?" he asked hopefully.

"No, not around there. It doesn't matter, does it? I just didn't want you to worry if you called up and no one was home."

"Do you have the phone number out there? Can I talk to the kids?"

"They're in the car. We're just on our way now."

"Do you have a phone number—?"

"No. I don't know what it is. We'll call you if we're not too busy."

"Ann, you have no right to—I have a right to talk to them, and you have no right to take them to a place where I don't know the phone number," he said, suddenly angry. "You have no right—"

"Well, since you're too busy for them—"

"I told you, I'm here on work. And I *have* been—"

"Don't you yell at me. Don't you ever yell at me, you—"

"I'm not yelling, but you have no right—"

She hung up.

He went swimming to douse his anger. He was only good for about ten minutes. The sparkling crystal-blue waves were well-water cold, delved by the storm from the deeps of the Lake, with a kind of raw, deep-sea alienness. It was like swimming in the cold blue of the sky, or the depthless swells of the open ocean. When he came back in the telephone was ringing again.

It was Dr. Maureen Allison, of Dr. Adam Burschevsky's

Sensory Reorientation lab. "Sorry for the late notice, but my husband and I are having a get-together this evening—people from the Institute, mostly—and we wanted to know if you could come. Brad wants to meet you; he's read your books."

4

Ivywood Drive ran parallel to the Lake through thick woods, and now and then you could see the water down a long wooded slope, and the lights of houses among the trees in the evening. There was a yacht club at the end of the road, Maureen had told him, and if you got to it you had gone too far. Wayne didn't get to it, but the fact that it was there reinforced the feeling that Ivywood Drive was a kind of paradise, one of whose celestial aspects was that everyone was rich, lights hanging among the trees on quiet evenings in the windows of big houses where lovely blonde girls grew into their twenties, the reflection of this world in their blue and green eyes saturating it with radiance, portals as they were to the numenal realm.

He turned at a mailbox marked Tollaksen/Allison and descended a hundred feet of drive overhung by trees to a large, remodeled Victorian house. The wraparound porch had been changed along the right side to a roofless deck hung with colored Chinese lanterns in the pinkish-blue dusk. Wayne self-consciously climbed the steps to it. He felt underdressed, as he always did at parties, but somehow the writer's uniform of jeans and T-shirt—over which he had put on an old suit jacket for the occasion—had gotten such a hold on him that he felt conspicuous and pretentious wearing anything else.

At the back of the house the deck widened to 30 feet, and the Chinese lanterns glowed in imitation of the maraschino sun hovering in blue-grey haze over the Lake. People sitting and standing were red-tinted silhouettes against the sunset, and there was the hum of conversation and laughter, low, jazzy music. The air was still and cool, with the waxy citrus smell of citronella candles. Wayne went forward and leaned on the deck railing. The deck stood above a last slope grown with ivy and day lilies before it flattened into coarse beach grass and sand, surf breaking a hundred feet away. In the blue atmosphere his residual anger from the phone call with Ann seemed to drain away into sadness. Nothing he could do. Had to let go.

"Oh, Mr. Dolan, you *are* here. I didn't see you come in." He turned to see Maureen Allison looking flushed and happy, holding a glass.

Was he hungry? Did he want a drink? There were so many people who wanted to meet him. She led him among the chatting and laughing groups, put her hand on the arm of a very big man in a white linen suit without a tie. "I'd like you to meet my husband, Brad Tollaksen. Brad, this is Wayne Dolan, the science fiction writer."

Brad Tollaksen had shoulder-length blond hair, a tanned, clean-shaven face, and thoughtful eyes. His hand was big, bony, and strong.

"Hey, I read *The Blue Messiah* and *Hammer of God*," he said. "Great books."

Wayne mumbled abashedly because, of course, they weren't, and it was astonishing to meet someone who had even read them. "Are you at the Institute too?" he got out politely.

"No."

"Oh, bullshit," Maureen said, turning to Wayne, half-laughing. "He's just ashamed to be what he is. He works for Dr. Helios, who isn't here, but maybe you've met her . . . ?"

"No, but I've met some of the other doctors," Wayne said.

Brad laughed.

"Who?" Maureen asked.

"A Dr. Daniels."

"He seems a little odd at first," said Maureen. "He's a lapsed Mormon, tormented by doubts. But he's one of the best scientists at the Institute."

"Then there's this Dr. What's-his-name, Carvery, the Nobel prize winner. Jumped down my throat when I asked him why he believed in God, and I saw a Ouija board in his office."

"A Ouija board?" His hosts' eyes sparkled with the pleasure of gossip.

"Yeah, on his desk."

"Another fruitcake," said Brad.

"Did he talk about his research?" Maureen asked.

"No. He just told me that there's only one question worth asking: what happens after we die. He's very intense about it."

"He's intense, all right. He's in his office all night and at the hospice all day. Never talks to anyone, and if he does it's like an answering service. Come over here." Maureen led him to a table covered with food while Brad went to change the CD. Wayne piled a plate with potato salad, deviled eggs, crackers with smelly cheese, Greek

olives, sliced apples. "He's scoured the whole country for
terminally ill psychics, people who appear able to mentally influence dice trials. It's a slight influence, but apparently statistically significant. He's found three—an
old man and two old women. He's brought them to the
Bernard Lentin Center, a high-class hospice north of
here. In exchange for the best dying care available,
they've agreed to participate in his research. He goes up
there every day with a dice-throwing machine and an assistant to record the trials, and throws dice by their bed-
sides. He plans to keep going up there and throwing for a
week after each of them passes away, and they're supposed to try to influence the dice just like before, if
they're anywhere around. And if the dice throws keep
deviating from chance, he thinks he'll have proven
there's an afterlife. Oh, here's Adam."

Maureen conducted Wayne toward a tall, patrician
man with a large, intelligent nose and silver-grey hair in a
ponytail standing in conversation with two young women.

"Adam, I'd like you to meet Wayne Dolan; Wayne,
Dr. Adam Burschevsky, my boss."

"Ah, the writer," said Burschevsky, pleased, as if he
was well aware of Wayne's books and reputation. Wayne
shook an expressive, long-fingered hand, flattered in spite
of himself. "Maureen—who ought to be *my* boss, for all
of our relative intelligence—has told me about you."

Wayne had been greatly interested in Dr. Burschevsky's
Sensory Reorientation device. Dr. Burschevsky looked
forward to discussing that and other projects in depth
with him, and in exchange learning more about the writing craft. Back at the food tables, Wayne accepted a cold
beer from Maureen. His hands full, she walked him over
to a big rattan chair and deposited him on soft cushions,
telling him to call her if he needed anything.

He ate, looking around, trying to imprint some faces,

get a feel for scientists' body language at parties. Suddenly voices were raised nearby. A group of eight or ten people had made a circle of chairs and a sofa by the deck railing. One of them was Ray Daniels' big, owl-like assistant Tom, who sat leaning forward, eyes wide open. Daniels himself stood against the railing, dressed in his black jeans and shirt. Wayne didn't recognize anyone else except the jowled, tonsured, unhealthy-looking man who had slammed his laboratory door in Rilfsbane's face on Wayne's first tour of the Institute. He was listening to a small, dark-skinned man sitting in the middle of the sofa between two others, who, however, had edged away to the ends as if to give him room.

The small man was saying: "It doesn't make sense that such a belief would conferred a survival advantage in a world where it doesn't correspond to reality, eh. It's just self-contradictory."

"Not at all," the tonsured man said coolly. He sat in a chair on the opposite side of the circle. Unlike most of the other guests he was dressed in a suit and tie, expensive-looking but unable to disguise the soft, unhealthy body that bulged out over the belt and in the pant legs. He had small feet in soft leather loafers. His face was aggressive but controlled, cerebral. "Such a belief performs a whole host of adaptive functions, even if it's not valid, Samir. Like the belief that garbage caused Plague in the Middle Ages: it protected those who held it because they kept away from garbage, which bred rats, which *did* cause plague. So there you have a belief that gave those who held it a reproductive advantage, *even though it was false*."

"So tell me what advantage a false belief in God gives," said the man he had called Samir, leaning forward sullenly but attentively.

"For one thing it gives a reason to live. It protects the self-conscious and reflective human animal from the realization that it's going to die. Lower animals don't have the self-consciousness to understand that, so they don't need religion. Humans who believe they have a divine soul get comfort, strength to go on, to struggle and overcome odds. A second thing it gives is a built-in social hierarchy: the priest and the king are God's representatives on Earth, so they're to be obeyed blindly. A primitive society organized like that has a tremendous advantage over one where it's every man for himself. It's no wonder that societies that believe in God have flourished all over the world."

"But it's just the opposite, eh," said Samir heatedly. He had a strange accent, half Canadian, half something Eastern. "Worship of God, the building of churches, spending time on religious ceremonies, support of a clerical class, restrictions on otherwise advantageous behavior because of moral rules, are all *drags* on a society, putting it at a great reproductive *dis*advantage. And also, why should the idea that you're going to die be depressing in a Darwinist universe? Why wouldn't you be happy as long as you had reproduced, knowing that your DNA would be preserved? Why would you need to believe in a divine soul for comfort?"

"Because your brain is hardwired that way," barked the tonsured man, suddenly leaning forward and glaring at Samir like a guided missile honing in. "That's why Hall's research is crucial, absolutely central. Because it shows that the region of the temporal lobe that makes people believe is like the appendix or the pineal gland: an evolutionary dead end."

"What bullshit," Samir said. "All real perceptions are mediated by brain structures."

"But—you have to—he said—methodological—wait! wait!" a hubbub of voices came from the onlookers, and the tonsured man could be heard repeating loudly: "Absolutely critical. Absolutely critical," while Samir's angry voice was repeating: "Such bullshit, man."

Maureen Allison's voice rang out above the others: "—we don't *know* what Hall's research is going to show because he isn't done yet." Wayne saw her standing behind someone's chair.

"That's right," said Samir loudly. "That's right."

"Oh, come on, Maureen," said the tonsured man. "His chimpanzees *improve* task performance, *improve* mating success, *improve*—"

"Even if it makes people stop believing in God, it proves nothing," said Samir excitedly. "It simply means that his virus has damaged an important part of the brain responsible for—"

"But didn't you hear me, I said it *improves*—" the tonsured man snapped, grabbing the arms of his chair as if to jump out of it at Samir, but the rest of his words were covered by more hubbub, including laughter. More people were gathering around the circle now.

"I don't see how he's going to extend his research to humans," said Daniels' soft voice, which was somehow audible over the hubbub, and somehow hushed it, as if Daniels was someone to whom people habitually listened. "How's he going to get subjects?"

"Volunteers," grunted the tonsured man, "the way you usually get subjects." He raised his hand as if signaling that he would be one.

"But you're no good as a volunteer," said Daniels. "You already don't believe in God. And nobody who *does* believe is going to let Hall near them with his vaccine, since they're going to be afraid it will deprive them of their religion."

"But those people *have* to participate, for the advancement of science," barked the tonsured man.

"Never," snapped Samir. "I don't know anyone who's going to let Hall damage his brain in order to prove some insane—"

"If you don't participate, don't call yourself a scientist," the tonsured man yelled above the renewed hubbub, suddenly enraged. "Don't ever call yourself a scientist, Samir!"

"I'm a better scientist than you any day!" Samir shouted back furiously.

Suddenly the music got twice as loud and Brad Tollaksen in his white linen suit seized his wife and began to ballroom dance with her. There was laughter, catcalls. The circle broke up, and more people were dancing. Faces relaxed, bodies undulated. Between the figures Wayne could see the tonsured man, still seated, face raised laughing and talking to someone, his words drowned by music.

—

That night Wayne dreamed again. He was walking along the ancient, dark stone wall of a castle. As he walked, the wall seemed to get older and older, the stone brown and sandpapery, and it seemed that sticking out of it at intervals were the single legs of animals: sheep and oxen and goats. A huge portcullis in the wall was closed, but a small, rough wooden door next to it stood open. He went through that into a low, narrow stone passage lit by candles. The passage was full of billowing smoke. After stumbling along for a while, he found that the smoke was coming from an arched doorway, within which was a big, dark, dingy room with a huge table. Three Arthurian wizards were leaning over a tureen on the table, waving their hands over it in magical gestures, and the water in the tureen was giving off the smoke. As Wayne came nearer he saw that the water was bubbling, and that the wizards were skimming the bubbles off, and that the bubbles were made of shiny stone, like marbles. Each one had a number on it, and as he watched, the oldest wizard held eight of them up to him in succession, showing him the numbers *3 - 0 - 1 - 6 - 2 - 4 - 1 - 5.*

Four dreams in a row, was the first thought he had when he woke at 9:30 the next morning with a dry mouth and an angry little headache already beginning to swell and writhe inside his right temple from last night's beers. Four dreams in a row with the account number 30162415.

The morning was overcast, almost chilly, a brisk wind from the Lake carrying a few raindrops, and the Lake itself muscular and silty grey, roaring with white breakers under the vast solid grey of the sky. He checked Bolling's machine but there was no message from Ann and the children. Anger stirred in him, but he went out to wade in the surf in swimming trunks and a long-sleeved T-shirt that the wind fluttered along with his hair. A warm undertow dragged at his ankles. The grey, rushing landscape and clean breath of vast, distant sky and water seemed to revive him, scouring out his headache and fatigue and all other signs of mortality.

Five thousand dollars. Five thousand dollars would be a fifth of the advance money he had chiseled out of Astrid. But what if this was something real? Four dreams in a row was extraordinary, though it could be just some fixation of his unconscious. But what if it was a real dream Indian offering real mystical knowledge? It seemed bizarre, but on the other hand, if it *was* real it would be exactly what he had to have, he realized suddenly, stopping in his tracks, water washing around his feet, perhaps the only thing that could save him. And wasn't that at least some evidence that it was real, if there was a need that only it could fill? And could he really afford not to find out, crawl to his grave wondering whether there might have been an exit?

Besides, all of this had put another angle for the book into his head. He had first intended to write about the Deriwelle Institute, and then about the Institute and the quasi-mystical landscape around it; but now he saw that this was still too narrow. The real story widened out into his whole life—his middle-aged suffering and confusion in the Mid-Atlantic Region, his trip to the Institute, the beach house, St. Clair, the dreams of the Indian and the bank account number. Every book needed a protagonist, and Wayne Dolan would be the protagonist of this one. And what would a protagonist do if he had serial mystical dreams urging him to deposit $5,000 in a local bank to receive secret spiritual teachings from a numenal Indian?

And on top of everything, he realized with both a lifting and a sinking feeling, it was likely that the dream number didn't correspond to any real account at the Farmers' & Merchants' Bank at all; if it was all a figment of his unconscious that would be too much of a coincidence. So he probably wouldn't lose his money anyway; it would just be a grand gesture.

From somewhere above him the surge of an engine was carried by the wind. He had walked a hundred yards and was now below the neighboring house he had glimpsed among the trees from his kitchen window; it stood atop the wooded bluff, modernistic and cedar-sided, its wooden beach steps swooping in a long perspective to the sand ten yards from him. A moving truck was backing toward the house along a road invisible from where Wayne stood. Neighbors were apparently moving in or out. Wayne vaguely hoped it was out. Humans could only spoil the quiet, vast landscape.

—

The St. Clair Public Library looked like a small 1950s version of a Roman temple, with pillars and high, dusty windows, sandwiched between a drab Motor Vehicles Administration building and the County Clerk's office. It was old enough so that the stone steps were worn a little round, and the entrance had the sharp, musty smell of old stone. Inside, two huge ancient females dozed at a huge ancient desk, and behind them the hush of the books on tall metal stands receded into dimness, absorbing noise like soundproofing.

There was an actual card catalogue. It took Wayne a few minutes to figure out how to use it. The books on "Blue Water Indians—Religion" were in section JR771.

The narrow JR700–799 aisle felt as if no one had visited it for years. The books on Blue Water history and customs were greyed with age; their bindings crackled and exhaled puffs of dust when he opened them. In the obsolete typeface of *The Indians of South Western Michigan*, Wayne found the index entry: "Dreams, Blue Water Shamans." He turned to the referenced page with tingling hands.

> The Blue Water medicine men or Shamans were held in awe by the populace in part because of their supposed abilities of dreaming. According to this belief, these Shamans were able to meet and talk to, in dreams, legendary Shamans who had lived at a time when the power of the Shamans was much greater, and thus to obtain advice and teaching from them. It was said also that the Shamans cultivated the ability to live in both dreams and waking at once, and that this was a sacred state, in which

they were able to see the spirit world and exercise extraordinary powers. It was also believed that in this state they were led to the things and people destiny had picked out for them.

Wayne stood holding the book, his hair prickling on his head. Account number 30162415, he repeated to himself, to make sure he hadn't forgotten it.

The St. Clair Farmers' & Merchants' Bank was in another dull, 1950s pseudo-classical building complete with grooved pilasters and curly capitals of molded cement. In contrast to the windy grey day, inside it was still and bright, with marble floors and wood paneling, the tellers up high behind a tall counter faced with polished stone. The lady at Wayne's window looked in her early sixties, grey hair immaculately done, wearing an obsolete smart tweed suit with a brooch, like a kindly first-grade teacher turned professional. When Wayne asked if he could check on the existence of a particular account number and who it belonged to, she told him the bank wasn't allowed to give out that information, and continued to smile as he shakily wrote out a check For Deposit in account 30162415. She glanced it over, stamped it, put it in a drawer, and smiled some more.

Outside, Wayne stood on the steps of the bank, fighting the urge to run back and tell the nice first-grade teacher he had made a mistake. But almost certainly he would get a polite call from the bank tomorrow informing him that his check could not be debited; he had written Bolling's telephone number on it for that very purpose. And anyway, now he was a protagonist, he thought with a flicker of exultation: intrepid, inquisitive, probing into the deep places of the human soul for the answers to the riddles of existence.

A man in a grey raincoat came out of a narrow shop half a block down the street and walked quickly in Wayne's direction, holding the brim of a felt hat against the wind. As he approached, Wayne recognized the dark, serious, sunken-eyed face of Dr. Edmund Carvery, Senior Research Fellow at the Deriwelle Institute. Suddenly awkward, he started casting around for some appropriate greeting, but Carvery walked right past, not noticing him. He was visibly upset: his lips moved and his downcast eyes tracked back and forth blindly. He got into a grey BMW and pulled away.

Curiosity came over Wayne. He went down to the door from which Dr. Carvery had emerged. It was painted a peeling black, sandwiched between a bookstore and an antique shop; through a pane of glass Wayne could see dusty steps leading up. A sign above the door showed a hand with an eye in the palm, and the ornate words: "Madame Bakila, Psychic Readings."

—

The dirt parking lot next to the county highway looked mysterious and significant in the grey afternoon, with hissing greenish shadows under trees swaying and fluttering in the wind, as if Wayne's deposit of the $5,000 had somehow brought them to life, like a right move in a computer game vivifying a previously inert landscape. Up on the Mound the wind was stronger, almost chilly, and the vast roar of the Lake came up from all around. Below the grey sky the grey water was chopped with fast-moving waves out to the horizon.

The boulder's sandpapery surface was neutral in temperature. As Wayne leaned against it the wind seemed to diminish, as if the rock created an aerodynamic shelter. He squirmed, adjusted his position, trying to get comfortable. When he had fallen asleep up here before it had been in warm sunlight, and without the excitement of having just paid his $5,000 secret knowledge fee. He closed his eyes and tried to relax, but the wind eddied around him uncomfortably, and the roar of the Lake was intrusive. After a few minutes he got up. There was no prospect of falling asleep up here today. He gazed out above the swaying and hissing forest that fell to the surf, and across the roaring expanse of water toward the invisible source of the wind.

5

After the argument at Maureen Allison's party Wayne had talked to Ray Daniels, who had seemed relieved to fade into the background and discuss science fiction, and Daniels had told him to come over to the lab any time. Wayne was pleased: here he was attending parties and meeting the Institute scientists socially, just like the real Tracy Kidder. After leaving Shaman's Mound he drove to the Deriwelle Institute's Building B. The guard studied his ID and waved him in. The building seemed empty, quiet. Daniels' lab door was open. Wayne peered in diffidently.

Four people sat at a small table by the far wall of the lab, heads bowed, faces grave: Daniels, his big, owl-like assistant Tom, the small, dark man, and the pudgy, tonsured man with whom he had argued at the party last night, and whose own lab was a few steps down the hall. All looked chastened, as if they had decided to make up, no one wanting to meet the others' eyes. The thought even crossed Wayne's mind that they were having some kind of prayer meeting, until he saw that each of them held a hand of playing cards.

The tonsured man threw down some cards vigorously. "Two," he said. Daniels shot him replacements from the top of a deck.

Wayne knocked gently and came in. All the men's eyes came up. They had stacks of quarters in front of them on the table.

"Hi!" said the small, dark man enthusiastically.

"Excellent," said Daniels.

"Who the fuck is this?" asked the tonsured man.

"The science fiction writer," Daniels told him.

Wayne grinned shyly. "I brought you some books," he said to Daniels, holding them up. "Hope I'm not interrupting."

"Not at all, man," said the small man. His use of the idiom in his Canadian-foreign accent sounded only slightly stilted, as if he had been talking to the natives long enough that it had become second nature to him.

"You play poker?" asked Daniels.

"Jesus," said the tonsured man, looking at Wayne unpleasantly.

Wayne weaved among the desks, cluttered worktables, and instrument carts. He put the three paperbacks he had brought on the table in front of Daniels.

"Excellent," Daniels said again shyly.

Wayne could see that Tom held two twos and two nines. "I know the game," he said.

"Pull up a chair," said Daniels.

"Oh, fuck this," said the tonsured man angrily, and threw down his cards. He started to scrape his quarters into his hand.

Then everyone was full of distressed expostulation, Wayne apologizing for interrupting, the tonsured man sulkily making marginally polite excuses without meeting Wayne's eyes, pouring his quarters, which he seemed to have more of than anyone else, into his suit-jacket pocket and walking briskly out, not heeding the calls and exclamations of his friends.

After he was gone the others grinned at each other. "Drensler's excitable," said Daniels to Wayne. "You want to play?"

Wayne sat in the seat warm from Drensler's soft body.

"Samir Farris," said Daniels, nodding toward the small, dark man. "Wayne Dolan."

Wayne and Samir Farris shook hands. Up close, Farris had a handsome hooked nose, shiny black eyes behind thick glasses, and perfect teeth shown in a wide, delighted smile.

"Oh yes, yes, they told me about you. A novelist, eh? Really glad to meet you." It was somehow impossible to believe that any of this was insincere; Dr. Farris seemed often on the verge of breaking into delighted laughter, but the friendly expression in the black eyes alternated with an intermittent blankness, as if now and then complex thoughts carried him great distances, and at those moments he chewed the cuticles of his fingers nervously.

Wayne bought five dollars' worth of quarters from Daniels, and they played a few hands.

"So I never figured out exactly what it was you and that guy—" Wayne nodded toward the door "—were arguing about last night."

"We were arguing because he's an idiot," said Farris.

"He got kicked out of some religious order for having a bad temper," Daniels added. "I'm not allowed to say which."

"And now he's an atheist. I think it's revenge," said Farris, looking hopefully at Daniels.

Daniels threw two quarters into the pot.

"And he likes Ray Hall's research more than his

own," squeaked the owl-like Tom gleefully, tickled to be included in this gossip, looking searchingly into the faces of each of the other men.

"Ray Hall?"

"Raymond Hall," said Daniels. "He's the only real scientist at the Institute."

Farris laughed guiltily as if trying to suppress an uncontrollable amusement.

"What do you mean?"

"He's a Nobel winner, and he has an international reputation. If the Institute has any credibility at all, it's because of him. He gets a quarter of the annual hardware budget, on top of his government grants. Building A is all his, almost. He does molecular biology research: DNA. He's discovered the genetic basis for religion."

"He *claims* to have discovered a genetic basis for religion," said Farris. "But that's like saying you've discovered a genetic basis for believing the world is round. The fact is, there's a genetic basis for believing true propositions."

"What about this guy Edmund Carvery?" asked Wayne. "He's won a Nobel prize, and he believes in God, it seems like."

"He talked to you?" Daniels asked. They all looked at Wayne curiously.

"Yeah. Why?"

"He doesn't talk to anybody," said Daniels. "And he hasn't published since he's been here. I heard he had some kind of breakdown a couple of years ago. The rumor is that his scientific career is over, and the Administration has him here for his name."

Wayne hesitated. "I saw a Ouija board in his office."

A telephone somewhere in the lab rang ten times and quit.

"So which side are you on?" Wayne asked Daniels as

he replaced two of his cards. "You on the pro-God or anti-God team here at the Institute?"

Another phone somewhere in the laboratory started ringing.

"I better get that," said Daniels, and dodged among the tables, then started scrabbling around in the junk to find the phone.

"What kind of research do you do?" Wayne asked Farris while he was gone.

"It's something in developmental biology," said Farris vaguely, chewing the cuticle of his left little finger. His expression was deeply absent, as if the real locus of his research was another, mental dimension where no one else could follow him. "Mapping morphogenic fields, which are just a certain kind of attractor."

"He's trying to build a computer model of the soul," said Tom, studying his cards.

"Say what?"

"These mathematics," said Farris, "that biologists use to describe development, how embryos grow, for example, use 'attractors,' which are mathematical expressions describing something that guides things to their proper ends. Well, that was always thought to be the function of the soul in old times: a spiritual entity that surrounded a person or thing, guiding it. These attractors are supposed to exist in a 'vector field'; a kind of abstract mathematical realm that might possibly be like a spiritual realm, and our idea is: what if these mathematics are really describing what used to be called the soul? So we're trying to find an attractor that we can run forward beyond the final stages of life to see what comes afterward, if it's anything coherent."

"Whoa," said Wayne.

Daniels returned from his phone call. "That was

Allouette. Hall's giving the Convocation this week, and she wants to make sure I come. You should come, too," he said to Wayne. "You'll get to see the great Raymond Hall in action."

⏤

It was a hot, windless night, and he was running in the woods, the trees black clots and slashes against the grey-black of the sky. He had committed some terrible crime or escaped from prison and the police were after him, their dogs baying. He ran desperately until he came to the brink of the Lake bluff, stumbled and slid down it. The Lake washed gently on the sand, black in the moon-less night. Kicking off his shoes, he jumped into the wa-ter and swam.

Then it seemed that morning came, and the Lake had turned into a vast grey-green ocean, and he was swim-ming far out, out of sight of land, swimming up and down giant swells like hills gulping and gurgling around him, the water's cold, unknown depths beneath. And it seemed somehow that he had been swimming for days, or years even, or rather had passed some point in the ocean where time had begun all over again, his old life left behind, and he saw on the horizon a green line, which very slowly grew to the headlands of a continent, a new and utterly different land, sundered from the life he had left by impassable waters, and a fair wind blew from it, and on that wind he smelled the scent of green things growing.

⏤

He woke to a perfect summer's day. A tingling silence surrounded the beach house, and the sea smell and elec-tricity of the Lake were softened by a warm breeze and the scent of lilies. After swimming, Wayne sat in a lawn chair at the top of the bluff and worked at his laptop, pushing out of his mind the beauty of the morning, his loneliness for his children, the anxiety about his $5,000. Anyway, his dreams about the bank account number hadn't come back last night. Was that because he had—? He interrupted these thoughts for the twentieth time and went back to describing St. Clair.

It was midmorning when the boom of distant rock and roll pulled him out of the laptop. For a second he thought a car was approaching down his drive, but then he realized that the sound was coming from the house away along the bluff, his neighbors—who had moved in instead of out, apparently—and at that same second he saw, framed between gently fluttering branches, two figures walking down the beach.

They were still far off, but he could see that one had dark hair and the other blonde, and that both wore bikinis.

His new neighbors.

His heart jumped with apprehension, but the stronger force of middle-aged fear pulled him out of his chair. Bolling had said that in the fated life providential things happened. Wayne had had a feeling all along about Southwestern Michigan. Life, real life, was passing before him. He had only to stand up and grasp it. Jump this time when the portals of the numinous whirled by.

He stowed his laptop in the bedroom, and as he pulled on his damp cutoffs, the distant rock and roll coming through the window, the two girls walking up the beach, a feeling came over him as if he were a teenager again. This most recent day of sunlight might be happening 25 years ago, when rock and roll floated up the beach and bikinied girls sashayed along, and dim green shade under the bluff trees smelled of dampness and earth, and he was 18, climbing down cool flagstones, emerging onto the hot sun-blinding sand, the Lake glittering pale green.

The two girls had turned around and were walking away up the beach again. They hadn't seen him. He followed quickly, heart pounding. They were going slowly, the small surf washing around their feet; he caught up with them faster than he expected. He felt unprepared, naked, hollow-chested. They were barely fifteen feet ahead: he saw with a rush of fear and exultation that the one on the left had a long silver-gold braid that swung as she walked. The other's pageboy was an artificial purplish-auburn, sleek and lustrous as water.

"Hi," called Wayne. He tried to make his voice friendly and cheerful but it came out with a crack that he hoped was covered by the sound of the surf.

The two girls stopped and turned around in a single, quick motion.

They were very beautiful. The pageboy of the one on the right curled forward at her chin; her eyes were long and brown, her lips thin and sensitive, tanned skin freckled appealingly over her nose and cheekbones. She wore a gold thong bikini, and she was perfect: stomach flat, shoulders square, breasts round, hips slender, her whole body erect and effortlessly healthy and strong and young.

But the other one was like some kind of angel. Her deep blue eyes were like a shocking spark of electric ocean in her beautiful, pale, innocent face. The Lake seemed to fade to a cardboard counterfeit of water behind her, as if within her the sound of the ocean thrummed and its fresh wind blew. Her taut body was as perfect as the pageboy girl's but more beautiful because more unconscious, as if unaware of its beauty, and the unconsciousness of it seemed to have crept up into the ocean eyes, as if she were a force of nature, or as if from too much being looked at she had gone unconscious to hide herself. She was unknowing and beautiful, full of ocean, her body ivory and silver, an angel-pale spirit, but full of the awful unconscious grace of an animal.

The silky girl.

The two of them stood and looked at Wayne without a word and without moving, not afraid or startled, but watchful.

"Hi," he said, breathing hard, as if he had been running.

They looked at him without a word.

"I—I'm your neighbor from down the beach," he panted. "I mean up the bluff." He pointed behind him foolishly.

Neither of them moved or said a word. Their looks were flat, without either friendliness or anger, as if they were waiting for him to finish.

"I—I thought I would come down and say hello," he stuttered.

Their eyes had the seeing blankness you use on the wino panhandler at the subway.

"Did you—just move in?" he asked, cudgeling his brain for conversation.

No reaction.

"I'm Wayne." He held out his hand, taking half a step forward.

Not a flicker.

Humiliation suddenly choked him, stronger than he would have thought possible, as if the two of them were beating him savagely, though their expressions didn't change in the least.

"Well," he panted, "I guess I'll go back."

He turned around. His body felt bent over, as if he couldn't straighten it. When he looked back after a few steps, the two young women were walking up the beach again just as before, erect and beautiful, not even bothering to glance back.

—

When in doubt, work on the book, had always been his motto. And he wasn't really in doubt now: he needed to work. It was no slam on him that those two castrating bitches had blown him off without a word: who knew where people like that came from or what their story was. There was no need to worry about it; it was no reflection on his attractiveness or self-confidence or age, because their level of rudeness had gone way beyond anything that could be attributable to any of those things. The episode had even given him a grim feeling of satisfaction: he had weathered it; it hadn't hurt him. He would keep trying, keep putting himself in harm's way until he came up lucky. He was finally putting into practice the words of the philosopher Wayne Gretzky: "A hundred percent of the shots you don't take don't go in." Work on the book would reboot him, center him, drain out excess bile and phlegm, so that later he could go down to the St. Clair bars and try again.

But as the day went on a perverse sense of oppression visited him. He kept trying to immerse himself in the book but the feeling kept creeping back, as if the excess bile and phlegm hadn't all been drained out, as if he hadn't survived the castrating bitches as unscathed as he had thought. His mood had gone sour, self-flagellating. He started to obsess about his $5,000. The Farmers' & Merchants' Bank hadn't called him yet. Could it be that his money was gone? Had he actually done something so stupid? With his child-support payments and the rent on his Mid-Atlantic apartment he would be out of money soon enough, long before the advance on his next book, if any. Was it possible that there actually *was* an account number 30162415, and that whoever owned it wouldn't report $5,000 showing up from nowhere? Should he call right away and say that he had made an error? Would he be able to get his money back? But wouldn't that ruin the story value of what he had done—wouldn't even *worrying* about it ruin the story value, the intrepid questing hero sniveling about his child-support payments and rent?

The most important thing with the book was to get at the truth, he lectured himself. And the truth was that he wasn't the type to fork over $5,000 on a whim of his unconscious, even if it coincidentally resembled some historical Indian superstition. Maybe that was why he had never been successful with women: they smelled his caution and retentiveness—he wasn't the self-destructive, reckless type who could make them lose control, overmaster their instinctive female prudence, which was what everyone wanted in this tamed, Disneyfied, 401(k) world. Maybe that was also why he had never been successful as a writer: he didn't have the wildness it took to break new ground, contradict everything that had gone before, make something entirely new. He might have had it once, in his twenties, when he was too confused to put it to any use, but that was over. He was in his forties now, a cautious, slightly seedy middle-aged man, but without a family or savings or a respectable job, any of the things middle-aged men had that to some extent justified their dull, retentive caution. And that was the protagonist of his book about the Deriwelle Institute for the Technological Study of Religion; that was him.

He felt like standing up and throwing his laptop off the bluff, but he didn't. He clutched it instead, trying to make words come out of his fingers. Middle-age panic, which cannot be described to others, was creeping over him. He was still attractive and hunky, though greying around the edges perhaps. But in a few more years he would be down at the heels; the caution and slight seediness were just the thin end of the wedge. It was now or never to get some kind of life. The urge came over him to drive right now to St. Clair, go out on the public beaches where the bikinied girls sunned, or into the bars where the tanned, laughing tourist kids came for lunch, hungry from swimming and playing volleyball, the latest rock thumping in their jalopies and convertibles, their unconscious, beautiful bodies surrounded by the air and electricity of the Lake—

But he clung to the laptop, trying to make words come out of his fingers. He knew what writing novels was. He had managed to write five only by resisting all temptations except those associated with the laptop, sitting in his room and writing while he and Ann still lived together, hearing now and then vaguely through the door the sound of his children's sweet voices, but then silence.

And what was it all in aid of, he wondered. In his twenties he had imagined that while still young he would be famous and inwardly illumined, finding through his writing the secret door to the numenal world. But experience had turned those fantasies to dust, and now it seemed that all that was left was the labor, the daily work on his current book, whatever tinny, two-dimensional representation of reality he managed to cudgel out of his exhausted brain. It was like chasing one of those little dust whirlwinds that blow around on the sidewalk before a storm, around and around in tightening circles, chasing dust around and around until he too became dust. Meanwhile his children were growing up without him, he left behind, chasing dust round and round in tightening circles, as if perhaps just one more skillful twist, one more vigorous leap might get him in range, to finally catch it, finally be transformed into the young, wealthy literary lion and illumined sage of his early fantasies.

He was an addict, he realized; but his addiction was to dust, to nullitude, without even the momentary ecstasy of the normal, animal addictions. He would sit and struggle with his laptop, hunched over its little pale screen while this beautiful day lived and died, never to return, while he grew beyond the age where he could ever hope to have a lover, while his children grew up, forgetting him, while life slipped by, while empty Christmases came and went.

No wonder he was so easily preyed upon by delusions like the dream Indian offering a magic way out. Even now he could feel himself foolishly hoping it had not all been a fantasy—hoping not intrepidly, but desperately.

6

That evening the hissing of sprinklers came with preter-natural clarity in the soft, still air on the vast lawns of the Deriwelle Institute, a hot orange glow above the forest trees fading into dusk.

The Convocation Hall was the round building two hundred yards from Building B. Wayne had come early for the local color; he approached the half-grassy, half-craggy hill along an empty sidewalk. Close up the hall was high and domed, with decorative pilasters between tall windows. It had a slightly unreal, larger-than-life air to it, like a movie set. What looked like geomantic signs were carved into the stone arch above the huge front doors. Inside was a high-ceilinged reception room where two men in white tuxedos were setting up glasses and bottles on a long table. Beyond that was an auditorium with several hundred plush seats descending to a stage with a podium and projection screen. Dark blue curtains were drawn back from the tall windows. The ceiling rose to skylights and a high dome painted a velvety blue-black with tiny silver dots like stars. Around the dome's edges more geomantic characters were painted in gold, their bold, garish, runic shapes giving the place a slightly barbaric feel. More of Manson McDuck Deriwelle's bequest conditions, Wayne guessed. No wonder the Institute didn't have more heavy-hitter scientists, despite the brisk money they were paying.

Soon the distinguished audience began to arrive, and by ten minutes to the hour the place was alive with a low, excited hum, like before a new Star Wars movie, except that the program said this was Dr. Raymond Hall, Nobel Laureate and Past Francis Crick Distinguished Chair of Evolutionary and Molecular Biology at Harvard University, formerly of Princeton's Institute for Advanced Study and Cold Spring Harbor Laboratory, giving a Non-Technical Presentation for the Layman on His Research into the Genomic Basis of Religion. Samir Farris, Ray Daniels, Daniels' assistant Tom, and Eric Drensler sauntered down to center front seats just below the podium. Maureen Allison and Brad Tollaksen waved from across the amphitheater, where they were sitting next to an old woman whose cigarette gave off a lazy column of smoke next to the NO SMOKING sign.

Evening blue showed through the skylights, but as the natural light faded indirect lights around the walls gradually brightened, giving the place a plush, bluish glow like a high-class theater. Alan Rilfsbane and old Dr. Florisbund came in, conducting a couple of distinguished-looking individuals to whom Rilfsbane seemed to be talking nonstop, waving one hand gracefully and expansively.

Down the aisle now came half a dozen people, walking self-importantly in a rough cordon almost like security guards: three men and two women around a large man with glasses who carried some loose papers. The large man climbed up to the podium and tapped the microphone, eliciting huge thumps from overhead.

Wayne had taken a seat level with the podium and 25 feet away, so he was able to study Dr. Raymond Hall closely. Hall was perhaps in his mid or late 50s, wearing a dark suit of conservative cut, six-one and well built but getting thick-waisted, his large face smooth and unlined, dark hair neatly barbered. He had the smiling charisma of an important political figure, and his eyes behind large glasses showed a quirk of sardonic humor; yet at the same time it seemed to Wayne that there was a heaviness about him, as if he had had to face some unpleasant truths about life.

The conversation in the amphitheater subsided to a low hum. Hall leaned toward the microphone: "I haven't done this since my last teaching job. I'd hoped I had escaped from all that."

There was some laughter and a scattering of heartfelt applause.

"In fact, my natural trepidation at presenting my research to so sophisticated an audience was counter balanced only by my conditioned aversion to keeping you waiting longer than the grace period allowable for a full professor."

More laughter.

"I've been asked to give a talk on the research I've been privileged to carry out with support from NIH, the National Science Foundation, and the MacArthur Foundation, but mainly with facilities and resources provided by the Deriwelle Institute itself, for which I feel profoundly grateful. I can truthfully say that without the Institute's patronage—and without the assistance and creativity of many who are here tonight—I would never have been able to do this work. I hope the results will be considered some modest payback for your generous support."

There was an introductory pause. Words sprang up behind him on the big overhead screen: "Localization of Genomic Markers for Temporal Lobe 'Religion Centers' on the Long Arm of Human Chromosome 17." The footlights went dim.

"Ladies and gentlemen, I would like to present evidence that the gene governing the activation of the 'God module' area in the frontotemporal lobes is located on the long arm of human chromosome 17, more specifically at q20-21. The gene appears to work by governing the activation threshold of neurons via expression of serotonin and norepinephrine receptors. Using primate models, our research shows that the so-called God module area does indeed appear to condition religious belief and experience."

A familiar diagram appeared on the screen, like a cross between a cauliflower and a bicycle helmet. An arrow bearing the legend "Temporal Lobes" pointed to a bulb low down on the side. A crosshatched region toward the end of the bulb was labeled "God module."

"It has long been suspected that the predisposition to religion has a physiological basis, given its near universality in the human species. Even today, when scientific materialism has become the dominant intellectual paradigm, about 95 percent of the world's people are adherents to some religion, with 30 percent reporting mystical or religious experiences. This is true even in scientifically advanced countries like the United States. As far as we can tell, this 95 percent adherence level has remained constant throughout history, and our species appears always to have practiced religious observances. For example, around 60,000 years ago Neanderthal men buried their dead with flowers, and by 25,000 years ago Cro-Magnon humans had already devised elaborate forms of worship.

"Other evidence for a biological basis for religion comes from observations of certain brain disorders, which have among their symptoms a condition called 'hyper-religiosity,' an unusually intensified preoccupation with religion. The disorder best known to cause this is temporal lobe epilepsy, or TLE, which is basically an overstimulation of the neurons in the brain's temporal lobe. Building on this fact, Dr. Michael Persinger of Laurentian University in Ontario conducted studies during the 1980s showing that persons professing deep religious faith or claiming to have had mystical experiences often have other traits suggesting mild forms of TLE. His conclusion is that intense religious feelings and experiences are associated with epileptoid activity that overstimulates the temporal lobes. Similarly, Dr. Vilayanur Ramachandran at the University of California showed religious stimuli to intensely religious persons and TLE hyper-religious subjects, and used EEG measurements to localize the brain site activated in response: this was the frontal portion of the temporal lobes. Dr. Ramachandran has dubbed this area the 'God module'; he notes that it exists in everyone, but is simply abnormally stimulated in TLE by overfiring of neurons in the temporal lobes. Thus, in most of the religious but nonepileptic 95 percent of the population the module is still active, but simply at a lower level.

"Finally, Dr. Andrew Newberg at the University of Pennsylvania Medical School used high-resolution PET and SPECT blood flow maps to confirm that brain tissue in the 'God module' area fires intensely during religious episodes.

"So by the mid-1990s science had developed good evidence concerning what parts of the brain are responsible for religious belief. At roughly the same time, other research was suggesting the genetic underpinnings of these 'religious' brain structures. Wilhelmsen-Lynch Disease researchers, using standard linkage analysis, found that a chromosomal mutation at 17q21-q22 interfered with regulation of neurons in the frontal portion of the temporal lobes, resulting in hyperreligiosity. Here, then, was evidence that somewhere in the chromosomal region 17q21-q22 a regulatory factor was coded governing activation of the neurons in the 'God module.'

"Subsequently, we at the Institute made our own contribution. These were primate studies aimed at illuminating the activity of the religion module in humans.

"It is well-known that animals can display 'religious' behavior when randomly reinforced. For example, if pigeons are put in Skinner boxes and given random rewards in the form of food pellets, they develop ritualistic bobbing and weaving motions, as though trying to will the higher powers to deliver good fortune. More advanced protoreligious behavior has been observed by Goodall and Kohler in chimpanzees.

"Now, chimpanzees are only about 30 times more genetically dissimilar from human beings than white Europeans, black Africans, and Japanese are from each other, so they are a good model for investigating human behavior. Many of you may recall the three years during which Building A was equipped as a veritable zoo, with approximately 90 chimps participating in our experiments. I am sure that the Institute remembers the expense, which, however, it bore without complaint.

"In our experiments, we surgically inserted into the skulls of a test group of chimpanzees devices which, at random intervals, injected a mixture of morphine and psilocybin into their brains, a combination creating powerful feelings of peace together with religioform hallucinations and affect.

"By the end of six months, these chimpanzees had

evolved a set of ritual behaviors, apparently in response to the 'mystical' experiences provided to them. The details of the rituals are a fascinating subject in themselves, and my colleague Dr. Chu is preparing a series of papers on them; however, for our purposes it will suffice to observe that the rituals appeared calculated to propitiate or motivate whatever invisible powers were responsible for the 'mystical' experiences. PET and SPECT scans of the brains of the chimps when involved in their rituals showed intense firing patterns in an area of the primate brain roughly equivalent to the human temporal lobes." A lowbrow version of the cauliflower/bicycle helmet diagram now appeared on the screen, with a tiny patch low down colored red.

"Even more significant was what occurred when we allowed the altered chimps and a control group of intact chimps to mingle, combining their living facilities. Instead of the control group diluting the ritual practices of the altered group, many of them joined it, becoming, without any surgical modification, just as 'religious' as their cohorts. It was as if the altered group had 'converted' these nonaltered chimpanzees to their new 'religion.' And to top it off, these nonaltered 'religious' cohorts exhibited the same brain-activation patterns as the altered chimps during their participation in the rituals. In effect we appeared to have created a self-sustaining chimpanzee 'religion' using the simplest of methods."

Hall paused and drank water, as if to give the significance of his remarks a chance to sink in.

"It now remained only to identify the genes coding for the activity of this brain region. We removed tissue from the chimpanzee analogue of the 'God module' and used standard gene-engineering techniques to identify the DNA sequences expressed during the chimps' religious rituals."

Complicated figures and flow charts followed each other on the screen.

"We know that neurons in this part of the brain are switched 'on' and 'off' by serotonin and norepinephrine receptors. Now that we had identified the unique DNA codes in the chimpanzees' 'God modules,' we could use these codes as 'tags,' and engineer a gene producing proteins that switched 'off' the serotonin and norepinephrine receptors in the 'tagged' cells only." The accompanying slide showed a bulgy black molecule bumping aside a wimpy purple. "Thus, we now had a gene that would target 'God module' neurons, blocking their activation without injuring them in any way.

"We packaged this gene into a monkey retrovirus called SV40 and infected our 'religious' chimps. We predicted that the modified SV40 would graft our switch-off gene into the chimps' neurons, permanently shutting down their 'God modules.' And sure enough, the chimps infected with our 'God module neutralizing factor,' or GMNF, showed significant and progressive reductions in their religious behavior.

"The final stage of our research was to determine whether deactivation of the chimpanzees' 'God modules' resulted in any mental deficits or deterioration. To do this we gave our chimps a battery of tests. To our surprise, the GMNF-infected chimps did *better* on the tests than the nonaltered control group, and also did better on the tests than they themselves had done before being infected. The conclusion was inescapable that *genetic deactivation of the chimpanzee analogue of the human 'God module' had produced a significant improvement on tests involving the chimps' highest cerebral functioning.*"

Hall drank some water. The auditorium was dead silent in the dark.

"You can probably guess the rest of the story," he went on, though Wayne couldn't, not even vaguely. "We were fortunate to have access to the research team working on human Wilhelmsen-Lynch Disease. We synthesized DNA probes based on our chimpanzee sequences and used them in *in situ* hybridization at low stringency on chromosome 17q in samples of temporal lobe 'God module' brain tissue from human subjects who had died of WLD. The probes hybridized even at low temperature. We sequenced the portion of the chromosome where our probes had hybridized, and determined that the human genes for the 'God module' are similar to those of chimpanzees." The members of the audience around Wayne were watching Hall with grave attention, as if they understood exactly what he was talking about.

A slide with three bullets came up on the screen.

"So, what are our conclusions from this research?" Hall's arm stretched out, its silhouette indicating each bullet in turn. "First, that a well-defined cortical area in the frontal portion of the temporal lobes constitutes the physiological substrate for human religious behavior. Second, that the genetic coding for this cortical area is located on the long arm of chromosome 17, and can probably be manipulated through control of the expression of this gene or set of genes. And third, that deactivation of this cortical area, at least in chimpanzees, does not degrade, but on the contrary appears to enhance higher cerebral functioning.

"If anyone has questions, I would be glad to answer them now."

The lights came up, and, after a breathless second, the audience burst into prolonged applause. Wayne glanced across the auditorium at Daniels, Farris, and Drensler.

Drensler was applauding thunderously; Daniels was clapping politely; Farris sat without moving.

Hall looked around with a smile and drank water. The applause subsided finally, and was replaced by the hum of voices and the rustling of people who had sat still too long shifting in their chairs. While they were thus engaged, a skinny young man with a serious expression and a notebook stood up and said something that was lost in the general noise, which quickly subsided to let him say it again: "Jason Riverdale of the *St. Clair Post-Dispatch*. I was wondering, Dr. Hall, if you could give a clarification for the layman. Are you saying you've proved that religion is an illusion?"

There was a ripple of appreciative laughter and a small smattering of applause. The young man looked around with a grin.

Raymond Hall smiled indulgently. "Not at all."

"Can you clarify that for me, sir? Didn't you say that religion is a result of activity in part of the brain—?"

"There are two points here," Hall said. "First, religion has played a very important role in human evolution. Modern sociobiology teaches that religion was promoted by natural selection as a way of improving social cohesion and psychically strengthening believers against the fear of mortality. Primitive societies in which religious belief was widespread were more robust, gaining a reproductive advantage over nonreligious societies. So religion has been a very important factor in the fitness of the human species.

"Second, those who wish to square their religious faith with the results of our research can take comfort in the fact that perceptions of real things in the real world *always* take place via activation of parts of the brain. Thus, they would argue, the 'God module' is simply the part of the brain that is activated in perception of spiritual things. Yes. Dr. Drensler."

Drensler had vigorously raised his hand as Hall finished his answer.

"Your response to the distinguished representative of the press is certainly literally true as far as it goes," Drensler said. "Religious groups will certainly *take comfort* in your perceptual argument. But if I remember my brain physiology, the temporal lobe region you're talking about is remote from any of the brain's perceptual areas; in fact, it's smack in the middle of tertiary association cortex, isn't it, where thinking and fantasy occur? And my second point is, surely religious cognition should be a whole-brain phenomenon, if it is indeed the highest human activity, as is sometimes claimed. But instead, the research you've presented teaches us that it is actually relegated to a localized area of an archaic portion of the brain, like other powerful, primitive urges such as sex, aggression, and so on."

Hall looked uncomfortable, then smiled in spite of himself in response to a ripple of laughter through the auditorium. He chose his words carefully. "Leaving aside the value-laden descriptors, I can say that your physiological understanding agrees with my own. Dr. Helios." He pointed up toward the top of the auditorium before Drensler could follow up.

Dr. Helios was the chain-smoking old woman next to Maureen Allison and Brad Tollaksen, and who Wayne now remembered was Brad's boss. Her voice was dry and cracked, as if the cigarette smoke didn't agree with her. "Call me Jean." She had a faint Southwestern drawl.

"Jean," Hall corrected himself, nodding courteously.

"I'm just as interested as Dr. Drensler in flushing you out a little more. You've given us your experimental results and some conclusions that any undergraduate could draw. But what do you think is behind all this? What does your research say about human nature? About religion?"

"Well, I'm a scientist, not a theologian, so such speculations—"

"Bullshit," Dr. Helios' scratchy voice was even, without rancor. "I hereby bestow on you the title of theologian." Laughter from the audience. "No one who does years of research on religion does it without wondering what it means. I want to know what your personal conclusions are, not the journal-abstract pablum."

"Could you be a little more specific in your question?" Hall asked with courteous timidity, drawing more laughter.

"OK, let's start with the origin of the 'God module,' " said Helios, smoke dribbling from her mouth. "I understand the argument as to why such a structure would be selected for once it arose. But a brain structure arising by random mutation that predisposes one to believe in religion? That's like proposing a brain mutation that makes one believe in communism or the general theory of relativity, isn't it?"

"No, I don't think so," said Hall. "It's an excellent point, but I believe there is a plausible explanation for the evolution of the 'God module' based merely on the general evolution of the brain. Indeed, it may have been inevitable that nervous systems evolving along the lines taken by the human brain would evolve a 'God module' or something like it."

Helios waved her cigarette and nodded approvingly, signaling him to proceed.

"Two of the features of human intelligence that have given our species its enormous fitness advantage are first, our ability to abstract and generalize, and second, our obsession with meaning and pattern. The first quality, abstract thinking, allows us to group things into classes, and to think about large systems rather than just whatever happens to be in front of us. In fact, our ability to generalize is so powerful that we are even able to think about the concept of 'everything,' and to devise concepts like unified field theories to try to explain 'everything.' Now, this abstract thinking function is localized in the frontal portion of the brain. It is believed that one of our ancient ancestors underwent a mutation increasing the size of his frontal lobes, and the abstract-thinking ability this bestowed created a survival advantage so powerful that his offspring have inherited the Earth.

"As for the second ability, the drive to find pattern and meaning, this is known to be localized in the temporal lobes and the limbic system inside them. Again, this is a brain development resulting from some ancestral mutation, which bestows a powerful survival advantage because a compulsion to discover pattern and meaning results in the ability to control the environment once its underlying rules are discovered. This compulsion is the impetus for modern science and technology, which, again, have made us masters of the Earth.

"So far I have said nothing controversial. But what happens when these two characteristics collide in the brain, which I believe they have done, very literally? The brain evolves by mutation, just like every other part of the body, and one function may very well overlap with another, quite by chance, like speech and taste overlapping in the tongue. What happens if the brain tissue with the drive to generalize, to look at things as a whole, overlaps with the tissue obsessed with meaning and pattern? This overlap would create brain tissue functionally driven to find the meaning of things as a whole, global meaning, we may wish to call it. The Meaning of Everything; the Meaning of the Universe. This is religion. This is what all the religions have in common, whether they postulate a single god or many gods or no god, an afterlife or no afterlife, whatever their particular moral rules and metaphysical teachings. The one thing they all have in common is a belief that the universe, everything that happens, is not random or senseless—it has a deeper meaning. Everything Has a Meaning is the motto of the religious man. Global meaning—it may be hidden, may be incomprehensible to the human mind, but it is there. The adherence to this belief in the absence of any evidence—in fact, in the face of overwhelming evidence to the contrary—this is the hallmark of religion; it is also the hallmark of a genetically programmed disposition.

"And where in the brain would such an overlap of abstract-thinking neural tissue and meaning-seeking neural tissue take place? As I have mentioned, abstract thinking is localized in the frontal region and meaning is localized in the temporal region. What about the frontotemporal region, the frontal portion of the temporal lobes? This is where we would expect such an overlap to take place, since it is at the juncture of these two specialized areas. And, of course, this is just where Ramachandran's 'God module' area has been found."

There was a murmur from the audience, rising to enthusiastic applause.

"Fabulous. You're doing better now," said Jean Helios when the applause died down. "I knew there was something behind all the recombinant DNA mumbo jumbo. But I'll tell you what's wrong with it." She took a strong drag on her cigarette and dribbled out smoke as she talked. "The area of the temporal lobes you're talking about. Dr. Drensler is giving it short shrift: tertiary association cortex is where all the inputs from every part of the brain come together and get processed, so in fact it can be viewed as the 'highest' part of the brain, hierarchically. But Goldsmith and others have demonstrated that the frontotemporal region shows a characteristic pattern of heavy stripes of dopamine receptors. Now, typically dopamine receptors are inhibitory rather than excitatory. If your structural argument is valid, it looks to me like you've found a region that inhibits religious perceptions rather than vice versa."

"Yet that appears contrary to the experimental evidence," said Hall. "Overstimulation of these areas in TLE causes hyperreligiousity, for example."

"Yet atrophy of the same areas in WLD also causes hyperreligiousity."

"Well, but remember the primate studies—"

"You're talking about experiments on monkeys, eh!" came a voice from low down in the amphitheater. Samir Farris was waving his hand indignantly. "I object to the presumption that this has anything to do with human functioning. And, 'Everything Makes Sense' is the motto not only of the religious man, but also of the scientific man. The postulation that Everything Makes Sense is the foundation of our science. If the scientist can work from that assumption, why can't the religious man? This is an attack on religion based on a philosophical sleight of hand! The same modes of reasoning used by science are being held up to ridicule in a religious context!"

"I certainly don't mean to attack religion, Dr. Farris," said Hall. "However, I think the scientific and religious modes of reasoning are really quite different. Science focuses on specific, limited patterns within rigorous rules of reasoning—"

"That's not true," interjected Dr. Farris. "You yourself mentioned the unified field theories—"

"Let the man talk!" Eric Drensler said angrily from

three seats away. "This is a scientific meeting, not a free-for-all!"

"I'm just pointing out—" Hall said.

"What you're asking us to do is accept your characterization of *human* religion based on some monkey experiments that can never be tried on humans—"

"But that's where you're wrong, Samir!" Drensler yelled. "Didn't you hear him? He's isolated the regulatory genes that control the human 'God module.' It's a simple matter to package them into a human retrovirus to turn off the human temporal-lobe area that gives rise to religion. We *can* do the experiment—"

"It'll never happen! The government isn't going to let you cause viral brain damage in humans to test your—!"

"You refuse to put your beliefs to the test of science! You're using bureaucratic excuses to hold back science—!"

——

A Reception Following the Lecture was held in the big anteroom outside the auditorium, now brightly lit by chandeliers and filled with the hum of a hundred voices and the clink of glasses. Wayne stood shyly in a large group surrounding Raymond Hall, who held a glass of some masculine brown liquid and smiled politely and with intermediate attention at the babbling person ahead of Wayne, radiating charisma, patience, and courtesy.

The babbling person finally left off, and it was Wayne's turn. He stepped forward nervously and said: "Dr. Hall."

Hall gave him a bright, courteous smile. His hand was large and solid, but his shake was surprisingly light, as if he didn't want to touch you too much.

"I'm a guest here at the Institute."

"Welcome," said Hall. "I trust you don't find us too tedious?"

"Not at all. I'm a writer actually."

"Ah." Polite and noncommittal. The large, clear brown eyes behind the glasses rested alertly on Wayne, making him feel flattered and also that he shouldn't waste the famous man's time.

"Yes. I'm writing a book about the Institute."

"Ah, wonderful."

"I was fascinated by your talk tonight, with its implications for religion and so forth. I was wondering, it would be a great help to me to have a few minutes of your time to ask you some questions. Would it be possible for me to do a short interview?—not interview, really," he stumbled on when he saw that the word seemed to pain Hall, "more just a discussion of your ideas. Sometime. Not now, of course," he finished stupidly.

Hall's bright smile stayed on automatic. "I'm afraid my schedule is terrible for the next few months," he said politely. "I really doubt it would be possible."

"It would only take half an hour." Wayne was aware that other supplicants were pressing around him for a chance to talk to the big laureate.

"I'm afraid—But I'm here now; is there anything I could—?"

Wayne cudgeled his brain. He could see Hall's eyes beginning to withdraw, move politely to the next appealing face at Wayne's elbow. "Well—well, do you believe in God?" he stammered desperately, unable to think of anything else, and anyway it was what he really wanted to know.

"No, I do not myself," said Hall, almost too earnestly, "though I respect those who do. Some of the finest scientists of my acquaintance are religious men, and I understand and value the perspective they bring to our discipline." He looked at Wayne with earnest seriousness for just long enough to be credible, then put his hand out again. His handshake this time ended in a subtle gesture of disengagement: a small extension of the arm and release of Wayne's hand with all his fingers splayed out. He was now turning his smiling, polite attention to the next person. Wayne backed up in embarrassment and confusion, the person slotting in front of him and beginning to talk in a high, elaborately casual singsong.

7

Out in the warm, cricket-trilled night the lights of the Institute glowed yellow over the vague contours of dark lawn and trees. Wayne walked along the sidewalk behind some scientists who were laughing and talking as if they had been to a party. His short talk with Hall had left him feeling deflated, foolish, small, like an hysterical fan wasting the time of a celebrity. The moment he opened the door of his old Honda, it occurred to him to wonder also about Hall's lecture.

The sense that everything was tied into some greater pattern, some higher meaning, was an illusion, an accident of neural architecture, was what Hall had said, finally. This soft night, his divorce, his children growing up without him, he growing old without them, his struggles with his books, the silky girl—no higher meaning.

He drove home, trying to decipher a numbness that had settled into his chest. Why should this bother him now? Scientific materialism had been around for a century and a half; he had learned it in school. Had it just come home to him in his sober middle age what it really meant?

Lying in bed later he found himself listening attentively to the slow wash of the surf in the gentle air. No higher meaning. His life an infinitesimal spark of light in an infinite darkness, so small in comparison that it was essentially nonexistent, he was essentially already dead.

—

After that the night passed fitfully, Wayne never fully waking but riding on surges of feeling—sorrow, anger, regret—that made him toss and turn, sometimes gasp for breath. After a seeming eternity this passed, and he sank down, deep, deep down, into the paralysis of deep, dark sleep, and in that subterranean darkness he had another dream.

It seemed a long, deep dream; the profoundest dream he had ever had. In it the Indian in the blue-green reception room explained everything. He sat in the chair on the other side of the little table and explained to Wayne the meaning of life, what had gone wrong and where it was leading, explained carefully to him the mechanics of what had been lost and why, and how to get back; and he promised to help him. It was all very simple and made perfect sense, yet it was very, very profound, satisfying, and self-evidently correct. And when Wayne woke in the bright, damp morning, shafts of early sunlight making faint rays in the humidity and sparkling in dew on the lawn, the air smelling like the morning of a sea-journey, he was filled with a feeling that seemed to come back to him through long years of memory, though from when he couldn't remember. It seemed the opposite of the feeling he had fallen asleep with, as if his sleep had been a mirror, reflecting him into a different world. His chest was bursting with warm excitement like youth and hope and the knowledge that anything was possible. The path to the fated life, perhaps even to the far green continent, was open. It was all just a matter of knowledge, and now the knowledge had been given to him. It had all been *real*, the dreams at Shaman's Mound, the dreams of the account number, the $5,000. It was a miracle, he told himself as he sat up in bed, rubbing his eyes, and incredibly it had happened to him, Wayne Dolan. His life was going to start over again. It wasn't too late. He had the strength to do what was needed, and the Indian, incredibly, in exchange for the $5,000, was going to help him.

He cast his mind back to the dream, to savor it, hold it in his consciousness like a jewel, to say to himself again the words that still seemed to be ringing in his auditory cortex, the last words the Indian had said just a minute ago before he woke up, and which summed up the whole teaching and wisdom of the dream. He quieted his mind, quieted his excitement with an effort, let the memory well up in him.

"Life is like an onion."

Yes, that was it. It was so deep, summarizing in just a handful of words everything the Indian had told him—

But—

A doubt hit him. He was just now coming awake, he realized: his waking up a minute ago had been a dream as well, or a half-dream, though the morning out the window looked just as he had seen it. So perhaps he had been both dreaming and looking out the window at the same time somehow. But as waking came into his mind, the sinuous, feeling-soaked, antinomian logic of dreams receding, "Life is like an onion" sounded rather less profound. He must have gotten it wrong: what the Indian had told him was intensely important and sensible. He cast his mind back again to retrieve it.

"Life is like an onion."

Yes, that was what the Indian had said: it still rang in

his ears, as if he had just finished hearing the Indian's strong, gravelly voice.

A chill began to creep through the bright, healing gladness. Of course, sometimes dreams that seemed profound and rational were completely senseless when you woke up—

But this was the antidote to his whole wasted life, his divorce, the loss of his children, his lousy books, cheap fantasies, his fear of women, to all the science that proved there was no God and no deeper meaning. Wasn't it? His memory of the dream was fading now; he had the image of the Indian sitting in the plastic chair, his inscrutable face, powerful nose, string tie—but the rest was hazy. All he could remember now of what the Indian had said was "Life is like an onion."

He lay back on his pillows, the cynicism of modern life coming to his aid, like a blank, grey, humorous wall coming down to shut out the pain of disillusionment, of having his deep, numinous dream proved vacuous. At least he could laugh at himself. And he could put it in his book; he had had a dream that explained everything, redeemed everything, and its message was: "Life is like an onion."

In a minute he got out of bed, feeling grimly cheerful. It was real life distilled into a short episode. A metaphor or something for the book. Paradise lost.

He threw on clothes and went downstairs to the kitchen. "Life is like an onion." That was a good one. The dream had almost completely gone now, the wall of humorous cynicism, the antidote to pain, also shutting out the feeling of numen, the awe and credulity that were the dream's natural habitat, and without which it dried up and died like a fish out of water. The sunlight out the windows had changed subtly too; it had a tired look now, as if a darkness had crept into the pure, humid brightness of it, as if Wayne's eyes were darkened rooms out of which he saw the sunlight through a narrow chink in a curtain.

The darkness of depression, he thought; the penalty for getting off your medication of cynicism, for letting your psychic blood sugar get out of control, letting yourself get picked up so you could be dropped. Like falling in love with a beautiful woman you know is going to break your heart. He got cornflakes from the kitchen cupboard, milk from the refrigerator. Or maybe it was the darkness of middle age, the deep fatigue of living, a fatigue that made you sometimes understand why people died: they just got tired in the end, very, very tired, and decided to lie down and chuck it.

He tried to shake off the feeling. He was a novelist, after all, and a novelist was a hero; this was grist for his mill. A metaphor or something. He sprinkled sugar on his cornflakes. But before he could get the first spoonful of the ambrosia to his mouth, words came into his mind, clear as day now.

"The world is like an onion."

Yes, that was it—that was exactly it: not "Life is like an onion." And now that the exact, accurate rendition of what the Indian had told him came into his mind, it seemed to draw after it other words: "Sometimes we cross boundaries, enter into another skin of the onion—another world, superficially like this one, but not the same." The words were in the Indian's strong, gravelly voice; he remembered them suddenly from the dream, and how the Indian had looked at him steadily and seriously.

Wayne put the spoon of cornflakes back into the bowl. But it was no good; he couldn't remember any more. His grasping consciousness just seemed to send the dream-substance whirling away like handfuls of mist.

But as he was rinsing his bowl and spoon at the sink

another fragment in the Indian's voice came back to him. "—most important—the interpenetration of dreams and waking—"

———

The Building B guard had now seen Wayne enough times that he buzzed open the door and waved him through with a bored look. When Maureen Allison answered his knock in her lab coat she looked surprised for a moment, but then smiled.

"Sorry, I should have called," said Wayne. "Is Dr. Burschevsky in? He said I could come talk to him."

"He's just out of the tank," she said. "He's been in since before dawn. He's on the patio recording his experiences." She looked curiously at Wayne's urgent face. "Shall I tell him you want to interview him for your book?"

"Well—yes."

"I'll go see." She went into the back room. A couple of minutes later she reappeared and beckoned.

The Sensory Reorientation machine looked potent and alive this morning, the transparent tank half-full of water, LCDs and dials lit, the big room full of the subtle ionic smell of electronic equipment. A door was open at the rear, and bright sunlight and the singing of birds came through it. Maureen led Wayne outside. There was a flagstone patio in a small wild garden surrounded by tall, untrimmed hedges and young trees. Dr. Adam Burschevsky sat in a cast-iron garden chair wearing a long white bathrobe, his long silver hair drying on his shoulders, his patrician face relaxed and almost sleepy, taking in the sunlight, yet in an odd way focused, as if he was so intelligent that even in utter restfulness he could debate a whole roomful of ordinary people and win.

"Mr. Dolan," he said as Wayne came out onto the patio, making a motion as if to stand up, but instead just leaning forward slightly and putting out his long, intelligent hand. Wayne shook it. "What a pleasant surprise." He gave his warm smile.

"Is now a good time?" asked Wayne. "I guess you've been up since—"

"Perfect. I never feel better than when I come out of the tank. It's one of the benefits of meditation, you know. No one would want to become enlightened if it didn't feel so good." His smile was luminous and kind. He motioned Wayne to a chair. Maureen excused herself and went back in to finish shutting down the machine. "Maureen says you want to talk to me about my work."

"Well—yes. I hope it's no trouble." He imagined that if he let Burschevsky talk he would be able to slip in his questions about his dreams gracefully. Burschevsky, the renowned mysticism researcher, should know what to make of them if anyone did.

Burschevsky put his hands in the pockets of his robe. "Not at all. In fact, I welcome the publicity. Never believe a scientist who claims to be disinterested in his results. Scientists are generally pimply, anal-retentive kids who never get any dates, so they get Ph.D.'s instead, and then get their psychic income sneering at challenges to the status quo of which they are now the high priests. One such challenge is my own crusade to discredit this wrong-headed approach to science called 'physicalism': the notion that everything has some physical explanation." He leaned back comfortably in his chair.

"For example, the idea that consciousness can be explained as some property of matter. That makes no more sense than explaining, say, time as a property of matter. There is no evidence at all that consciousness/intelligence isn't a primitive characteristic of the universe, which froze out of the Big Bang along with mass/energy and space-time.

"But you may ask, hasn't science found purely physical explanations for everything that's been studied so far? Aren't we betting against the odds when we cherish the belief that someday, somewhere, the scientists will find something they can't explain with physical causes?"

Wayne might have asked that, but he had begun to feel peculiar. A sensation had come over him that he couldn't remember ever having had before, yet which seemed intimately familiar, like a lullaby your mother used to sing before the time of memory. It was as though some quality of the light had changed, until it seemed that the world changed too, and instead of a patio behind a modern laboratory building they sat in the jewel-bright garden of a fairy tale, the brilliant sunlight falling on a man in pure white with long silver hair, and all around gemlike colors remembered from a garden long ago, which Wayne had been waiting all his life to see again.

He shifted in his chair, took a deep breath, and blinked his eyes to dispel the disorientation, tried to focus on what Burschevsky was saying.

". . . In fact, non-physicalist explanations are actively excluded from consideration as 'unscientific.' Take neo-Darwinism, for example, a theory that fits the data so poorly that even after 150 years thousands of biologists do little else than try to come up with mechanisms for how the theory could possibly give rise to the world we see.

"The problem is in their methodology, of course. They start by assuming a physicalist origin for life and then look for the best possible physicalist explanation. Obviously, proceeding from there to the conclusion that they have proved that life arose from purely physical causes is circular. Yet woe betide any who point this out."

He, Burschevsky, the little garden, were part of a

story, and a silent witness watched them, as if a consciousness walked invisibly in the sunlight dappling through the slightly moving leaves of the trees—

". . . Mysticism is the sincerest form of empiricism. The mystic defies all theories, all expectations, all socially acceptable and scientifically prescribed perceptions; he sees something that doesn't fit anyone's preconceptions, even his own. Mysticism is the antidote to dogmatism, which limits acceptable perceptions to those that support the accepted paradigm. Are you all right, Wayne?"

Wayne had put his hand to his face dizzily. In the thick wash of sunlight a scrap of dream had come to him, and he strained to hear the Indian's gravelly voice: ". . . things defined as unreal can only be seen in a place where we allow ourselves to see unreal things . . ."

He glanced up to see Burschevsky watching him curiously. He rubbed his eyes and shook his head to clear it. "Sorry," he mumbled. "I—I'm feeling a little—strange."

"Are you ill?" Burschevsky asked with a shade of impatience.

"No—I don't think so. I just had a—kind of a flashback or something. A dream came back to me for a second. Some words. Can I tell you about something?" So much for a graceful transition. Wayne rubbed his hands over his face vigorously to clear his head. "Sorry to interrupt your—what you were telling me, but this has been puzzling me, and now—"

"Certainly. Go ahead," said Burschevsky politely, but he didn't seem too pleased at the interruption of his spiel—perhaps particularly because he sensed that Wayne had been about to call it that.

So Wayne told him about his dreams at Shaman's Mound, the dreams with the bank account number, how he had deposited the $5,000, and finally his dream of last night and the fragments of it that had come back to him. "And just now you were talking and—and somehow it felt for a minute as if I was *in* a dream, but awake too. And then I seemed to remember some more words from the dream, that seemed to go along with what you were saying. Something like "you can only see things that you have defined as unreal in a state where you let yourself see unreal things," or something like that. And that's dreams, isn't it? Is he—does that mean that in dreams you can see real things that you've defined as unreal?"

Wayne's explanation didn't seem to improve Burschevsky's mood. The nostrils in his long, patrician nose seemed a little pinched. "You're staying in Alphonse Bolling's house, you said?"

"Yes."

"Then I would be careful of whatever 'extra-normal perceptions' you seem to experience. Bolling is obsessed with his subliminal sensory technology research, and he isn't too scrupulous about how he comes by experimental subjects. A mystical experience in which you are asked to deposit $5,000—!" Burschevsky laughed shortly. "It may be too well hidden for you to find without actually tearing down the walls, but I would guess that Dr. Bolling has some of his precious subliminal hardware installed, and you are receiving messages from it. These messages would likely show up mostly in your dreams, where material excluded from daytime consciousness often surfaces. Bolling." He shook his head sadly. "You might consider finding another place to live. And now, if you'll excuse me, I need to change." He stood up. "Thank you for coming to see me; I hope we can talk again sometime."

—

Bolling *had* offered to let him stay at his house with unusual alacrity, Wayne reflected as he drove back down
the county highway in the bright sunlight. Had he been
eager for an unsuspecting research subject? Wasn't that a
more plausible explanation than a dream Indian who demanded money for spirit-guide help? A fury came over
him suddenly, a futile rage. If he had squandered his
$5,000 and his credulity for nothing more than that, if
Bolling had tricked him—

At the beach house he dialed the telephone number in
Europe Bolling had left, ready to spit his rage into the
man's ear, let him stutter out his explanation. But the
phone rang unendingly with an old-fashioned sound, not
even a message machine picking up. Wayne spent the rest
of the morning going carefully through the house, looking for signs of subliminal sensory technology, standing
on chairs and examining the upper corners of the rooms,
feeling for wires under the carpeting, tapping the walls
for hollow spaces or hidden speakers, looking in closets
and crawl spaces for anything like the console he had
seen in Bolling's office. He could find nothing.

—

That night he had a dream that seemed unusually clear
and bright-colored, almost as if he was awake inside it,
but sinuous with the feelings of the far continent. He
drove on a winding road over thickly forested hills, the
ocean showing occasionally between vine-hung trees to
his right. A long way from anywhere he came upon a
house with a yard grown so wild that it was hard to tell
where it ended and the woods began; ivy grew shaggily
in place of a lawn, mingling at its edges with the forest
leaves and overhanging the mossy retaining wall along

the road. The house itself was dark weathered brick, set so close around with huge oaks that it looked almost like a natural outcropping of rock. Brick steps led to the front door. On a middle step, in the damp, quiet evening the forest made of afternoon still shimmering on the ocean, he saw a woman, her eyes in evening light glistening, skin glowing faintly against the forest's slow brown and green decay, motionless, as if time had frozen, she caught on the steps like a fly in amber.

And he knew it was Her, and that he had indeed come to the other world, the far green continent.

Sometime earlier or later in the night, in an unconnected time, it seemed, the Indian's face had appeared, his gravelly voice gently urging: "Look at your hands. Look at your hands." And the thought came to Wayne: ". . . the interpenetration of dreams and waking . . ."

⎯

He woke with a luminous warmth inside his chest, the exaltation and feeling of deep mystery and inkling of immortality he got on those rare occasions when he dreamed of the far continent. He sat up. The morning was grey, humid, cool, with the smell of leaf mold and the sound of waves coming softly through his window, and another sound too: the distant thump of rock and roll.

He got up stiffly and went downstairs, looked out his kitchen window.

On the deck of the neighboring house half a dozen women appeared to be dancing naked.

Wayne squinted his eyes acutely, then ran upstairs for his glasses. Yes—they were too far away for a good look, but except for one T-shirt and a cowboy hat, they seemed to be completely nude.

His heart pounded suddenly. Sometimes a man knows what he has to do. And the dream of Her—had it been a sign from the numinous realm or his own subconscious? That today was the day to break out of the rut he had worn deep for too many years? Some fate had planted half a dozen wild women right next door to him, one of whom at least resembled the silky girl. He had to go. The worst they could do was ignore him again. He ran back upstairs and put on cutoffs and a T-shirt, then looked at himself in the mirror, rubbing the remaining sleep out of his eyes. There was the touch of grey in the hair, the lines at the corners of his eyes and mouth, but he filled the T-shirt well, and with a certain reckless derangement in his eyes he guessed he looked quite sexy.

He went downstairs and slipped on his beat-up tennis shoes, strode out the front door, then came back in and took from the kitchen cabinet a bottle of wine. Napa Ridge Merlot; he had bought it against an occasion much more modest, but it was perfect for this one. He strode out again feeling masculine and potent; carrying a bottle of wine to the house of a bunch of naked girls at 6:30 A.M. had a certain swagger to it.

The county highway was quiet and damp in the still morning, barely a leaf stirring; he drove a hundred yards, then turned down the next gravel drive toward the Lake. The house at the end of it was bigger and fancier than Bolling's, cedar-sided, the windows tall and narrow, skylights in the broad, shallow roof. Wayne's hands were tingling as he got out of the car. He could hear the rock and roll thumping around back, some kind of Euro dance music with heavy bass and drum-machine riffs.

The front door faced the gravel drive, tucked between flower beds and evergreen bushes. With a supreme effort Wayne approached and pressed the doorbell, heard it *bing-bong* inside against the thump of music.

He waited, stomach quivering, thighs trembling. Nothing happened for what seemed a long time.

He rang again. Same torturous result. At first he felt relieved, until he realized that if no one came he would have to go around to the back where they were dancing.

So he rang the doorbell again, and this time, only a few seconds later, someone came. Through the narrow window to his left he caught a quick motion, as if someone was running lightly, childishly. Then a woman opened the door.

She was naked. She had a mass of curly black hair gathered at the back of her head, a few ringlets hanging over her alabaster shoulders, and a smudge of black at her crotch. She kept her left hand on the doorknob and her right on the jamb, holding her as she leaned out slightly, breasts thrust out casually, inquisitively, almost childishly. She was very beautiful. She had perfect, delicate features, and her shoulders and hips and the curve of her stomach were slim and healthy and young. Her eyes were large and black, and looking in them Wayne realized that she hadn't gotten up early to dance with her sisters in the dawn, but had been up all night, probably with chemical assistance. Her face was slack, her breath faintly alcoholic.

Faced with this vision of decadence and beauty, all the swashbuckling lines he had practiced on his short drive seemed choked out of him. For several seconds he just stared. Then with a supreme effort he waved the bottle of wine toward her, and said: "I'm—I'm your neighbor—"

She closed the door. She didn't slam it, and there was no sign of anger or fear in her slack, occluded face. She just closed it softly and quickly, as if eager to get back to dancing, and he saw the shadow of her body pass the window again.

He stood there holding the bottle, his mouth open to finish his sentence. And suddenly pouring into him came fury—fury at the *rudeness* of these beautiful, speechless,

contemptuous girls, at their insensitivity, perhaps just because he wasn't cool or young or wild—

He put out his thumb to push the doorbell furiously,
keep pushing it so that its languid ring would keep *bing-
bonging* over and over against their rock and roll, but suddenly he reflected that they might call the police, and that
it wouldn't look too good if they did, a middle-aged man
brandishing a bottle of wine and ringing harassingly at the
door of college-age girls at 6:30 in the morning.

He turned away, and at that split second he knew that
they had beaten him, and that they always would. He
didn't have the wild, heedless streak that would let him
go after what he wanted without fear, or dance naked
and wanton on his deck over the Lake at dawn; he was
full of fear and caution and calculation. He was filled
with a sudden, intense self-loathing that almost made
him fall. *Old*, he told himself, *decrepit, afraid. Dirty old
man, lecher, creep.* He felt an overwhelming urge to
smash the wine bottle down onto a rock, but his caution
won out and he held it in his tingling hand as he struggled back into his car.

He didn't go back to Bolling's, but followed the county
highway, an ache in his chest and stomach driving out
thought. *Old. Afraid.* This day passing, and he couldn't—
Could never— Life passing by, and he— This day of days,
whirling in a little vortex of dust. The morning was growing brighter, the sun cutting at a steep, yellow angle
through the humidity, sparkling in dew on the grassy
shoulder. He drove slowly, tiredly. On an impulse he
turned left at a narrow asphalt road, without any idea
where he was going. A few trailer-sized houses with small,
mossy lawns nestled under the trees at first, but soon the

road was flanked only by tall woods and a wire fence, which finally gave way to an old-fashioned iron fence, and beyond it gravestones and memorials.

This suited his mood. He pulled over by the cemetery gate. A grey BMW was parked down the shoulder, but otherwise there was no sign of living humans. The air was still, a little misty under the trees but shot with sunlight among the graves, and there was the faint, sharp tang of forest mulch. The gate moaned as Wayne pushed it open, and then the quietness was so complete that he could hear the swish of his feet in the cemetery grass, which looked like it was mown, but not too often. It was easy to believe that people were buried and laid to rest here: a certain watchfulness in the silent, vaguely autumnal sunlight seemed to keep an almost cheerful vigil, and their names were carved on the headstones, weather-worn and leaning, dating back a hundred years.

Wayne walked among them, touching some, reading names and dates. They soothed him, whether with their intimation of the triviality of earthly problems, or their inert, democratic receptivity, or just their quietness. The cemetery was bigger than it looked from the road, stretching back between the woods into a newer section with asphalt walks and upright headstones in rows. Wayne had come over a little hill and was approaching a stand of trees that had been left among the graves when he heard something, a sound of living feet among all this impersonal memory.

He paused, looking around, not wanting to intrude on anyone's lamentations, and not in a mood to be seen himself. The sound seemed to come again from beyond the trees.

The walk ran next to the trees; he could take cover by straying from it no more than three feet, not really skulking, but standing behind a wide trunk—

Just in time. A man was coming along the walk. He wore a grey felt hat and a grey raincoat that looked wrinkled and damp, as if he had been outdoors long enough for the dew to settle on him. With surprise Wayne recognized Dr. Edmund Carvery. His eyes were bleared and colorless, face grey and sagging, as if some quality of death had crept into his body from the graves, or as if he had been awake all night engaged in some inner struggle. His cheeks seemed damp, but whether with tears or sweat or dew, Wayne couldn't tell. He walked with a limp, as if his legs hurt, making Wayne wonder if he had been kneeling for a long time. As he passed Wayne's tree he rubbed a trembling hand across his face. Then he limped resolutely on, until Wayne lost sight of him among the graves, a shaft of yellow sunlight growing in the clearing like a rehearsal for the Resurrection.

8

When Wayne got back to the beach house it was nearly 8:30, and there was no sign of the girls or any sound of rock and roll. The Lake was a velvet silver-blue roiled by the surf at its near edge to greenish-brown and white. His walk in the graveyard had somehow made the events of the morning part of his book, and he took advantage of this by sitting under the bluff trees with his laptop for several hours. Six naked beauties dancing in the dawn, two Nobel laureates, one a hardened materialist, the other obsessed with the occult—

It was almost noon when an impulse struck him. He went inside and called the Deriwelle Institute, asked for Dr. Carvery's office. The number rang twelve times before he hung up. After thinking about it for a minute, he went and got in his car. Carvery struck him as someone who wouldn't necessarily answer his phone, but who, if Wayne showed up at his door, might talk, explain about the Ouija board and the psychic reader and the cemetery vigil.

The sun was bright on the highway winding over the wooded hills along the Lake, quiet and still, like a deserted movie set flooded with sunlight. The woods were giving way to fields on his left when the deserted, waiting feeling seemed to intensify suddenly. It was as though he were a character in a movie driving down that county highway, part of a story that hadn't happened yet in the stillness and waiting sunlight. It was a feeling like the one he had gotten in Adam Burschevsky's patio garden.

He was nearing Ivywood Drive, and the sight of the turnoff intoxicated him somehow. Ivywood Drive with the lights of the houses down the bluff among the trees in the quiet, windless evening—a place for the beginning of a story. If he turned on Ivywood Drive, turned on it right now, he might find the thread of that story.

He turned on Ivywood Drive.

The intoxication came over him twice as strong. Yes. This was the moment when the narrative opened, when Chapter One joined the protagonist in the forty-third year of his seemingly pointless life, driving on a wooded road above the Lake Michigan bluffs. He felt the world wide around him, still and vast and bright, holding his story in this sunlight and dappled shade as he drove under the trees. His body suddenly was full of the sinuous, unrefusable feelings of the far, green continent—could he perhaps have traveled there somehow? The thought made the hair prickle on his head. Why not? He went there in dreams, transported in the twinkling of a dreaming eye, or sometimes he saw it from afar, misty and green across a vast strait, the living wind blowing from it. Why not now, when he was awake?

The road wound along, ivy overhanging a three-foot retaining wall on his left, the Lake showing now and then between ivy-hung branches to his right. No houses were in sight, and he felt a long way from anywhere, yet something was strangely familiar.

And suddenly he hit the brakes, so hard that the tires squealed despite his slow speed. He barely had the presence of mind to pull off the road before he got out of the car, gaping.

Ivy grew on the rising ground beyond the retaining wall, mingling at its edges with the forest leaves and climbing several huge oaks growing in a wide, rough circle. Set among those oaks had been a house, a house of dark, weathered brick, almost like a natural outcropping of rock. Brick steps had led to the front door. He wondered when only for a split second. *This was where he had seen the house in his dream,* just exactly here—he recognized everything about it, the ivy, the retaining wall, the oaks—except here there was no house, and that had been on the far continent, and there it had been the damp, quiet evening the forest made of afternoon still shimmering on the ocean, while here it was bright and silent midday—

He caught a movement out of his left eye and jumped backward, realizing it was a car. He had been standing nearly in the middle of the road. The car slowed cautiously, and now it pulled up to him. The window slid down and a woman looked at him from the driver's seat, leaning over slightly so she could see his face.

"Are you all right?" she asked. "Do you need help?"

She had exquisite eyes, which he could see in the car's dim interior were blue-green; her skin was delicate and pale, her fingers long and shapely; her mouth quirked in a little smile, as if in amusement.

"No," he managed to stutter.

She paused just a second looking at him, then nodded; then the eyes were hooded with long-lashed lids, and the window slid up, and the car moved off.

Wayne stared after it, not breathing.

—her eyes in evening light glistening, skin glowing faintly against the forest's slow brown and green decay, motionless, as if time had frozen, she caught on the steps like a fly in amber—

Her.

And he had said "no" like an idiot when the only thing he really wanted in this whole world, in all the worlds, of all things the only precious—

And She was here, *here,* in this place somehow, which had been transmuted somehow to the far green continent from which the living wind blew, making all the world live—

He scrambled into his car and screeched his tires taking off after her.

He jumped over a rise, then over the next little hill and around a sharp bend, fishtailing. No sign of the car. It had to be just ahead—she hadn't been going fast. He sped up, careening dangerously—still no sign. Ivywood Drive rejoined the county highway after the yacht club, near the St. Clair River—but he should catch her before then. "No"—damn him for a fool! He rocketed past the yacht club. He was trying to remember now exactly what kind of car she had been driving—big, new, and expensive, and some pale color.

The stop sign at the county highway came rocketing toward him, and he could suddenly smell the earthy, wet, effluvial smell of the river. He stopped with a terrible screeching and jerk of gravity. He sat at the stop sign craning his neck up and down the highway, the acrid smoke of burned rubber coming in his window. He had lost her. But his heart was pounding with excitement. He had *seen* Her, She was somewhere in this waking world. *She was real.* The thought made wild electricity run through his body, and his hair stood up on end.

And in that second of wild exhilaration, as if dislodged by the currents rushing through him, a fragment of the Indian's words whirled upward out of the darkness where the memories of dreams are kept: "... what is real doesn't disappear however much you ignore it ..."

—

There was what you were taught was real, and then there was what was real. Cats reared in all-vertical environments were blind to horizontal lines; primitives who had never seen TV were unable to decipher the pictures on it. Maybe humans reared with a conventional worldview wouldn't be able to recognize sensory input inconsistent with it.

Yet what was real didn't disappear however much you ignored it. Its signals would still come to the senses. Wayne was walking on the beach in the blinding, crystalline afternoon, sparkling pale blue surf washing around his ankles, cries of seagulls above, the Lake breeze cooling the heat of the sun on his head and shoulders. He had looked out before he had come down to make sure none of the neighbor girls were walking. He had concluded that they were models or actresses from some great City who had chipped in for a vacation far from cameras and the public, and who resented the peering eyes of anyone.

If what was real was ignored by a mind that didn't think it was real, what would happen? You would have to see it sooner or later because it was present to your senses. But if you were bone-deep sure it wasn't real you would have to see it in a way that didn't suggest that it was; either you would see it when you were awake and call it a hallucination, or your mind would save it and only allow it to register when you were dreaming, because in dreams you could both see things with great conviction and later deny that they were real. "You can only see unreal things in a state you have defined as unreal," the Indian's gravelly voice seemed to have told Wayne. But it made sense, especially if the difference between the defined real world and the real real world was something subtle. It would be hard to ignore an elephant or a brick wall and then see it later as a dream. But if it was something subtle—certain connections between events, for example, strings of coincidences; or feeling tones that were projected around certain people or places, as they were in dreams; or what if the perceptions required simultaneous apprehension of a wide number and range of inputs simultaneously, of the kind a person concentrating on one or two tasks would probably miss? Was it possible that such subtle perceptions or connections, absorbed but repressed by waking consciousness, could form patterns in the unconscious and then emerge in dreams? The thought made his heart pound with excitement. Was the far green continent real? And Her? Was it possible that he actually *lived* in the far green continent, but in a state of unconsciousness, of oblivion to all but the tiny worries he leaned over so intently every day and every waking minute? Was that what the Indian had meant by "the world is like an onion"? Perhaps a subtle move from one skin to a deeper one, while keeping you physically in the same place, would land you in an entirely different reality.

He stood still and looked up from his thoughts, tried to peer out weak-eyed from the papoose of thought woven about him by long years of weary thinking. What he saw did nothing to dissuade him of his ideas. The sun, diamond-hot in a pale blue sky misted at its edges with humidity, pale blue-silver water washing cool around his feet, the Lake bluff vast and green and brown, its infinitely fine detail fading into the white mist of distance miles and miles away, quiet and still in the sunlight, and in the middle air gulls sailed and mewed.

But then he felt a familiar sinking, like ballast being taken on to stabilize his flying mind. The form and voice of Dr. Raymond Hall in the darkened Institute auditorium, silhouetted against illuminated diagrams. Wayne had had some random, epilepsy-like overfiring in his temporal lobes which had cast upon whatever happened to be in front of him an air of intense, profound meaning—that was the explanation Hall would give for the episode on Ivywood Drive. And wasn't it after all the most plausible explanation? After driving around St. Clair for half an hour looking for Her he had returned to the place he thought he had recognized from his dream, but by that time the immense bliss and certainty were gone, ebbing with the neural firing that had produced them; it had been just a place by the side of the road.

Yet all mental states were underlain by neural states, he fought back desperately. Who was to say which neural state let you perceive real reality? Mustn't it be that the answer was an *integration* of both states, a higher synthesis? What good were dreams alone, unfocused, fragmentary, unlived? What good was waking consciousness, ashen, narrow, impoverished? "The interpenetration of dreams and waking," the dream Indian had said. Did he mean that the integration of these two brain states was the way back to real reality? Could the Indian actually be sending him these experiences somehow, prodding Wayne's waking and dreaming brain states together from somewhere inside? Wayne could remember the Indian urging him to look at his hands in one dream; was that one of the exercises of the "interpenetration of dreams and waking," bringing waking volition into dreams?

A nice New Age hodgepodge, he told himself as he climbed Bolling's cool, damp flagstones in leaf-mold-smelling shade. Part Castaneda, part pop Vedanta, part Black Elk, and all constructed around a handful of disconnected phrases from a dream. For one thing, what in the world would a dream Indian do with $5,000? And for another, why should *he*, Wayne Dolan, have been singled out for such teachings? It was like a fairy tale, and one where he was the hero, suggesting infantile fantasy. On the other hand, he had the sneaking suspicion that he need not necessarily be flattered by his selection. Perhaps he had been predisposed to this program because of his extreme ineptitude at living, which had made him long ago begin delving into his dreams for the ingredients of life. But that also brought you full circle back to suspicion, since this might be just the next deterioration in some progressive psychological disease.

⸻

"This—kind of feeling comes over me," he said to Ray Daniels. "Like a feeling of ecstasy, but very quiet. It's like—" he tried to silence himself, think back to what it really had been like on Ivywood Drive and in Burschevsky's garden. "It's like everything around you has this depth—every little thing, every leaf, every rock has this great depth of implication, dimensions. And then it's like there's an *intelligence* pervading everything, which you're part of, and yet it's hidden from you—I don't know how else to describe it. And there's a feeling of mystery, like the world is beautiful and mysterious and vast and deep, profound. Like it all means something. It has this deep meaning, and you have this sense that everything's going to be all right. Oh, and that you can't die."

He looked sheepishly at Daniels sitting on a stool at one of his lab worktables, mild eyes studying him. Tom sat on the other side taking notes with intense concentration. "It's like being awake but dreaming at the same time. That's why it reminded me of your research."

"We should make him up a cap," Daniels said to Tom apologetically.

Tom giggled excitedly and started to rummage in a drawer, taking out small electronic things and lengths of fine wire.

"So what do you think it is?" Wayne asked anxiously.

"Sounds like a temporal-lobe event," said Daniels. "The limbic system governs judgments about significance, and it's inside the temporal lobes, so if you have intense temporal-lobe firing you can get these feelings of truth, beauty, and profundity."

"So what I saw wasn't real." Anxiety filled his viscera like cold jelly.

"All experiences are associated with brain states," said Daniels. "I measure brain states. As to what's real and what's not, I can't tell you that."

Wayne still stared at him.

"The limbic system's job is to tell you when something is significant," Daniels explained. "If what you're looking at seems significant, the limbic system fires. If the limbic system fires, what you're looking at seems significant. What *really is* significant—that's philosophy, not science."

But he watched Wayne alertly, as if to see if he had understood, if he was now a member of the same fraternity of doubt as Daniels himself.

—

That night Wayne dreamed he stood on a bouldered slope grown with cedars. Stars shone large and humid in the black sky, and there was a mist near the ground, the peaks and slopes of a craggy mountain landscape thrusting out of it. Straight ahead of him, a quarter mile distant, an observatory stood on top of a crag, light from the slit in its round roof tinting the mist; a quarter mile beyond that another observatory on a higher crag lit the mist also. But beyond the far observatory Wayne could see nothing, as if the world came to an end there, the mountains falling in bottomless precipices into mist. Then he knew that he had come to the edge of the other continent, where it falls away into mist, and where, if you look long and hard, you can see the vague shores of our own world in the distance.

—

The next couple of days Wayne interviewed members of a team of cosmologists, particle physicists, and religious scholars who were trying to anthropomorphize the Big Bang and the physical laws to give people a scientifically accurate image of the Source of Life to worship. He caught Maureen Allison and Brad Tollaksen for coffee, spent time writing, and now and then heard rock and roll down the bluff or watched a couple of the model-beauties walk on the beach. He had a telephone argument with Ann's lawyer in the Mid-Atlantic Region, who assured him that Ann had no obligation to tell him her phone number on vacation. He was tempted to call his own lawyer, but he didn't think he could afford that. At other times he wore the cap Daniels had given him and kept a lookout for what he thought of as the signs of an impending "integration of dreams and waking," but the memory of his experiences seemed to ebb, and even another drive along Ivywood could do no more than stir twinges. He ransacked the local library and bookstores for more about the Blue Water shamans, without luck. The books he found on mystical dream experiences were either obvious malarkey or the same ones he had read in his youth. The weather was hot and increasingly humid, and he swam several times a day.

On the third afternoon he was working the laptop in the shade of one of the bluff trees, squinting up now and then across the quiet, greenish-blue Lake into a haze of bright humidity, when he got a phone call from Ray Daniels.

"We're playing cards tonight at the lab. You want to come over? About 8:00?"

About 8:00 the sun was approaching the Lake in a flare of orange-red. The breeze through the car windows cooled Wayne's sweat-dampened T-shirt. Crickets trilled the blue air gathering under trees on the rich, trimmed lawns of the Deriwelle Institute. The guard buzzed him into Building B, and he sauntered down to the lab.

Daniels, Farris, and the indefatigable Tom were at the card table.

"Hi!" said Farris, eyes widening with delight, as if Wayne had just come in on a plane from Africa.

"Drensler's on his way," said Daniels. "He's having an argument with Coberg about some physics thing. They were almost biting each other this afternoon."

"That's all Drensler does is argue," said Tom, giggling, eyes sparkling with happiness at making small talk in this fabulously distinguished company.

Wayne took one of the two empty chairs, got out his two rolls of quarters, and Daniels shuffled the deck.

"I thought Mormons weren't supposed to play cards," Wayne said as Daniels dealt.

"Neither are Jehovah's Witnesses," said Daniels.

"Shut up, man," said Farris comfortably, studying his hand.

"You guys hungry?" asked Daniels rearranging his cards. "What kind of pizza do you want? I heard one of Carvery's psychic subjects died a couple of days ago."

"Hot peppers," said Farris. "Is that right?"

"Anchovy. And I heard he's getting statistically significant results from his dice trials, half a percent better than chance, and that he's been there for all three shifts of trials every day since the old lady died, and not sleeping," said Tom.

"You don't say," said Farris interestedly, throwing down two cards and studying their replacements.

"They say he looks like a zombie. The people who work for him are worried he's going to fall down on his face and die of heart failure. But they don't want to say anything to the Administration because people think he's a nut already."

"But that means—does that mean there's life after death?" asked Wayne. He had two twos and two sevens. He threw down the odd card and got back another seven.

"What kind of pizza do you want?" asked Daniels.

"I can go with hot pepper and anchovy," said Wayne. "But that was the result Carvery predicted if there was life after death, right?"

"There is life after death, man," said Farris, throwing two quarters onto the table.

"Tell us about it before Eric gets here," said Daniels. "Anybody want Coke? Pepsi?"

"Cream soda," said Tom.

"Raspberry spritzer," said Farris.

"Dr Pepper," said Wayne. "Were the dice trials conducted at the graveyard? I saw Carvery coming out of a graveyard near here a couple of days ago, early in the morning—he looked like a corpse himself."

The other men glanced at him curiously. Wayne won the hand with his full house.

"What were you doing at the graveyard early in the morning?" asked Daniels.

Wayne told them. Starting out with the girls dancing naked on their porch, he had their complete attention. Eric Drensler strode into the lab and slammed the door in the middle of the story.

"Why do they let these fucking morons into the Institute?" he yelled. His face was mottled red and grey. "All they do is give us a bad name, these *fucking— cocksucking—stupid—morons*!" The last four words were screamed, and Drensler took off his suit jacket and threw it savagely to the floor.

"Hey, Eric, you've got to hear this," said Daniels in his quiet, breathy voice.

"I don't want to hear anything, especially from this— this—" Drensler was glaring at Wayne alarmingly, eyes protruding as if a pressure in his head would pop them out.

"No, you've got to hear this," said Daniels. "I mean it."

"You're the moron, eh," said Farris, studying his cards.

Drensler strode toward Farris, hands clawed. "I've had enough from you!" he screamed. "I told you *never, ever—!*"

Then Daniels and Tom were up restraining Drensler, who was screaming curses at Farris and struggling, and Farris was saying that he guessed Coberg had won the argument, and there was foam on Drensler's lips. It took them ten minutes to calm him down, which they accomplished by letting him scream that Coberg was a moron, and Daniels making covert gestures to Farris to stop provoking him. Then the pizza came and they sat him in front of his paper plate and grape soda, and he chewed and sipped limply, clutching his cards in one hand, until a normal color started to come back into his face.

"Now start again with your story," Daniels said to Wayne, and Wayne started again. As soon as he described the six naked girls Drensler fixed him with a sharp glance. "This is where?" he interrupted. "At a beach house a few miles north of here?"

"Yeah, next door to Alphonse Bolling's place," said Wayne.

As he went on, Drensler continued to watch him sharply, but not with the prurient interest of the others, Wayne thought. Just before the part where he rang the naked girls' doorbell, Wayne artfully broke off and went back to describe his first meeting with the two girls on the beach. He left out the part about one of them being the silky girl with the ocean eyes, though the thought of her made his heart speed up. When he came back and described the girl who had answered the door naked he was gratified by salacious cries of wonder. But Drensler was still looking at him with a strange expression.

"These girls," he said to Wayne, "they are very beautiful?"

"Unbelievably gorgeous," said Wayne, flushed with storytelling triumph. "As beautiful as the galaxies, the ocean—"

"You would have intercourse with them if they were willing?"

"You've got to be kidding. I'd— I'd—"

He was supported by excited yells from Daniels, Tom, and Farris.

But Drensler sat back with what looked like satisfaction. Had Wayne been less distracted with artistic success, he might have wondered if Drensler knew something about the girls himself.

———

By the time the card game broke up it was midnight. Drensler had left early, Farris had gone to call his parents in California, and Tom and Daniels were throwing away the cans and pizza boxes, so Wayne walked out to his car alone in a heavy mist that made halos around Building B's doorlamps. His footsteps on the parking lot were muffled. He had his hand on his car door when he glanced up across the wide grounds of the Institute. Then he stood up and stared.

Fog had filled the hollows of the sloping grounds with a blanket of ethereal white. Two hundred yards away the Convocation Hall rose above the mist on its crag, and two hundred yards beyond that the other round building. Lights were on in both, tinting the mist through their skylights, and looking at them a sudden intense recognition went through him. *His dream of the observatories*— And all at once, without knowing how, he stood there, stood on the sloping ground of the far continent, looking across the mist at the last two crags at the edge of the world, the observatories sending their light up into the black heavens, stood in the fated life, in the mysterious eye of the world—

And in that moment he understood something. He wasn't Wayne Dolan, aging, divorced small-time science fiction writer who lived in a suffocating apartment in the Mid-Atlantic Region, not really. In the far green continent he was a young prince, handsome and wealthy, betrothed to Her, the goddess-angel, and he had come out to explore the mysteries of his vast realm, to reap the vast and intoxicating perceptions that were the ultimate goal of all things, to perceive the intricate interweaving of stories that made the world, and the apprehension of which was beyond every other desire. He was exalted, deathless. He had youth with no end, vast estates with great gardens and lakes, the mysterious delight of silken days and nights like deep blue jewel boxes to keep the stars—

Then the vision faded, and he was back on the parking lot outside Building B of the Deriwelle Institute, looking at the two domed buildings in the mist, and groping in his mind for some half-remembered words of the dream Indian.

9

Wayne turned his car onto the county highway toward St. Clair, still shaken from his vision. He knew he wouldn't sleep if he went home, and a feeling was on him like the one he had had on Ivywood Drive. He was a man in a story. The night was murky and dark, but hidden somewhere in it was a treasure, a jewel that reflected all the world, the eye of a goddess, containing his deep desires, desires so deep he often didn't even know he had them, for the fated life, the world in which death was an illusion, the goddess-angel . . . He followed the feeling this time to St. Clair.

St. Clair was dark and closed up at this hour except for a few bars along the tourist streets near the top of the bluff. The only moving car he came across was a police cruiser making its slow rounds. He made his rounds.

Driving along one chiascuro street he saw a splash of light on the sidewalk, like a scene from an old detective movie. An all-night Laundromat, with a flyblown storefront showing faded signs and the backs of tacky plastic chairs. His intoxication had almost all worn off, and he was tired. The flow of story seemed to have dried up, ebbed on the tide of his neurochemical bliss, as if this Laundromat were its far shore. But the shabby detective-movie ambience of the place appealed to him. As he parked, a bit of mist even swirled in the yellow light from the window. He went in, just in case.

Inside the air was damp and warm, smelling of detergent and the exhalation of dryers. A woman sat in one of the plastic chairs reading a tattered *People* magazine, and for a second Wayne's heart leapt. Was it possible? But then he saw the crutches leaning next to her, saw her ugly, thick-soled shoe.

Two of the big dryers were going monotonously. Otherwise the place was empty.

Wayne sat in a row of chairs against the wall, behind the woman's row. He felt let down. His vision, the intoxication, were all gone. Fittingly ironic that his fiery neurochemical transient should have led him to a run-down Laundromat: there was something poetic about it. He could put it in the book. He looked around, forming a description of the place in his head.

The woman was turned sideways in her chair, leaning over her magazine. From here he couldn't see her clumsy black shoe, and it was almost possible to think she was beautiful. Her face was full, oval, pale, with a little acne, rusty black hair falling straight to strong, voluptuous shoulders, lips parted as she read. She wore a shabby work shirt rolled up at the cuffs, taut over large, round breasts.

She shifted in her seat, the motion suggesting a strength in her body—strong from using the crutches, he realized. Her concentration on the magazine seemed a little strange, as if the whole world had contracted to its pages, or as if it took her whole attention to spell out the words.

One of the big dryers switched off, cutting by half the booming hum in the place, the clothes behind its glass window tumbling slower and slower. The woman looked up and put her hand on the crutches, swung up onto them in a stiff, practiced motion. She crutched over to the dryer, opened it, got both crutches under her left arm, and with her right started tossing T-shirts, shorts, and other items into a plastic clothes basket on the floor. Wayne tried not to stare. Her profile was stiff with hostile indifference. She was aware of him now, ignoring him.

When the dryer was empty she stooped, keeping her left hand on the crutches for balance, and grabbed the clothes basket with her right, bending the top of it shut with a strong grip. Then she got the crutches under her arms again and went over to a high table near the windows, her right hand holding both the basket and the handle of the crutch, her face stiff with the effort. Wayne had to restrain himself from getting up to help her. As he watched her the hostility in her face increased—not, he thought, because he failed to help her, but for the opposite reason: because he saw her, witnessed her lameness and helplessness.

She banged the washing basket onto the table. He was fascinated with her now. Her upper body was very strong, and her right leg was long and filled the jean leg tautly as it ran down from shapely, hard hips, but the left leg with the thick-soled black shoe hung useless: thin, twisted, and too short, like a marionette's leg when the string is let go. And the face was beautiful and angry, with acne and no makeup, the beautiful thick hair dull from some cheap shampoo and chopped off carelessly. She leaned against the table, and with her free right hand, helped slightly by the left, which had to hold on to the crutches, she began taking things out of the clothes basket and folding them sloppily and quickly.

One of the angry motions of her hand upset the basket, sending everything spilling to the dirty Laundromat floor.

Wayne stood up almost involuntarily, then after a millisecond decided it was the right thing to do. Perhaps he already wanted to rescue her; and anyway, he couldn't very well just sit there and watch her struggle. He went around the row of plastic chairs, but before he could bend down to help her pick up the clothes she turned on him, pointing one of her crutches threateningly into his face. Her face was white with rage.

"Get back!" she gritted.

He stopped, staring at her.

"Get back!" The crutch trembled, but her face daunted him. He stepped back with an impression of transparent eyes full of hate. Ignoring him again she painfully lowered herself, leaning on the crutches heavily with her left hand, and gathered up the clothes clumsily with her right, her strong leg crouching, the other sliding along the floor to the side like an inanimate thing. Then she bent the basket closed in her right hand and stood up. She was breathing hard, strong breasts rising and falling under the cheap shirt. She slammed the basket onto the table and started to take the clothes out and fold them again, hands trembling. Wayne retreated to his chair.

A mutter of thunder came from outside, and then another, louder.

The woman's other dryer stopped. She took her clothes basket to it and repeated the same clumsy ritual. A couple of times he thought her body shook as with a sob, but she made no sound, and when she turned again her face was dry. Her hands were still trembling as she folded the clothes on the table, her face set and angry, as if fighting some pain, and he noticed her fingers: long, somehow vulnerable. His chest ached watching her, but he couldn't look away.

When she was done folding she slid the piles of clothes into a stained laundry bag, pulled the drawstring tight, drew it through the handles of her clothes basket, then put the drawstring around her neck so that the laundry bag and basket hung down her back. Then she got the crutches under her arms and hobbled awkwardly to the door, balancing the bag on her back, still utterly ignoring Wayne. It struck him suddenly that she did her laundry after midnight so no one would see her; so no one would pity her or try to help.

Thunder boomed, and a spatter of rain hit the door as the woman wrestled her bag and basket through it, getting stuck for a moment halfway. A gust of shockingly fresh air blew into the Laundromat. The door closed.

Wayne waited fifteen seconds, then followed her, ashamed but unable to let her go.

Thunder boomed in the grey-black sky, and raindrops spattered the sidewalk. There was a smell of ozone in the suddenly gusty air, shreds of fog blowing. The dark shape of the woman hunched away up the sidewalk 20 yards from him.

By the time Wayne got his car started and pulled up level with her the rain had begun to come down in earnest, so when he opened the passenger window and called out, "Can I give you a lift?" there was ample excuse for it; he might have been an upright citizen offering to help a handicapped neighbor.

She was already wet; if she walked much farther her laundry bag and its contents would be soaked. Yet her face in the glow of Wayne's headlights seemed convulsed with rage as she turned on him, mouth open to shout some obscenity.

She slipped. As she turned toward him one of her crutches slid out sideways on the wet sidewalk. She caught herself with a wrenching jerk, her whole body straining. Then with a trembling effort she straightened herself, pulling the crutch back in so that it supported her again, the laundry bag swaying like a millstone around her neck.

Wayne put the car in neutral and slammed out. He was almost ready to forcibly drag her to it, but he didn't have to. A strong gust teeming with water struck them just as he got to her, knocking her off-balance again, the swinging bag around her neck dragging her sideways in the sudden downpour, so that when he shot out his hand it met hers, and her cold fingers closed on it in an involuntary gesture of intimacy and dependence.

In the rain she twisted painfully, a crutch clattering to the sidewalk. Wayne's left hand went under her armpit or she would have fallen; and without meaning to he felt her muscles and her softness and her desperation, and without meaning to he let the feeling go deep into him.

He squatted to grab her crutch, then kept hold of her arm as she came with him to the car, feeling her muscles tensing and relaxing. He yanked the passenger door wide, pulled the laundry bag off her and put it at her feet as she got in, sliding the crutches behind her head into the back seat. Then he ran around to the driver's side, the rain chill and clean and full of its celestial smell of sky, and then they were in the intimate space the front seats of cars make in a thunderstorm.

"Wet," he said happily, rubbing water from his face.

She didn't answer. Wayne saw with satisfaction that though she was wet she wasn't soaked, and the laundry bag's greasy surface seemed to have repelled most of the rain.

"I'm Wayne," he said, turning the wipers on high.

She said nothing. Her face was ashen, stiff.

"You all right? Didn't twist anything, did you?"

She shook her head.

"Where do you live? I'll drive you."

"That way," she said evenly.

He drove slowly along the rain-rushing street. Lightning glared and there was a heavy crash of thunder.

"Quite a storm. Came up suddenly."

"Left here."

He turned. At the woman's monosyllable he pulled up by a dingy two-story apartment house, bare bulb burning on a porch at the top of four wooden steps. She opened her door almost before the car stopped moving. Wayne jumped out and carried the laundry bag and basket up the steps and put them by the peeling front door, then went back down quick enough to take her crutches out and help her from the passenger seat.

She pulled away from him and climbed the steps carefully and dully, as people on crutches climb steps, and leaned down near the door to grab the laundry stuff.

"You going to be OK now?" he asked from the bottom of the steps in the rain.

The door swung closed behind her.

—

The storm blew itself out in the night, and next morning the sky was clear baby-blue and the sunlight crystalline, looking, as it shone on the stirring leaves, like the sunlight on postcards from the Caribbean. The Lake was metallic blue with a chilly, maritime-looking chop, and the breeze from it was cool. Wayne woke up late with a stiff neck, skipped his morning swim, ate cornflakes, and then sat at the top of the bluff and tried to write. But he couldn't concentrate. A feeling in his chest kept bringing the memory of his vision and the image of the crippled woman, her body twisting painfully in the rain, her strong, cold hand, the feel of the muscles and flesh under her arm. Around noon he gave up arguing with himself about how little sense it made. After all, it had been his plan all along to meet women in St. Clair, and was it possible that this one had something to do with his vision? The dirt road was damp from the night's rain and no dust rose under his wheels, but the county highway was dry, and the sunlight fell on a quiet countryside smelling of freshly watered fields.

In daylight St. Clair was a different town, and it took him a while to find the apartment house. Rain and darkness had lent it an air of mystery and beauty; in the bright early afternoon it was merely squalid. Its grey pebbled stucco was cracked, grey paint peeling on the front steps, door, and porch, the tiny lawn worn to hard dirt. A window on the second floor was propped open with a beer bottle, and the half-drawn shade had a brown stain. The tinny sound of a radio playing country music came from somewhere. On the front porch a very old man sat in a weathered wooden chair, his skin waxy pink, a few strands of greasy hair across his scalp, a week's growth of white beard on his face. His huge blue pop eyes followed with idiotic alarm as Wayne crossed the creaking boards.

Inside, a narrow, dim hall that smelled of stale cooking ran back to the stairs. There was an unmarked apartment door on each side. From behind one came country music; from the other the sound of a baby crying. Wayne climbed the stairs.

At the top was another narrow hall with a threadbare runner and a small window at each end. There were two more apartments up there, both silent. Wayne hesitated, then knocked at the door on the right, which was closer.

There was a pause, then a woman's voice said: "Come."

His heart was pounding, but not deafeningly, not as hard as it had pounded for the girls down the beach; maybe it was because she was crippled, flawed, not perfect like the silky girl, or maybe it was because he somehow already knew she was his—

He opened the door.

There was a small, slovenly living room with unmatched furniture. The woman stood in a doorway to the left, leaning on her crutches. She was wearing the same uniform as last night, jeans and a man's work shirt, the taut, threadbare cotton suggesting nakedness underneath.

She looked at him blankly for a moment, and then her face wrinkled in a frown. It flashed on him that she had been expecting someone else.

" 'The fuck you want?"

"I met you last night. I'm the guy who brought you home."

"Yeah." She seemed to flare with anger, as if the memory of her shame enraged her. "So what do you need, a medal, motherfucker?"

"Motherfucker" rolled off her tongue as if she used it a lot, so that he could imagine her sunk in a chair in this sleazy living room with her drug friends and calling people "motherfucker" in a raucous, laughing voice. The word and image made him flush with anger.

He chose his words carefully. "I don't need a medal. I wanted to meet you."

"So now you met me, you can go back to wherever you came from," she said, her beautiful face twisting in irritable fury. "Don't let the door hit you on the way out."

Her rage was intimidating, and without the witticisms

he might actually have left, but instead he stood in the doorway angrily.

Now she crutched toward him truculently, and as she came he finally saw her eyes. They were a beautiful emerald-green, but the pupils were shrunken to pinpricks.

"I told you to get out," she yelled in a brassy, practiced voice.

Yelling and truculent she seemed big, as big as he was. He took a step backward.

A movement behind him in the hall made him start, turn.

A man stood there. He was small and slim, wearing jeans and cowboy boots, an open leather vest over a faded blue work shirt. He had a dark reddish goatee and his head looked almost shaved, but there seemed to be a shadow around his face, like a memory of long hair that had just been cut. His muddy eyes looked steadily at Wayne.

"There a problem, Fredrick?" he asked softly.

There was a darkness about him, a kind of dirtiness, though there was no sign that he hadn't washed; it was a kind of dirtiness under the skin, or a shadow from the long, greasy, nonexistent hair; the darkness of it showed clearly the folds of his face, making it look oddly craggy.

"I was just trying to get Mr. Smith here the fuck out of my apartment," said the woman.

"Who *is* Mr. Smith?"

"Some asshole who gave me a ride home from the Laundromat last night and comes around now and wants his reward."

The darkened man looked up at Wayne with a strange, comprehending smile, as if he understood sickos. "You want your reward, Fredrick, is that right? Why'd you take a ride with him?" he asked the woman without looking at her.

"It was raining, King. Fucking pouring."

He was smiling up at Wayne. "You gave her a ride, Fredrick? Saved the lady in distress? And now you want your reward." He nodded his head, satisfied. He dug in the pocket of his jeans, came up with some bills and peeled off a twenty. He held it out to Wayne. "There you go, Fredrick."

Wayne just stared at him, fascinated and sickened and a little afraid. The man had a soft, drugged self-assurance that suggested criminal.

"Come on, take it, Fredrick. Before you go on your way."

"Give it to me if he doesn't want it," said the woman.

Wayne turned away from them, brushed past the man, and went down the stairs.

" 'Bye, Fredrick," said the man mock-wistfully behind him, and the woman laughed.

Outside the afternoon sunlight was bright and crystalline, but for a moment it made him feel sick, physically nauseous, as if it had reacted violently with the squalid darkness of the apartment-house hall and the small, darkened man. The leaves of elm trees made luminous shade on Wayne's car, and the cool freshness of the Lake was like a brief smell of some celestial autumn. He sat in the car pulling himself together, hearing the tinny strains of country music and looking up at what he thought must be the woman's window on the second floor, propped open with the bottle.

Sitting there he heard her cry out, one clear, sharp, animal cry of pain and pleasure. His breath caught, and there was a strange feeling in his chest, as if something red-hot had been poked inside him under anaesthesia. He had a sudden nauseous, hungry feeling, like low blood sugar. The hands with which he started the car were sweating and unsteady.

How it happened he could never exactly remember, nor figure out how one frame of mind could change so seamlessly to another so utterly different, nor even how the world itself could hold two frames so different, in effect two different worlds, thought they looked the same. But hadn't the Indian said "different layers of an onion"? Was that what he had meant?

All Wayne could remember clearly afterward was that he drove. The sick, hungry feeling propelled him, and he drove, taking one turn and then another on the narrow shady and sunny streets of St. Clair until he was outside of town on a little country road. It twisted and turned over small hills, now flanked by woods, now by fallow fields overgrown with weeds and tussocky grass. He met no one, saw no sign of humans except occasionally a small house with a shaded garden. The afternoon was quiet, sleepy, yet watchful, as if some retiring consciousness lurked in the sunlight falling on the gently moving leaves, the fields baking in the still air. He passed under some power lines that marched across the countryside on their huge metal towers. At one point it all seemed so beautiful and somehow otherworldly that he pulled over and parked under some willows overhanging the road, got out to walk. The shade was almost cool, just a hint of the electric air of the Lake cutting the smell of warm earth and mulch and vegetation, but when he emerged from under the trees the sun fell on him like warm iron.

The road went over a rise in a patch of woods, then ran down into a dell, the woods drawing away. His shoes scuffed on the warm asphalt, a few birds singing, locusts buzzing in coarse grass where sumac bushes grew with their royal purple blossoms.

The sunlight had gotten inside his head, filling him with its quietness and consciousness and with strange thoughts. The deserted and absolutely obscure feeling of the road gave him the notion somehow that beyond the top of the next rise there was nothing, that the world ended there, fell away abruptly in cliffs far down beyond sight into bright, cloudy sky.

He reached the top of the rise. No, the earth continued a little farther still, down into another dell, quiet and still and sunny.

If he kept walking in this quiet, sunny, obscure corner of the world, where would he get to? he wondered. Not back to the interstate highways, the rest stops, and finally the Mid-Atlantic Region; that seemed impossible: this was different from the world he had lived in for so long. No, he corrected himself, it wasn't a different world *physically*; it was more that if you returned to the interstates and rest stops and Mid-Atlantic Region from here, everything would be the same but completely different.

As if to confirm this, a vision came over him. There was a rest stop along the interstate, characterless and of no particular location, and it was raining, the world deep, luminous grey afternoon, the rain warm, and he had stopped to use the bathroom and stretch his legs, the whine of the interstate coming from two hundred feet away past the mown and anonymous grounds as cars and trucks roared by on their way to nowhere he knew, and he was traveling a long way but it meant nothing, and in the gloom of the rest stop building, looking at the highway map posted there, was She, wearing a raincoat, and as She turned to him he saw in her green eyes the world reflected, and this quiet, green, obscure landscape he walked through now, wondering.

There were answers in this world somewhere. He could feel it. Somewhere in this world was buried the thing he had been looking for all his life, though he had no idea what it could be.

At the top of the next rise the road curved through a thick, shady wood, then sloped down again, and in the cool, aromatic shade a new life seemed to be waiting for him. He came out from among the trees and the road began to climb again steeply, and at the top of this rise was a house. A cottage, rather, with a bright little garden around it, shaded by big trees. There was a white picket fence, a walk of stepping-stones nearly overgrown with grass leading from the gate to the cottage door. The cottage was old-fashioned and quaint, painted white, with window boxes, and it was perched at the top of the rise somehow precariously, as if attached to this world only tenuously, and when Wayne came up nearly level with it he stopped short, heart beating.

He knew this cottage intimately, though he couldn't remember ever having seen it before. It was a cottage from a fairy tale, and in it lived a little old man and a little old woman, and in the earth of that garden one could find jewels buried, and beyond it, just beyond the rise whose top it guarded, just out of his sight, the world fell away in great vistas of orchard cliffs, falling farther and farther and steeper and steeper to unguessed slopes vaster than the Himalayas, the air clear and crisp, and then beyond the gulf into which the ground fell, rising dim and far like a mountain out of the ocean, was the other world, the far green continent from which the wind blew that gave life, and the celestial rains, and this was the place, the secret, obscure, quiet place where this world came closest to that continent, and it was guarded by this little cottage, and he had found it.

He stood and stared, his mind flaring like a bonfire. He could go through that gate, go up to the door along the overgrown walk and knock, and the little old man would answer. It was all clear to him now, all clear, and now he saw it, he was at the very lip of that other world.

But he didn't need to go to the door, to look over the top of the rise. He stood here and he *knew*. It was all clear to him now. *And that was enough.* There was no hurry. He had been put in this world, on *this* side, for a purpose, and this world was beautiful, beautiful and mysterious, and things were hidden in it, clues, jewels of great price, like the gems buried in the earth of the cottage garden. He would stay in this world a little longer before he changed. He would plunge back into it now that his new perspective had cleared his eyes, showed him what he had been looking for, had showed him that he was safe, that nothing could ever really harm him because he could never die, and the far green continent nearly touched this world at this secret, obscure place he had found, just where no one would have suspected, and that was all he needed to know. He would go back into the fascinating, tangled skein of stories that was this world, play his part; and on some dim, luminous rainy afternoon at an obscure interstate rest stop, the warm drops falling through the sky reflecting in their limpid, celestial curvature the world spread out below, or on some misty, smoky night as he walked along a street, or on some quiet country road with sunlight lying still and conscious on everything, he would find Her, who had played hide-and-seek with him through all the stories and seeming difficulties of this world, and She would look in his eyes, and he would be consumed, carried away to the far green continent.

Satisfied, and yet filled with a yearning that it seemed would explode his body, he turned around and started back down the road without even one glance over the top of the rise. He would come back later if he needed to; this was enough for now. He had *seen*, and the flame of his vision had been all he could desire.

He walked, exulting, eyes blind with his visions, revelations coming from all sides, from where they lived in rocks and trees, in the air and sunlight and the road. He walked until he saw his car waiting patiently like a good and obedient animal under the willows, and he got in and turned around and drove back to St. Clair.

———

The interpenetration of dreams and waking, he thought exultantly as he drove through St. Clair in the sun-bleached and slowly ripening end of afternoon, slowed by many stoplights. The dream cottage with the old man and old woman, where fairy-tale clouds floated down the orchard cliffs to the gulf at the edge of the world—

Somehow the Indian had to be sending him these experiences, or guiding him to them from inside. Which meant that it was all *real*: the dreams at Shaman's Mound, the illuminations and visions, his luminous sense of happiness and hope in the morning. As he thought this, the luminous feeling started to creep into his chest again, as if his belief in its reality was a permission for it to exist, which had been destroyed by his previous doubts. It was real, and so was the little cottage, he thought with a chill, a trembling in the stomach, as if he had gotten up one morning and found himself in heaven. He had seen it while awake: he was awake now, and he hadn't fallen asleep this afternoon; he could trace his waking consciousness without interruption all the way from the squalid apartment house on Elm Street to the cottage and back here again to St. Clair.

And yet, he thought a little more soberly, was it possible? There was no place on this earth where the world ended, where the land dropped off into sky and a celestial continent loomed in the distance as across an expanse of ocean. That was dream stuff. The world was round. And people—philosophers, and later scientists—had been looking for a break in the prosaic fabric of this world—in effect, for the celestial—for thousands of years, but had found only dust and ashes.

A vague, familiar anxiety woke in his chest. Something unusual had happened to him, certainly, but had it been anything more than a hallucination?—not even a hallucination, since he hadn't actually *seen* anything, but a delusion, some brain transient known to modern science and common in psychiatric wards, which had convinced him that some of the dust and ashes, a house in some woods outside a small Southwestern Michigan town, was in fact a door to the other world. He looked around: the rich, fruity colors of late afternoon coming after a sun-blinded day seemed somehow deeper, more intense than usual, like the colors of things in the aftermath of an LSD trip. Was that a signal that something had gone wrong in his brain? Could it even have been an actual acid flashback, going all the way back to the recreations of his youth?

A sudden hunger woke in him to see the little cottage again, to examine it and knock on the door, and this time to look over the top of the rise.

St. Clair, with its elderly buildings and molasses traffic lights, was a town that cried out for U-turns not to be executed, but Wayne did one anyway. No doubt it would just be a little cottage near the top of a hill in some woods, like the place on Ivywood Drive had turned out to be just a patch of ground. But somehow he traveled to the far continent while remaining in this world when he had these "interpenetration" experiences; that was what the Indian had been trying to say with his metaphor about the onion. Wayne's hands on the steering wheel were sweaty.

He took a left on Linden Street, which had brought him back into town. Afternoon was cooling into evening on hedges, lawns, and elderly houses. The sound of children yelling somewhere came with the cool smell of cut grass, bringing to Wayne a sudden memory of running home at dusk, cheeks hot and hair sweaty, to see his mother in an obsolete hairdo standing on the front porch and calling him. A small, wistful sadness came for a moment to mingle with his haste, but then it was lost, left behind again, put aside as a man puts aside things that entangle him, with eyes averted.

There was a small park, then some empty lots, a tiny, elderly shopping center, a gas station, and then, quite abruptly, St. Clair came to an end, a last leaning stop sign standing at a crossroad flanked by bushes and unmown grass. Wayne now went slowly despite his impatience, looking in the dusk for a left-hand turn on a road whose name he couldn't remember.

He found what he thought was the turn, took it, and went slowly between thick woods with crickets singing and the damp smell of vegetation. It didn't seem familiar; of course everything looked different in the dark, but somewhere along here was a right turn—

He went another couple of miles before he realized that he was lost. He wasn't going to be able to find the road in the dark. He would have to come back tomorrow. He put his hand up to brush his hair away from his forehead, and touched the brim of a baseball cap.

10

"Temporal-lobe event," said Daniels next morning, studying the squiggles and numerical readouts clustered around a brain diagram on a screen at one of his lab worktables. "What time was your experience?"

"About 4:00," said Wayne. "I forgot to check exactly."

"That corresponds," said Daniels, clicking the mouse and typing, eyes on the screen. The diagram showed a spot of hot red low down on the right side, with a penumbra of orange and yellow around it.

"Does that mean what I saw was a delusion?" asked Wayne, though he knew what Daniels' answer would be. "An artifact of abnormal brain functioning?"

"I don't know," said Daniels. "I'm a scientist, not a philosopher."

"You're so fucking modest," said Wayne bitterly. "A lot of guys at the Institute are willing to tell me what everything means."

"Yeah," said Daniels softly, looking at him. "You better ask them."

"I don't like their answers."

"That's the problem with science."

Wayne studied him, his baby-brown eyes, the acne scars on his gaunt cheeks. "So what's your take? Is religion hooey or isn't it? What happens to us when we die?"

"I don't know."

"I can't use that for the book. Too wishy-washy."

Daniels gave him a small, sad smile.

—

When he got back to Bolling's house there was a message on the answering machine. At first there was a rustling of someone fumbling the telephone, and then a small voice said: "Hello? Hello?" anxiously, and then started to cry. "Daddy's not talking."

Danny. Wayne held the telephone tight. Alice's faint voice came soothingly from off receiver: "It's just a message. It's a recording. Don't worry. Tell Daddy what—come on, talk in here."

And Danny's voice again, very loud, his breath hissing on the mouthpiece. "Daddy, come home."

"Tell him all the flowers bloom, like you told me," said Alice's voice.

"All the flowers bloom. I love you till all the flowers bloom, Daddy," said Danny.

Then there was more rustling, and then Alice's voice, loud and a little strained. "Isn't that cute, Daddy? Danny thought of it all by himself. We were talking about you, and I said I loved you until the end of the whole universe, and Danny said he loved you until all the flowers bloom." Then sadly, "Daddy, when are you coming back? I haven't forgotten you, but Danny has, Mama says. Mama says we're at the beach and we don't have to think of you at all, but I want to think of you. I wonder when you're coming back, Daddy."

He called them at Ann's house, but of course there was no answer.

He had to go back to the Mid-Atlantic Region, he knew; but the thought of his apartment and his aimless, impoverished life there plunged him into despair. The celestial half-world of the Lake, the Shaman's Mound, the silky girl in the house down the bluff, the little cottage on the rise were *here*. And then he thought of the crippled woman in St. Clair.

⎯

The apartment house on Elm Street looked squalid and unhappy, like a neurosis in the middle of the healthy St. Clair summer, or the embassy of Hell in paradise. The awful old man was gone from the porch and there was no country music or crying of children, only the boom of TVs as he entered the sour-smelling hall. Upstairs was quiet. This was stupid: she had told him to go away, and her boyfriend might be here. But a strange certainty was upon him, and the words of the philosopher Wayne Gretzky rang in his head: "A hundred percent of the shots you don't take don't go in."

His knuckles fell heavily on the door, too loud and self-confident. She would guess he was scared.

The door opened.

The woman was dressed as he had seen her twice, in jeans and a cotton shirt, but her hair was uncombed and she looked sleepy, docile. The apartment behind her was dim, as if all the blinds were down. The pupils of her eyes were huge, their black eating up almost all the green. It took her a few seconds to recognize him.

"Didn't I tell you to get lost yesterday?" she said, rousing herself to be angry as if by an act of will. There was a TV slanginess to her manner, as if whatever drug she was on banished human feeling, leaving only a hip coolness to function as her personality.

"Yes."

She made a move to close the door, but he stuck his foot in it.

Now she was belligerent. "You fuck with me and my friends'll mess you up," she snarled into his face, without fear and still without real anger, but just pure dominance. "You want me to call them?" She half turned.

"No," he said.

"Then get the fuck—"

"I want to take you out. I want you to go to dinner with me," he said too quickly.

She laughed in his face. Not with amusement, but again just with dominance. She was full of something that made her able to do that, work herself like a machine to achieve dominance. He could see her thinking, see the cogs in the machine going round coldly.

"You a cop?" she asked.

He had heard about this. If you were a cop and you lied about it, the criminal could avoid conviction by pleading entrapment. "No."

"You got money?"

"Some."

She pulled the door open and gestured him in with a long, graceful hand.

He stepped in tensely, half-expecting the little man King to be standing somewhere with a weapon. He wasn't. The tiny living room looked even more depressing in the dull grey light through closed shades, and there was a humid, sweaty smell. A small TV was on with the sound muted, and a couple of dirty bed pillows were crushed on the sofa as if the woman had been lying on them.

She said: "Two hundred dollars." Her fingers twisted

the top button of her work shirt, and her breath had speeded up suddenly, breasts rising and falling in excitement. But not for him, he knew—for the two hundred dollars, which could buy her who knew how much more of whatever she was on.

"I don't have that much cash on me," he said, trying to get his bearings.

"Go get it."

"You're worth more than that."

For the first time she seemed to really look at him, frowning as if trying to see him through a haze of drugs and coolness and hate.

"So give me more," she said finally.

"Patience," he said. "I want to take you to dinner."

She thought about that. He could see the cold wheels going round.

" 'The fuck are you, anyway?"

"Fredrick."

She didn't even smile. "How much will you give me to go to dinner?" she asked finally, shrewdly.

Anger and shame came over him, but something, some certainty told him he had won, to be patient, to heed the words of Wayne Gretzky.

"Fifty dollars," he said.

"Give it to me."

He hesitated. "I'll give you twenty-five now and twenty-five after."

She should have been angry at that, offended, but she wasn't. She held out her hand.

He had intended to do some shopping, so he had enough cash to give her fifty dollars and still buy dinner. He pulled his wad out and peeled off a twenty and a five. She put them in the pocket of her jeans, then stood looking at him.

"OK?" he asked. "My car is downstairs."

She hung back suspiciously. "You'll drive me back too?"

"Of course." A vague sadness came over him from somewhere. "Jesus, do you go out with guys that don't drive you home?"

She colored suddenly, and he thought something cut through her drugged coolness—shame.

She brought sunglasses and a small purse. The purse was tasteful, its sophistication out of place against her working-class clothes. The sunglasses were so dark he couldn't tell what she was looking at.

He drove to one of the tourist places a block off the Lake bluff. She crutched past him awkwardly when he opened the door, looking away, as if she wasn't used to people holding doors for her. A feeling came over him suddenly, irrationally, of hot pride. The woman was a low-class prostitute and drug addict, but even with her shabby clothes and ridiculous sunglasses, her acne and shaggy hair, heads turned in the restaurant and didn't turn away even when they saw the crutches and the withered leg. It had been a long time since he had been on a date, he realized.

The hostess tried to take them to a window table but Wayne pointed to a dim booth in the back, figuring the drawn shades in the woman's apartment had been for her dilated pupils. When the hostess had gone, the woman lit a cigarette.

"I think this is the nonsmoking section."

"Who gives a fuck?"

Conversational icebreaker.

"What's your name?" he tried again. Then, suddenly irritated: "Could you take off the sunglasses? Or the fucking sunglasses, if that makes you feel more at home?"

She looked across at him as if deciding whether to be

angry, then slowly took off the sunglasses. Her eyes, smoky green in the dimness, seemed surprisingly vulnerable after the sleek black plastic. The pupils were still big but not huge.

The eyes made him recalibrate. "I'm Wayne," he said gently, as if trying not to scare some fierce, timid animal.

It took her a minute. She blew smoke across the table, head turned so that it didn't go straight into his face, and so she wasn't looking at him. Indifferently: "Gail."

"I'm a writer."

She glanced at him then, just for a second, as if she wanted to see this guy who said he was a writer, check whether he was telling the truth. Then she studied the restaurant indifferently again. "OK."

He followed up on his advantage. But delicately, carefully, trying to feel exactly the right words, as he did when he was writing, except here he had to push them out of his mouth instead of his fingers.

"I'm in St. Clair working on a book," he said slowly. "And I saw you. And you're—very beautiful. Numinously beautiful."

She glanced at him again and tried to sneer, then looked back at the restaurant. Was there the slightest tremor in her cigarette?

Then she surprised him. She asked, still casually: "What's 'numinously beautiful'?"

He was tempted to say "I don't know; I just made it up," but that wouldn't do here. This was no witty literary person to whom the irony would seem delicious, but a kind of primitive or animal, easily angered and scared.

So he said slowly and seriously, trying to catch the corners of her eyes: "Something—or someone—whose beauty fills you with imaginings. As if she isn't just herself, but *means* something, whose beauty *means* something."

A bright-eyed waitress chose this moment to pop over and wonder perkily what she could get for them this evening.

Gail ordered steak, cooked rare, and a bottle of sweet wine. The waitress brought the wine and poured half a glass for her to sample, but Gail drank it thirstily in a gulp. The waitress left the bottle, and Gail poured herself another glass. When she looked at him again the "numinously beautiful" moment had passed. Conversational gambits passed through his mind. What did she do for a living? No: the answer was probably unfortunate. Was she from this area originally? No: too stock and wimpy.

"Are you from this area originally?"

She gave him a real sneer this time. "That's a real cool pickup line."

"My pickup line was to offer you fifty dollars," he snapped back before he could help it.

Brief rage passed over her face; then she adopted her cold, dominant expression, eyes narrowed. "You ain't paid me, neither," she said with a loud, hard twang. "Where's the rest of my money?"

"After you eat. Don't you want your steak?"

She sat back and looked at him with a hard smile, in control again, though now with an edge of real hostility and irritability. He sat miserably, looking around. Why had he done this? He should just give her the $25 and get up and leave. But he had promised to drive her home. He should just get up and walk out, and to hell with the ride home and the $25; but he couldn't do that. All the inevitability he had felt, the certainty—an illusion, a trick of the hormones and the—what was it called?—the limbic system, to ensure that men pursued women beyond all reason, groveled, lied, betrayed themselves, just to capture and possess women, to ensure the survival of the species. A cruel system, overriding reason, decency, self-respect.

"So, you didn't tell me if you're from here originally," he said after he had calmed down a little. Might as well at least laugh at himself, play the ironic sophisticate slyly poking fun at the low-class whore, try to salvage a bit of his dignity.

It only seemed to enrage her, as if she understood what he was doing. "You shut the fuck up," she said, pointing at him with the hand holding her wine glass. It was trembling slightly. "I told you I'd eat with you, but I'm not going to sit here and listen to your faggot conversation and smell the come on your breath."

She said it kind of loud. People at a couple of tables close by looked around.

She took another long drink.

"You can get it down faster if you take it straight from the bottle," he said, trembling with anger.

She spat it at him. She actually spat half a cup of wine straight into his face, and splattered the rest of her glass on him too.

"I told you to *shut the fuck up*!" she yelled, face contorted with rage. "I told you I don't want to smell the *come* on your breath!"

The restaurant had gone silent. Wayne stood up, wringing the wine off his hands, wiping it from his face with his napkin. He got out of the booth and walked away between faces staring up at him from the tables.

"Hey! *Hey!* Where's my twenty-five dollars, you queer? You owe me twenty-five dollars! You owe me twenty-five—"

In the silence of the restaurant he could hear the clunk as she stood up on her crutches, and as he stopped at the podium to pay the horrified hostess he could see her from the corner of his eye coming after him, wobbling drunkenly.

From the corner of his eye he saw her fall. He didn't see how, but she had just drunk half a bottle of wine on top of her drugs, and her crutch might have hit some-body's chair. People were jumping up, and by the time he got back to her two men were leaning over her. Her with-ered leg was twisted grotesquely backward. Looking at it made him feel sick.

"God damn!" she was whispering. "Oh, God damn!"

"Lift her up," Wayne said, trembling, putting out his hands. "Gently. Watch her leg."

He and the two men carefully lifted her to a standing position. Her face was white and twisted with agony, eyes closed, and she was still whispering "Oh God damn, Oh God." She couldn't stand by herself.

"Can you help me?" Wayne asked the men. He put his arm around her, and one of them did the same on the other side, and they carried her, her good leg pumping blindly as if she was trying to walk. The second man car-ried her crutches and opened the door.

Wayne fumbled with his car keys while the men held her. He reclined the front passenger seat, and they put her in. Wayne clumsily fastened the seat belt around her.

"You don't think she needs an ambulance?" asked one of the men anxiously.

"I'll take her to the hospital." Wayne shook the two men's hands, a sob rising in his throat. As he pulled away from the curb he saw their backs, bent with shock, going back in through the restaurant door.

Gail was panting, lips parted, tears running down her cheeks.

"I'll have you at the hospital in five minutes," said Wayne.

"No. Take me home." Her voice was throaty with pain. "I need to go home."

"I'll take you home, but I want to make sure nothing's broken or—"

"No. No hospital. Take me home."

"Gail—"

"I'll be okay. Take me home."

"Gail—"

"They'll put me in jail, don't you understand?" she sobbed desperately, suddenly. "I need to go home. I *need* to go *home*."

"OK," he said after a minute, shaken. She was right. If she was as full of drugs as she looked a hospital blood test would be enough to convict her.

He pulled up to her apartment house in a flaming purple sunset. He held her crutches in his left hand and put his right arm around her. She leaned heavily on him, the softness and strength of her body and the bitter smell of pain and sweat giving him a strange sad feeling. She gasped with every step, and it was slow going up the stairs. The booming of televisions seemed all around them in the dark. When they got to her door she banged it open, pulled the crutches from him with trembling hands, and struggled gasping into the dark behind the silent TV whose moving pictures lit the living room dim grey, only a hint of deep red and purple showing by the windows where sunset leaked around the shades.

Wayne came slowly into the stuffy apartment; it struck him that he should make sure she wasn't too badly injured. On the TV someone was juggling, with cuts to the glad face of a talk-show host. There was a shut door behind the TV in the darkness.

He listened at the door. Silence under the dull TV boom from the next apartment. Then someone started to throw up, vomit splashing into a toilet. Wayne's heart sped up. She was in the bathroom going into shock or vomiting from concussion; he had to take her to the hospital despite everything, maybe to save her life. He listened. There was no retching or sounds of agony, just the thorough and systematic emptying of a stomach. Then the sounds stopped, and in a minute the toilet flushed. Then water was turned on, and someone gargled.

Heroin. It was heroin, he realized with a sinking feeling, consulting the encyclopedic drug knowledge people of his generation had grown up with; heroin, the glazed-eyed nurse, the powdered paradise, the drug that made you throw up when you shot it, and made your pupils big, and made you irritable and angry when you needed more—

When she opened the door and came out of the bathroom he was pretending to watch the TV.

"You still here?" she asked, and her voice was dull and sleepy, without a trace of pain. In the TV light he saw that her pupils had eaten up her eyes, giving her the strange, blind look.

She crutched to the greasy sofa, her face smooth and unlined. Her left cuff was unbuttoned. She lowered herself onto the bed pillows with a sigh, breasts shifting under her shirt.

"Go away," she said without looking at him.

11

The next afternoon Wayne took Linden Street out of town and was soon in the countryside, following narrow roads between dusty, sun-bright trees and tussocky fields buzzing with insects. At first he was confident he was on the right road, but soon realized he had taken a wrong turn. He retraced his path; there were the electric transmission towers marching along through a firebreak that rolled up and down hill over the countryside until it was lost in the distance. He turned his car there, raising a plume of dust, and started again. This time he took a later left, but soon it crossed a shallow stream in the woods. There had been no stream on the way to the cottage. He retraced his path again.

Starting again from the transmission lines he took his first right instead of left, figuring he had misremembered the sequence of turns. This seemed hopeful at first, and he thought he recognized a sharp corner with pine trees on one side and a rusty, overgrown barbed-wire fence on the other, but soon he was unsure again. He took another left, then tried a right, but one road ended at a farmer's track and another wound back to a county route with two lanes and a median.

In the end, after two hours of driving, he decided that his memory was too poor to find his way. He would have to use the brute force method: get a map and drive down all the roads around here one at a time until he found the cottage. Unless it was something that could only be seen in the intersection of dreams and waking, which had been sent to him by the legendary shamans for a payment of $5,000. But in the bright sunlight his sense of reality rebelled at this thought.

He drove back to St. Clair, a thought coming back to him ripening to an impulse. The crippled, crazy heroin addict Gail. He had seen her on the night of his vision of the far continent; a residue or penumbra of the vision had seemed to lead him to St. Clair, to the Laundromat. Had he been "led to the people and things destiny had picked out for him" as the library book had said the ancient shamans believed? Or was it a lot of malarkey, a coincidence invested with the aura of providence by epileptoid firing in his brain?

However you looked at it, the realization hit him almost with a sense of shame that he wanted to see her. She was a drug addict, defective, and probably mentally disturbed. She had humiliated and abused him on their "date." Was his self-esteem so low that he wanted more of that kind of treatment? It was a Jungian paradox: he, Wayne Dolan, consumed by fantasies of the perfect silky girl and of Her who lived in the other world, now wanted to see this twisted, raging, defective woman.

Anyway, he had good enough reason to visit her just one more time, he told himself. It would be the decent thing to do to make sure she was all right after her fall, see if she needed anything. And he *was* writing a book here, after all. The more colorful characters he ran across the better.

On another impulse he stopped at the grocery store and bought her some food, nothing elaborate, but plenty of sweets. He had heard that heroin addicts liked sweets. He picked up a bottle of wine as he passed that shelf but after a moment's thought put it back.

There was the sound of TV from inside her apartment. It got turned low when he knocked, and after he knocked a second time the door opened and she leaned on the jamb tiredly. She looked wrinkled and wan, as if she had slept in her clothes, and as if she could use some groceries. A regret went through him that he hadn't bought healthier food.

They looked at each other for a minute. Then the bag crackled as he held it up. "I got you some groceries."

She looked at him deadpan for another minute. Then she took the bag from his hands and closed the door in his face.

He leaned on the jamb sadly. In about two minutes the door opened again.

He came in. The shades were half up so that it was almost bright in the room. She was on the sofa, sitting against her soiled bed pillows. The carton of donuts he had brought was open and two donuts were gone already; she was chewing another ravenously.

He came over slowly, cautiously sat on the sofa as far away from her as possible. For a few minutes he watched her eat donuts as if she was starving.

"How's your leg?" he asked finally.

She looked up at him as if she had just noticed him. "I spit on you yesterday and called you a faggot." Her voice was low, subdued.

"Yes."

"So what are you doing back here?"

"I'd like to take you to dinner again."

"After I spit on you and called you a faggot and told you I didn't want to smell the come on your breath?" she asked with heated incredulity, as if angry at him for being so stupid.

"Yes."

She picked up another donut delicately between her thumb and forefinger, bit it with thoughtful relish, looking away from him. "It's going to cost you. And you'll get hurt in the end. Hurt bad."

"I know," he said, realizing that she was right. Tears stung his eyes. He suddenly put his trembling hands on her shoulders, tried to kiss her mouth full of donut.

She pushed him off, pushed his hands away, but not angrily, just in a businesslike way, almost distractedly.

"Do you have your two hundred dollars?"

"No."

"Then you can't touch me. You understand?" She looked into his eyes suddenly, with surprising earnestness and seriousness.

"Yes."

"You can take me to dinner tonight. I'll only charge you twenty-five dollars because of the groceries. But go away now. Come back at nine."

———

He went home and showered, put on his tightest jeans, newest T-shirt, and best old suit jacket. Back in St. Clair, he restrained himself from buying a bottle of champagne. Chocolates and flowers were too corny. He walked up and down the tourist streets, looking in the shop windows for just the right thing. Finally he saw in a jeweler's window a bright, heavy sterling silver chain. It cost him sixty-five dollars, but it was perfect: plain and powerful and beautiful.

When the last intense red sliver of sun disappeared into the blue-grey horizon it was five minutes to nine. Wayne drove to the apartment house, hands sweating, the painful stimulus of last night giving him a Pavlovian aversion despite his desire. It was a sign that he shouldn't be here, he argued with himself: the whole purpose of his life was to find and marry the silky girl; at this very moment he should be laying his plans, preparing himself. But when Gail opened the apartment door he was somewhat reassured. She had put on fresh jeans and a man's dress shirt that her breasts filled tautly, her hair was brushed, and she seemed to be wearing makeup. Her eyes looked almost human. Her face gave a little quirk, like the beginning of a smile.

He said, awkwardly: "I brought you something."

He held up the midnight-blue case as she leaned on her crutches. She took the necklace out with one hand, held it up. Her eyes when she glanced at him were full of pain. She said nothing, but put the necklace over her head, shaking her hair to get it free, and let it fall onto her neck and inside her shirt. She looked at him again, sadly and defiantly.

Tears stung his eyes. He had two hundred dollars in his back pocket, separate from his other money, but he left it there now, secret. He held the apartment door for her.

He had reservations at a nice place with a terrace, so they sat under trees hung with dim lights in the warm, still night air. She ordered steak and wine again, giving him her little quirk of an almost-smile. He decided to be brave. When the waitress had gone, he clasped his hands under his chin and said: "So, are you from this area originally?"

The quirk turned into a real smile. She was very beautiful. "No," she said.

"Will you marry me?"

This time she laughed, a quick, beautiful, ironic laugh from her beautiful throat. "What is it with you? I haven't exactly been charming to you."

Her eyes were shining, and her voice had lost its gutter brassiness; it was soft, almost educated. Had she gotten just the right dose of her medicine? he wondered. Or was it a matter of timing: past the sleepy stage but not yet to the itchy, irritable, craving stage? Either way, he could almost have been out to dinner with an ordinary woman in her late twenties.

"You're maddeningly beautiful. And also, I guess there's more to you than meets the eye."

She was suspicious. "Like what?"

"Like I don't know. You tell me. Obviously you're not the typical—" He stopped, aware of his blunder.

"Typical what?"

Somehow he knew she would be able to smell phoniness, like an animal or a child. He looked into her eyes and, after a pause, said seriously: "Drug addict. Prostitute."

It shook her. She looked straight at him, and then her beautiful green eyes filled with tears. For a second her mouth twisted and he thought she was going to start screaming curses and spitting at him again. But instead one of the tears spilled down her cheek.

"Fuck you, Fredrick," she sobbed suddenly, quietly.

"I don't understand," he said shakily. "I don't understand how someone like you could end up—like this."

"Someone like me," she sobbed, looking around to see if anyone was watching her. Her eyes were haunted. "What do you know about *me*?" Her voice was contemptuous, and the last word grated with rage.

"Nothing. Nothing." He hung his head in sorrow and shame. Then he looked up at her. "Tell me."

"Take me home," she said. "You can keep your twenty-five dollars. And this." She fumbled in her collar for the necklace.

"No. Please."

Angrily: "Yes. Now. Or do want me to spit on you again?"

"I don't care." She looked at him for a split second then, and he followed up on his advantage. "I think I'm in love with you."

The shake in his voice was real, and she was like an animal or a child; she could tell. She stopped and looked at him. He put his hand on hers across the table. It was hot, moist, as if flushed with her crying. She pulled it away.

"Find some nice straight girl with nice straight legs, Fredrick. You and me got nothing to talk about." Her voice was hard. She put her hand out for her crutches.

Time to try his ace card. He pulled out the two-hundred dollar bills, laid them on the table in front of her.

She looked down at them in surprise, then up at him with a contempt that he thought was mixed with misery, then down at them again. Finally, she licked her lips and said in her hardest, slangiest voice, a small, fierce smile on her face: "Well, you got to take me home first, Fredrick. We can't do it here."

"No." He kept his hand palm down on the bills, half covering them. "This isn't for that. I want you to tell me about yourself."

She looked up at him, her hardness troubled by doubt.

"I want you to tell me about yourself. From the time you were a little girl. How you got to be like this. That's what this money is for."

She looked down at the bills, shaking her head, not so much in refusal, he thought, as in confusion.

"Then you can have the two hundred dollars. And then if you want I'll take you home."

She looked up at him suspiciously, almost fearfully. "What do you want to know?"

"Everything."

"You bastard," she said in a low, angry voice. "You stupid bastard."

Just then their food came, a slim, polite Latin boy laying it before them gently, glancing curiously at the bills on the table. He poured Gail a glass of wine and she drank it with a shaking hand, then started on her bloody steak, sawing it with her knife, not looking at Wayne. Wayne ate slowly, watching her. As she ate and drank she seemed to become calmer, as if alcohol and protein were a stopgap substitute for her drug.

Finally she started to talk, still without looking at Wayne, still sawing and chewing and drinking, talking in jerky sentences between mouthfuls. Her voice was dark, not quite sullen.

"My father made me the way I am. When I was a little girl he did an experiment on me, and it made me this way."

"What?" said Wayne, shocked.

"He was a scientist—is a scientist. A famous fucking scientist at this Institute place near here. And everybody thinks he's such a fucking great man. And he's just a fucking pig. He did this to me. When I was a little girl he gave me a shot. I remember it. He told me it would be good for me, like a vitamin. I trusted him, looked up to him like a god. He held my hand while he gave it to me. If it was so fucking good, why didn't he take it himself? He gave it to me, used me as a guinea pig. And after that I was all twisted, ruined. My leg didn't grow anymore, and I grew up twisted inside, dark."

Wayne felt sick. He put a forkful of pasta back onto his plate. "You're kidding."

"I'm not kidding. And he's a millionaire. He works at this fucking Institute place and they pay him millions. And you know what he gives me? Nothing. *Nada.* He wouldn't give me anything to save my life. He pretends I don't exist, doesn't want any of his great scientist friends to know I exist, or anyone else. But they're going to know I exist. Oh, yeah, they're going to know. If he doesn't do right by me. If he doesn't give me what he owes me for doing this to me." She looked up at Wayne now, and her eyes were hot, obsessed, like the eyes of a crazy person.

"I tried to sue him, but my lawyer double-crossed me. Told me I wouldn't be able to prove that he had given me the shot, or that the shot did this to me. But I know it did. And he's going to pay me, or else all his great, big friends and the whole world are going to find out what he did. That's why I moved out here after him. I want him to know he's never going to get rid of me until he pays me, and the day is coming when I'm going to expose him if he doesn't."

Wayne was sitting back in his chair watching her helplessly. "But—who is he?" he asked. "What's his name?"

"What difference does that make to you?"

"I'm—I'm writing a book about the Institute. That's why I'm in town. I know a lot of the Institute people."

She studied him with renewed interest. Finally she said: "Raymond Hall. Dr. Raymond Hall, Ph.D., big fucking Nobel prize winner."

⬤

The story hadn't seemed to affect her appetite, but Wayne felt queasy. He asked her questions, watching her eat and drink in her ravenous, animal way. Her mother had died when she was two. She had been seven when her father had given her the shot; they had lived in Princeton, in a nice house with trees in the yard and a picket fence; she was vague about what had been in the shot: some kind of serum that was supposed to make her smarter or something. After dinner she had a huge ice cream, which she dispatched with as much gusto as the steak, still drinking, but after that she seemed to get irritable, chafing under his questions, though her hand greedily devoured the two hundred-dollar bills when he pushed them toward her. Her pupils were getting small now, and she was restless, face greyish with a sheen of sweat, as if nauseated by her huge, rich meal.

"I have to go home," she said finally. "Take me home."

He caught her mood of urgency and took her home. Night was deep blue as he pulled up by the apartment house, streetlights half-shaded by the big, untrimmed trees. She ignored him as he followed her slowly up the stairs in stuffy darkness. She banged into the apartment, headed for the bathroom without a word, banged the door closed behind her. He shut the apartment door and sat on the sofa in the light of a tattered table lamp.

After a minute he could hear her rummaging loudly in the bathroom, and then she screamed. He jumped off the sofa and she burst out of the bathroom, seeming to leap across the living room at him despite her crutches. She stood in front of him trembling, pinprick eyes wide, sweating face contorted.

"What did you do with my stash, you bastard?" she screamed at him. "What did you do with it?"

"What? What are you—?"

"Don't give me that shit!" she shrieked in insane rage, and her clawed hand grabbed his collar. "What did you do with it?"

"How could I have done anything with it? You saw me when I was up here. I never went in there."

"Don't give me that you fucking—!"

"Don't yell at Fredrick," came a low, earnest voice from Wayne's left. "He said he don't know anything about your scag."

Wayne and Gail jerked around. The man King was standing in the dark kitchen doorway watching them calmly. He was dressed exactly as before, in jeans, work shirt, vest, and cowboy boots.

"Don't you believe Fredrick?" he said to their surprised faces. "He just told you he don't know anything about your scag."

"King," said Gail anxiously.

"Yeah, man," said King, his voice mellow.

"You—you took my stash? I didn't know you were coming up, why didn't you call me, man? I—I need it right now, King."

"You going to talk like that in front of this narc? Why don't you just sign a confession?"

She waved her hand impatiently. "He's no narc, he's just some poor sucker wants my ass."

"You give it to him?"

"No. Look, man, I need my stuff, bad. Can I have it?" She crutched over to him and put out her hand appealingly. She was an inch or two shorter than he was.

"I flushed it, baby. You know I don't approve of shit like that. And neither does Fredrick. I *know* Fredrick wouldn't like you to be using, so I flushed it."

"You didn't." Her voice shook hard.

"Yeah, I did," he said, looking into her face with slow relish. "What you going to do, call the cops? Why don't you call them?" He paused, watching her. Her eyes were down, searching blindly for nothing. "And now that you're hanging with Fredrick, you don't need that kind of shit anymore. You don't need me, neither. I was just kind of getting you ready for your new life."

"King, this fool is nobody. He wants to give me money to sit across from him at restaurants, and I take it. OK? I haven't fucked him, and I'm not going to. I still love *you*, baby. I need you." Her voice trembled as if she meant it, meant it desperately.

"Nah, you don't need me no more." He looked at her sweating face with his sadistic smile. "You got Fredrick. I'll see you around."

He started to move toward the door.

"King!" she grabbed his arm. Her voice was desperate, harsh with fear. "I need it, baby. You *get the fuck out* of here!" she screamed at Wayne, turning toward him as if just remembering he was there. Her face was frightening, scraped raw, eyes red, mouth drawn wide with fear and hunger.

"No, let him stay a minute," said King, glancing at Wayne. "I want to show him something." He looked back at Gail. "You want it, baby?" he murmured.

"Yes." She was sobbing now, her hand still on his wrist.

"How much?"

"I told you—"

"OK." He shook off her hand. Then he reached down and undid his jeans. They were the kind that buttoned, and he undid each button slowly, watching her face.

Wayne was paralyzed. He was bigger than King and he could beat him, beat his sadistic, dominant face until it was broken, until the man was unconscious or dead— But Gail had told him to get out; she needed this man for drugs; if he beat up King she would be cut off, and it would be his fault. And who knew what King could do to him, what weapons or friends he had. He couldn't do anything to King. But he had to at least get out, get out of there. But what if King hurt her? And a kind of hypnotic, fascinated horror was on him now, as King unbuttoned his pants, watching Gail watch his hands.

The jeans came open, revealing sparse, reddish pubic hair and a short, thick penis, ruddy as if from hard use, pulsing slowly erect like a thick, blind, sluggish worm seeking some carrion that was its food.

"You need me, baby?" asked King. "Show me. Show me how much you need me."

She hesitated, turning half toward Wayne again, but this time her eyes were down, her face white. Then she turned back to King, and with a glance at his face she slowly lowered herself on her crutches until she was kneeling in front of him. He pulled the crutches away so that they fell down on each side with a thump, and she held on to his hips to steady herself. He pulled her hands away and lowered her the rest of the way. She gasped as weight went onto her withered leg. Then she took his penis in her mouth, tongue first, pushing herself forward until the whole, thick, ruddy worm was inside her mouth and throat, her eyes closed, one of her hands holding his hairy testicles, rolling them slowly in her fingers, the other on his hip to steady herself.

"Yeahhh, that's nice, baby," he said. "Now take off your shirt. I want to see your nips while you do that. I bet Fredrick would like to see them too."

Without opening her eyes she fumbled at the buttons on her shirt, undid them each clumsily, then pulled the shirt aside roughly so that it slid down her arms, her breasts exposed, shockingly naked and beautiful, the nipples small and perfect. Then she put the hand back to him, working his penis in and out of her mouth, sucking it with little gulps in her throat, eyes closed, breasts wagging slightly. The silver chain Wayne had given her lay around her neck and down onto her breasts, and King took it and twisted it until it choked her, biting into the flesh of her neck like a leash, and she choked, but just kept moving her head back and forth, sucking.

King's body was shaken by her mouth as if by a powerful force, and he gasped, but his chin was lifted, half-closed eyes looking down at Wayne, a frown of exaggerated dominance on his face that would have been comical had it not been so horrible.

Wayne's hands and stomach were shaking, his palms slick. He was sick and light-headed, dizzy, numb inside, full of something that might have been rage or arousal or nausea if he had been able to feel it. With a huge effort he moved toward the door, slowly at first, dragging himself, but as he went the urgency of his movement increased, so that he was running by the time he reached it, and slamming it behind him ran down the stairs desperately in the dark, stumbling on his own feet, and out into the cool, aromatic night.

As he ran to his car her small, sharp animal cries of pain came from the upstairs window, again and again. He started the car, slammed it into gear, and roared away as fast as he could go.

He drove with all his windows open, drove aimlessly and fast on country roads, the sweet, deep blue air of the summer night blowing on him and slowly soothing his trembling and nausea. Still, it was two hours before he could turn his car around and try to find St. Clair again in the night, and another hour before he pulled up in front of the apartment house.

Its windows were dark, except one lit by a blue-grey glow. He climbed the stairs silently, listened at the apartment door. Only the murmur of TV. He opened the door without knocking.

She lay propped on the sofa, facing the TV. He sat on the edge of the sofa and put his hands on her shoulders. One side of her mouth was swollen, a little dried blood at the corner of the lips, and around her neck was an ugly welt. Her eyes on him were all pupil, large and velvet.

He put his arms around her, her breasts warm against him, her lips warm and moist and passive beneath his. She pushed him away, but without anger. Her voice was sleepy, relaxed, docile: "Go away. I'm OK. It doesn't hurt me. Go away."

A tiny glint of reflected TV light caught his eye. The silver necklace he had bought her, broken now, was clasped in her hand.

12

When Wayne woke up next morning exhausted from feverish dreams, the sun was shining on smooth green swells. No model-beauties were on the beach, so he took a swim to wash off the trauma of the night. The air held an overripe humidity, the water tepid in the oblique yellow sunlight falling between the bluff trees, and the swells were round and murky, a kind of comfortable primordial soup. The blue of the sky shaded into the morning grey of distance on the Lake horizon.

Wayne swam until he was calm, washed clean of earthly attachments. Gail Hall was nothing to him, after all, despite the impression she had made; he could return to his solitariness, forget her depravity and beauty and desperation except as food for his book. At most she had been a detour from his pursuit of the silky girl. A familiar feeling, a thrill of excitement, fear, yearning, and depression came over him at the thought of the girl down the beach, her warm, small body and beating heart.

He went in for some cornflakes.

After two bowls of the ambrosia he composed himself and picked up the kitchen phone. Whatever else happened, a writer couldn't afford to ignore grist for his mill. A courteous, quiet-voiced man answered at Deriwelle Laboratory Building A.

"I'm sorry, Dr. Hall is in conference," he told Wayne. "May I take your number?"

"Well, actually, if there's any way I could speak with him—"

"I'll certainly give him the message as soon as he's free."

"It's somewhat urgent," Wayne said in his best bland but portentous voice. "I really think he would want to talk to me right away."

"If you'll give me the substance of it, I'll be sure to give him a detailed—"

"It's—sensitive. Of a personal nature."

The man hesitated.

"A family issue," Wayne added.

"Let me see if Dr. Hall can break free for a moment."

There were two minutes of silence, and then Raymond Hall's heavy, authoritative voice. "Hello?"

"Dr. Hall? This is Wayne Dolan. The writer. We met the other night at your Convocation. At the reception afterward."

"Yes, and how may I help you?" The undertone of impatience and distaste was thinly disguised.

"Well, I've just been doing some research for my book on the Deriwelle Institute," Wayne drawled, "and I came across a source I wanted to cross-check with you."

"I see. I'm sorry, Mr. Dolan, but as I believe I told you—"

"Her name is Gail Hall," said Wayne. "She indicated that she's your daughter."

Silence on the other end of the phone.

"As I think I may have mentioned at the reception, I hope in my book to take an in-depth look at the Institute and the people who work there. But, of course, I want to be as fair as possible. Ms. Hall has given me some—leads, but I wanted to make sure I confirmed them with you to ensure, you know . . ."

"Yes. Yes, of course, I appreciate that." Hall's voice was now cautious, attentive. He paused. "I think I may have a cancellation in my schedule this afternoon. Would you like to come down to the lab then?"

——

By two o'clock the day had turned hot, and the vast, emerald Institute grounds seemed washed pale by the sunlight. Wayne took the unaccustomed avenue down to Laboratory Building A, which was set back almost against the forest. The guards who buzzed the door open and directed him to step through the metal-detector were more numerous, burlier, and more police-serious than the guards at Building B. Classified recombinant DNA research went on here, he remembered. One of the guards escorted him down a quiet, industrial-plush hall to a door with a pebbled-glass window.

Inside, the decor was the same industrial-plush as the hallway. A smoothly groomed man with the soft, courteous voice Wayne had heard on the phone told him that Dr. Hall would be right with him.

Wayne sat in a soft armchair, feeling the way you do in the dentist's waiting room. The Hall family generally made him very nervous, he reflected. At five minutes past two an inner door opened and Dr. Hall appeared in a starched shirt and tie, handed a folder to the man at the desk, and turned to Wayne, a courteous, serious look on his large, handsome face, though still with an undertone of absence, as if much of his mind was preoccupied with deep matters. He gestured politely toward the open door and said to the secretary: "No calls."

This man was a Nobel prize-winning scientist, Wayne reminded himself as he sat in another armchair in front of a large, tidy desk in Hall's large, tidy office. Engaged in groundbreaking research. He knew things that Wayne could study for years without understanding. And he, Wayne Dolan, was here almost as a blackmailer, at best a tabloid newspaper hound of the kind that had hunted Princess Diana to her death. His hands were sweating enough to smudge his notes.

Hall settled himself in his chair, folded his hands on the desk, and looked at Wayne politely. Blinds were drawn over large windows, adjusted so that only a little sunlight entered. In the soft, bright illumination from expensive lamps, Hall's dark, bland eyes were hard to read behind their large glasses.

"So," he said. "What can I do for you, Mr. Dolan?"

"Well," said Wayne, flustered. The outline he had jotted down seemed vague suddenly, the questions he had written, and which he now surveyed, seeming either insupportably intrusive or laughably equivocal. "I—" It belatedly occurred to him that Hall would wonder how he had just happened to meet his daughter, and would assume that there had been prying and skulking involved. "Without meaning to—" No, don't be apologetic; the thing was to get Hall on the defensive at once, to control the interview.

Hall was watching him curiously, giving, without moving a muscle, the impression of a man looking at his watch.

"I talked to your daughter," Wayne finally blurted in what sounded to himself like a bleating voice.

Hall continued to watch him politely and blandly.

"Gail," said Wayne breathlessly, as if to establish that he knew her name. "With the crutches—" He made a gesture showing how crutches fit under a person's arms.

Hall nodded the slightest bit. It seemed he was aware that he had a daughter named Gail who used crutches.

"And how is Gail?" His voice was calm, solicitous, courteous.

"Not so good," said Wayne. "Not so good, and that's one of the things I came to ask you about."

Hall raised his eyebrows politely, noncommitally.

A sudden, head-clearing resentment woke in Wayne as he looked at the bland, pleasant face of this great man who sat in his plush office and asked about his crippled heroin-addict daughter like someone inquiring after a distant great-aunt.

"Yes. She blames you for some of her difficulties."

"For some?" asked Hall, a weariness entering his voice. "Or for all?"

He sighed and turned his gaze to the windows. If they hadn't been shaded he could have gazed out them wearily and sadly. Instead he turned his eyes back to Wayne.

"What's her story this month?" he asked. "What does she say I did to her?"

Wayne held his voice steady. "She says you gave her a shot when she was seven years old. Some kind of experimental serum. Except the experiment—wasn't a success."

"Did she tell you what was in this 'experimental serum'?"

"You did give her the shot, then?"

Hall studied him, as if trying to decide how to handle him. Finally, he said: "For certain reasons, I can't talk about that. But assuming there was a shot, does she know what was in it?"

"She didn't say, except to indicate that she blames it for her—problems."

"So she has no idea what she believes I gave her. Could it have been medicine? An inoculation, for example, to counteract a disease? I was a parent as well as a scientist, you know, at that time."

Wayne stayed silent. Gail *was* probably crazy. But the mention of her name and the vaguest hint at her story had changed Hall's mind about giving him an interview. If there was nothing to what she said, why had he done that?

As if reading his thoughts, Hall went on sadly: "Mr. Dolan, in Gail you see a tragedy, one of the two great tragedies of my life. The first was the death of my wife. Do you have children, Mr. Dolan? Can you imagine how it feels when your daughter hates you so much that you feel you have to be always on your guard? Gail is disturbed, Mr. Dolan. This is not the first time, not by a long, long shot, that she has tried to disrupt my life, besmirch my reputation with her wild accusations. It happened while I was still at Harvard, many times while I was at Cold Spring, and there was even an embarrassing incident when I was awarded the Nobel prize."

"And yet," said Wayne nervously, "according to your talk at the Convocation, you have been working on a kind of experimental serum for years, right?"

Anger now flashed through Hall's reserve. "An 'experimental serum' to improve the lot of mankind, Mr. Dolan. Not to injure or deform."

"But experimental serums don't always work the way they're supposed to. That's why they're experimental, right? I mean, how could you know that a serum might not injure or deform if it had never been tried before?"

Hall was shaking his head angrily. "No. I refuse to sit here and listen to this—this nonsense." He composed himself with an effort. "Now I want you to hear me, Mr. Dolan, because I'm only going to tell you this once. I don't have time to spend my entire career defending myself against delusional accusations. Perhaps you don't have the expertise to recognize the indicia of dementia and paranoia; I'm willing to give you the benefit of the doubt.

"People like you are suspicious of scientists. Because we work in ways you don't understand, because our discoveries upset the very foundations of your beliefs, because we occasionally seem to wield an uncanny power over nature, lay people suspect and dislike scientists. They ascribe to us a whole array of evil qualities, from arrogance to impiety to callousness. But I'm here to tell you, Mr. Dolan, that no father ever loved his daughter more than I loved Gail. She was all that was left to me after her mother died. If you had known her when she was a little girl—" Here he seemed choked by real emotion; but no tears came, and in a minute he went on. "I would never have done anything to hurt her. *Ever.* If I gave her this serum—and let's say, hypothetically, that I did—if I gave her a serum, it would never have been anything to hurt her, but only something to protect her, strengthen her. Yet now, to a mind ravaged by addiction and disease—you've seen her—which will seize upon anything to blame for its own condition, to avoid taking responsibility—that act of a father giving an inoculation to his daughter takes on a sinister meaning, it's twisted, brooded over through years, and finally made to look criminal." Hall's eyes were haunted, and his breathing had deepened.

"Protect her and strengthen her how?" asked Wayne.

"I beg your pardon?"

"Protect and strengthen her how? Not the stuff you're working on now, was it? Not your antireligious serum?" Hall was silent. "Not on a seven-year-old girl?"

A momentary, almost frightening gleam came into Hall's eyes.

"You can't be serious," said Wayne. His nervousness and righteous anger were gone now, replaced by a sinking queasiness. "You neutralized the part of her brain that gives higher meaning to things? A seven-year-old girl? Jesus."

"Gives the illusion of higher meaning," said Hall. "Obscures reality by providing a delusional system of higher meaning. Don't you understand? Didn't you hear my lecture?"

"But—even supposing that's true, couldn't—Jesus, a seven-year-old child—"

"A child will grow up stronger, will develop coping mechanisms based on reality-based cognition rather than on delusion."

"But look at her. And her leg—"

"That's just another sign of how much you don't understand," Hall said contemptuously. "It had nothing whatsoever to do with her leg. That's the motor cortex, a completely different area of the brain than the vaccine would affect. CNS motor paralysis diseases afflict a percentage of the population. To connect that with the vaccine is completely ridiculous. As to her other problems, addicts always blame some outside force that makes them powerless against their drug."

"But someone who doesn't believe there's any higher meaning to life—to counteract that despair—"

"Mr. Dolan." Hall was looking straight at him across the desk, and his anger seemed to have ebbed, replaced by a kind of sadness, as of a man who has come to grips with unpleasant truths. "Listen to me. No, please listen for a minute. I know you're upset about Gail, and you may not believe this, but I like that about you. Gail is my daughter, Mr. Dolan, despite everything, and someone who can see past her sickness and see her the way I remember her—" He looked down at the desk for a minute, as if overcome by strong emotion. "But let's try to talk sense to one another, see things more clearly. Do

you think scientists are immune from the lure, the seduc-
tion of higher meaning? That for some reason we're not
like other people, that we don't wish everything made
sense, that we could live forever in some kind of afterlife,
that the grotesque evils and insanity of this world had a
cosmic inner pattern and plan? We're human, Wayne—
I'm human. In fact, what do you think scientists have
been doing for the last five hundred years but looking for
that very inner pattern and plan, searching for it, from
Kepler, who scanned the heavens to find the workings of
the divine order, to Newton, who invented calculus and
physics for use in the religious treatise that was his life's
work, to Darwin, who searched living organisms for evidence of a creator? In fact, it is the *scientists* who are
the real devotees of higher meaning, and it is the scientists who would have found it if it existed. The early scientists were all monks and clergy, did you know that?
Science began as a religious exercise: it was believed that
the study of nature would reveal the hand of the Creator
and hints as to His divine plan. It was never suspected
that no sign of a God would ever be found at all, that
deep, rigorous study of nature over hundreds of years using incredibly sophisticated techniques would turn up
not one iota of evidence—not *one*, anywhere—that God
exists or that any greater intelligence of any kind exists,
but instead would show that everything works according
to mindless, mechanical laws, and that human consciousness is a fluke of the outworking of some of these
laws. From the farthest reaches of space to the tiniest
particles inside the atom, from sand to the most complicated living creatures, scientists have explored them
all, and no God has been found or even suggested—there
are only these mechanical laws as far as the eye can see.
This isn't some whim or premature conclusion or philo-

sophical sleight of hand. It is the result of five hundred years of concentrated study by thousands of the best minds of every generation, of millions of objective experiments, of painstaking replication of those experiments, of reasoning, predictions, testing and retesting of predictions, all of which has been gone over again and again by people of all backgrounds and biases, but most of whom, the vast majority of whom would much rather have concluded that there was a higher meaning. If there had been one there to find, we would have found it, we would have fallen on our knees before it, we to whom meaning, pattern is everything.

"But we didn't find it. Try as we could, we simply didn't find it. And, because we had vowed to serve the truth wherever it might lead, we had to admit that to ourselves. It simply wasn't there. You're an educated man; are you aware of any scientific theory that says, 'and at this point natural law stops and God takes over'?"

Wayne shook his head.

"Now, if as a scientist after long study you finally come to see this, contrary as it runs to your instincts and desires, if you have the courage and dedication to truth to face this, and if you also finally come to understand that the human compulsion to believe in a higher meaning is simply a primitive drive programmed by an ancient part of the brain, like sex or aggression, it might occur to you that the human race would be better off without it. Despite its importance in our evolutionary past, it appears to play no positive role in modern life. On the contrary, religious wars, fundamentalist intolerance, anti-intellectual dogmatism, are scourges on our race. If you thought that you had discovered a way to destroy the compulsion that leads to these things without damaging any other part of the brain or body, but if your discovery could work only on a *developing* brain because of the relatively primitive state of DNA technology at that time, and if there was a child you loved and to whom you wished to give this gift of truth, of clarity, of *reality*, what would you have done? To wait until the child was grown and could make her own decision would make no sense, since by that time the vaccine would no longer work. It was either give it to her without her consent or throw the gift away forever. Tell me, what would you have done?"

Hall's face was serious and solicitous, his attention focused on Wayne like a powerful magnetic field that Wayne could feel bending his mind, changing it. Against this strong current he found it difficult to think. "But what if—what if you were wrong?" he said slowly. "And how could you be sure you were right—really sure? If you were wrong and you gave it to her, you might just have screwed her up for life. I mean, you're not the only scientist in the world. Some very smart people have looked at the same data and come to the opposite conclusion. For instance, Dr. Carvery, right here at the Institute, believes in God and the soul and an afterlife."

Hall nodded sadly. "Yes. Dr. Carvery."

"He's a Nobel prize winner too, isn't he?"

"Yes. He was one of the most brilliant scientists I ever worked with. Ed Carvery and I were at Harvard together. But it's a sad story—another senseless, sad story. Several years ago his two-year-old daughter was killed in a car accident, and since then he hasn't been right in his mind. He doesn't sleep, and he's been involved with these parapsychology people." Hall waved his hand, as if trying to brush away something ugly and distressing. "His former colleagues have distanced themselves, and he was put on emeritus status at Harvard. The Institute was practically the only place he could go to do active research."

"But his research has been successful, they say. I heard that his dice-throwing results have shown a significant—"

Hall shook his head. "There was a statistical fluke the first couple of days," he said. "Then things evened out. If you don't believe me, go see him. Don't call him—he doesn't answer the phone: just go up to his office and knock. And tell him to get some sleep, for God's sake. He's been acting suicidal, they say." He shook his head again slowly, as if trying to shake off unhappy thoughts.

"But it's not only Carvery, is it? There are plenty of other scientists who believe in God. Dr. Farris, Burschevsky, maybe even Daniels, though he doesn't talk about it."

Hall shook his head. "Not Daniels."

"But the others. That old lady, what's her name? Remember the questions she was asking you at the Convocation?"

The strange gleam Wayne had seen before came into Hall's eyes, part anger, part something else. "They don't want to believe," he said in a strange voice. "They're Carverys, all Carverys at some level. They're not willing to face the truth. But they'll have no choice but to face it in the end."

The look and strange voice almost made Wayne believe for a minute that Hall had some kind of retribution planned for the refractory scientists, but then the man's tight control reasserted itself, and he was the sober, courteous scholar again.

"Well, but," said Wayne hesitantly. There was the old reluctance to talk about his own experiences, but this was probably the only shot he would get at Dr. Raymond Hall. "I've had some things happen to me that suggest—something going on that's not entirely, you know, within the realm of—of science."

"Yes," said Hall gently, encouraging him to continue.

So he did continue, haltingly at first, but then warming to his subject as Hall watched him with curious, engaged eyes. Wayne told him about his naps on the Shaman's Mound, the dream Indian, the $5,000, and his experiences of "interpenetration of dreams and waking," leaving out the details, the little cottage, the observatories in the mist, and the others, which somehow he just couldn't bring himself to tell. But at the end he had told Hall more than he had told anyone else, even Burschevsky, and he realized suddenly as he finished that he had opened himself to a refutation.

Which Hall gave him, but very gently.

"Wayne," he said. His hands were clasped on his desk, and the large, dark eyes behind the glasses were grave, almost warm. "Your experiences are"—he shook his head, searching for words—"powerful. Compelling. Seductive. When I listen to you, my own heart swells, cries out, wants to believe that this is real, that there is something beyond our world that can redeem us from death, from all the senselessness we have suffered, from all our inadequacies. And your experiences are genuine, I'm convinced of that. You *have* felt and seen all the things you've told me, without a doubt. But Wayne"—he leaned forward intensely—"*it isn't real.* I'm telling you this with not a trace of vindictiveness, but with pain, because it's important for you to know. There's a thumb-sized region on each of side of your brain that if I opened your skull and stimulated it with an electrical probe, you would have these same experiences. You would feel transported, illuminated, absolutely sure of the validity of your experience, but it would just be me with the electrical probe. What happens is, some abnormally strong firing of neurons in this part of your brain takes the place of that probe, and does exactly the same thing.

"Several million years ago some of our ancestors experienced an evolutionary spurt in brain growth over only a few thousand generations. As part of this spurt, and quite by chance, the part of the brain in charge of generalization overlapped with the part in charge of assigning meaning to things, and the result was a small region where these two functions converged, and the result was feelings of generalized meaning, meaning attaching not to particular things, but to *everything*.

"Those humans who had this mutation obtained a kind of inner strength, a willingness to fight seemingly overwhelming odds, since they were convinced that in the end everything would work out in a good and sensible way. And they tended to come together in groups centered around their religious feelings, and work for the good of the group. Both of these things gave them a powerful survival advantage over those without the brain mutation, and their offspring who inherited the mutation also survived disproportionately, until almost everyone had it.

"The experiences conferred by this brain feature are compelling, beautiful, numinous—they had to be to do their evolutionary job. *But they're not real.* They're like the hallucinations of a schizophrenic, which can be powerful and convincing, but are merely the product of abnormal brain functioning. In your case, for instance, your dream of this Indian and his demand for $5,000 has set up an autohypnotic state that apparently kindles these temporal-lobe epileptoid episodes. Do you see that?"

He studied Wayne, then went on.

"Look at it this way. Suppose that in this world we were all or nearly all schizophrenics, with roughly similar hallucinations. For years and years—centuries, perhaps—people would believe that these hallucinations were actually real, until finally perhaps a small group of schizophrenics with relatively more of their thinking functions intact decided to test the hallucinations. So they performed tests over hundreds of years, but not an iota could they find of any objective trace or evidence for the real, objective existence of the shared hallucinations: they showed up on no measuring devices and turned out to be completely unnecessary for the functioning of the world. Of course, the majority of people would still go on believing in the hallucinations, especially if they were pleasant ones. But finally the scientist-schizophrenics—for that is what they would be—would sadly conclude that in fact they were nothing but hallucinations.

"Now suppose someone came along with a cure for schizophrenia, a simple pill or injection that corrected the brain problems causing the disease. As soon as people learned that this cure was going to eliminate their beloved hallucinations, which had already been under attack by the small group of less-impaired scientists, of course there would be an outcry. It would be considered blasphemy, heresy. Some might theorize that what the pill or injection actually did was damage the brain so that it could no longer support the 'higher' perceptions comprising the hallucination. The more philosophically inclined might find ways to argue that the hallucinations were really real despite the fact that a correction of an imbalance in the brain would make them disappear.

"In time, however, a few courageous, truth-seeking souls might try the vaccine—and these would be rewarded by relief from the hallucinations. This would of course make them more intelligent and successful—like the monkeys in the study that I discussed at the Convocation—since they could deal more directly with reality, but this would still probably not be enough to convince the bulk of the population: they would continue to cling to their hallucinations, the only reality they had ever known.

"Of course, the brain abnormality we are talking about here is not schizophrenia, it is the generalization/meaning overlap area in the brain. The shared hallucination is the resulting belief in a higher power, a higher meaning."

He looked at Wayne as if wondering if he had understood.

Wayne could feel the ground slipping out from under his feet. It made so much sense; it was the only plausible explanation, wasn't it? "And so—so, what will the world look like to us if this 'shared hallucination' is removed? If you switch off that part of the brain?"

Hall's eyes were hot with interest. "It's hard to predict. A whole set of reality-based cognitions may be masked by the delusion-creating activity of the 'God module.' Perception is not a passive process in which we receive input from the outside world like camera lenses or microphones. The neural architecture of your brain determines what you see, hear, perceive. If we change this architecture, the way you perceive may change in radical ways. It may be that patterns, gestalts, paradigms, connections between things that have never been made before are just waiting to be discovered when we make this change. Or our perceptual filters may shift so that we actually literally see and hear things we have never seen or heard before."

Wayne's heart seemed to be beating quickly, whether from fear or Hall's infectious excitement, he couldn't tell. "And if people are determined to cling to their—hallucinations?"

Hall shrugged. "The custodians of this new knowledge would have a choice. They could decide either to wait thousands of generations until the brain changes they had caused in themselves and a few others spread through the population as a result of natural selection of the more intelligent and successful nonhallucinators. Or—" Hall shrugged again, but his eyes were still hot on Wayne.

"Or what you did to your daughter."

Hall frowned for a moment, but then said seriously: "I've tried to explain myself as well as I can. I can see you're interested in seeing the world clearly, but that you still have doubts. I'd like to be able to dispel those doubts, if I may. But only if you wish."

"Well—of course. That would be—"

"Good, then." Hall looked at his watch. "Oh, but look at the time. I'm afraid I can't spend any longer on this at the moment. But I have your permission to try to bring you round to my point of view at some later time?"

"Yes, certainly," said Wayne, flattered in spite of his upset, standing as Hall did so.

"Just one more thing," said Hall. "Speaking hypothetically, assuming there had been a shot, a vaccine—it didn't work. Our knowledge of DNA techniques in 1980 was far too primitive. The noninvasive testing I did later showed that the vaccine had not taken effect, had made no measurable changes. So Gail really can't blame her problems on the vaccine—assuming there was one."

The second-floor hallway of the Administration Building was silent, still, and somehow stuffy, probably a contrast to the summer day outside, but to Wayne it seemed to have a mausoleum-like atmosphere. Perhaps some air had seeped out under the door of Edmund Carvery's office, making the whole hallway dim and melancholy, because when Wayne, knocking twice and getting no answer, screwed up his courage and opened the door softly, the air that came out to meet him was sad and stifling, as if it had been breathed too many times, heaved forth in sobs or the faint gasps of despair.

He pushed the door just wide enough to put his head in. The office was dim and still, even more cluttered than he had seen it before, the blinds down over closed windows, and at first he thought it was empty. But then he saw that someone was sitting at the desk, sitting with his head down, as still as the cardboard boxes or piles of paper. For a second Wayne thought he was asleep, and then a blare of panic went through him as he remembered Hall's remark about suicide, but then Carvery stirred and looked up.

He looked terrible. Bleared bags hung under his blurry eyes in the grey skin of his face. He had lost weight, making his slightly saddle-shaped bald head look too big for him, and the narrow shoulders under his shirt and sweater were folded forward exhaustedly.

"Dr. Carvery?" Wayne said as gently as he could, and it came out sounding like a child's voice, piping and shaky. "Dr. Carvery, I hope you don't mind— Are you all right?"

Carvery's head dropped down again as if it were too heavy to hold up, and Wayne saw that he was staring at something on the desk. A photograph. The notion came over Wayne that he had been staring at it for hours.

Carvery made no protest, and after a second's hesitation Wayne came in, shutting the door silently on the fresh air of the hall. He stood looking at Carvery in the dim, chaotic office, and then overcome by curiosity, moved the two steps to the desk. He looked down at the photograph.

It was a little round-faced girl, smiling happily. Someone had made her pigtails, but one had come partway out, and dark baby-hair wisped down on one of her cheeks.

There was a long silence, and then Carvery spoke. His

voice was faint, abstracted, almost puzzled. "I used to tell her stories about what she would do when she grew up," he said. "Go to school, be a mama with her own children, live in a big nice house with cats and dogs, visit her mama and papa. And her eyes would get this far-off look, and she would smile, as if she could see all those things off in the distance."

"I'm so sorry," was all Wayne could think of to say. There was a long silence while Carvery stared down at the picture and Wayne tried to think of anything else. Finally he asked, very gently, in his piping voice: "How did your experiment work out? With the dice?"

Carvery smiled slightly and glanced up at Wayne. All the combative intellectual heat had gone out of him. His skinny hand picked up a sheaf of computer printouts and dropped them an inch back onto the desk. "I should have quit after the first forty six hours," he said, looking back down. "Then I would be almost sure now that I would see her again."

"But you might have been wrong."

Carvery shrugged. "What difference would it have made?"

Another long silence, which Wayne broke at last by saying: "Dr. Hall has been asking about you."

Carvery glanced up again vaguely. "It's very kind of him."

"He—he hopes—that you will seek help if it gets too—if you start feeling like—"

Carvery shook his head slowly. "I'm not going to kill myself, if that's what you're worried about. At least this way there's one of us to remember. If I died, and if there's nothing after, then it would all be gone, vanished, as if it had never been. At least this way there's one of us to remember."

"Have you ever thought of—of having another child?"

Carvery shook his head. "I might forget her then," he said. "And if I forget, and if there's nothing after, then there will be nothing left of her at all. Nothing."

He looked back down at the picture on the desk.

13

That night Wayne dreamed he was in the little blue-green office of the dream Indian, and the realization that he was there jolted him awake, but even awake he was still there, sitting in the plastic chair next to the table, and in the other chair sat the Indian, and the Indian nodded his stony, powerful head, and said, with apparent pride: "We are sponsoring the most important research at your Institute. We inspired it, and we are guiding it." He closed his eyes and nodded in stolid, unwavering certainty.

⸺

"Where have you been?" Gail demanded when she opened her apartment door to him the next day around noon.

That jolted him. He had been trying to figure out how to explain why he had come back at all. "Well—I—wasn't sure—you don't always act glad to see me."

They were standing in the middle of her tiny living

room, she staring at him truculently with small-pupiled eyes. "How much money do you have?"

"With me? Not—"

"Get me a thousand dollars."

"A thousand— Why? Are you—?"

"Go get it."

He opened his mouth to argue, then closed it. The thought crossed his mind that she was going to have sex with him. He had told her she was worth more than $200, and she was taking advantage of that. And now that he had said it he couldn't very well back down; not and keep seeing her. His heart pounded looking at her, part demon, part beautiful animal, part vulnerable woman. He still had almost $20,000 in the bank, even after his donation to the dream Indian, though that wouldn't last him until the book came out, even without the rent on his Mid-Atlantic apartment and his child support. To blow a thousand dollars on a—whatever she was—What if she asked for $2,000, or $5,000? That would be next. She would just keep asking until he said no, and then she would blow him off. She was probably giving it to her friend King, and the two of them were laughing.

He went and got the money. Drove to the Farmers' & Merchants' Bank and wrote a check. When he got back to the apartment he wasn't in a good mood. He noticed that Gail's pupils were larger now, but not enormous, as if she had given herself some medicine but not too much. He handed her the ten crisp hundred-dollar bills, and she shoved them into the back pocket of her jeans as if they were of no importance. Then she put her hand on his shoulder and kissed him. Her breasts were naked under the shirt, her lips warm and moist, and he was enfolded in her musky woman's smell, not too clean, her mouth tasting slightly minty, as if she had just brushed her teeth. It was just one kiss, and there was the barest touching of tongues, but when she pushed him away his heart was pounding, and her face was a little flushed. She looked at him searchingly, as if they had just done a desperate thing and she wanted to be sure she could trust him. What she saw evidently satisfied her, because she turned her face away and said casually: "I'm hungry."

—

"You're looking for what?" Gail asked him as they headed northeast on Linden Street after lunch, with a road map he had picked up at a gas station.

"A house. Cottage," he said awkwardly. "Up on a hill. A rise, like."

"Why?" She had on her black sunglasses, and he couldn't see her expression. "Who lives there?"

"I'm not sure, exactly. I found it the other day kind of by chance. I've been looking for it on and off since."

"Why?"

"I had kind of a— What you might call a—an unusual experience there." He described it to her. She was the only person he had told about it.

She studied him as he headed onto the narrow country road outside town, dusty green bushes and vine-hung trees pressing close on both sides. The day had turned hot and humid, with a whitish haze around the sun; it was hot in the car, but Wayne's air-conditioning wasn't working.

"A gateway to another world." she mused when he had finished.

"Well—I don't know."

"You're fucking crazy."

"Why?"

"There is no other world. There's just this fucking world."

"How do you know that?"

The black glasses were turned on him. "Look at me,"

she said. He looked at her. "If there was another world, don't you think I'd believe in it? I do my best to get as far away from this world as I can. Through the wonders of chemistry."

They rounded a curve, and there ahead were the power lines swooping between their metal towers. "This is where I lose track of which way I went," Wayne said. "Can you see where we are on the map?"

She opened it. "No. Yes. This is Old Lawrence Road, right? Yeah, I see it. So what now?"

"You mark where I drive, and if we don't find the cottage we come back here and start again and take a different route. You mark off each one of the routes so we can be sure we've covered them all. Sooner or later we'll find it."

She sighed, but took the red pen he handed her.

"So how do you know there's no other world, other than your chemistry world?" he asked, trying to keep her amused. Evidently this wasn't the most exciting date she had ever been on.

"Because there's no sign of one anywhere," she said, not quite angry. "Because if there was one, things would be—different."

"But I think I may have seen a sign of one."

"You were fucking hallucinating. Just another chemistry world."

"That's not fair, is it? You say there's no other world because there's no sign of one; I say I've seen a sign of one; you tell me I'm hallucinating. If there *were* a sign somewhere, you'd dismiss it as a hallucination."

"Look," she said turning on him again. "I'm familiar with—shall we call them 'different states of consciousness.' They come from little pills, powders, shots, things that go into your brain and affect how it works, so you feel good, or you see things that aren't there, or imagine that you're someone you aren't. But it's all temporary.

Because when the pill or powder or shot wears off, it's gone, you're back here again. See? You always end up back here, in this hellhole." Her forehead was creased. "The same thing can happen with chemicals your brain produces itself, if it's not working right. But unfortunately, this is what's real." She smacked the vinyl upholstery of her seat with her open hand.

Wayne took a right on a narrow blacktop, much cracked and patched. There were no signs of habitation. The branches of trees hung over the road, and in the white haze of the afternoon, which had thickened almost to greyness, it looked close and tunnel-like. "Crabb Lane," Wayne read off a rusted road sign.

Gail marked the map.

It was bumpy, so they had to drive slowly. Wayne could feel a waiting stillness in the air, and the leaves on the trees were still. Storm coming.

"Let's say you take a pill and hallucinate that you're seeing a tree," Wayne argued. "That doesn't mean that every time you see a tree it's a hallucination, does it? I mean, you might see a real tree."

"OK, well, you show me this other world," said Gail. "We won't take any pills or powders, and when I see it, I'll believe it."

Wayne thought about that. "Well, I'm not sure you could see it. I mean, seeing it seems to depend on—on being in a specific state of consciousness, and if you weren't in it, I don't think you could see it."

"So we would both be standing at the top of this hill looking down, and you would say, 'hey, look at that,' and I wouldn't be able to see anything?"

"Well—"

"That's a hallucination, Wayne."

It was the first time she had ever used his name, and he

turned and looked at her, warmth blossoming in his chest. But she was impassive in her black glasses.

"Maybe not," he said. "Maybe you would be the one hallucinating. Maybe we're all hallucinating when we're not in that state of consciousness."

The glasses looked steadily at him. "You know what you're doing? You're twisting your logic, stretching it every which way to justify the idea that there's this other world. You're using arguments you wouldn't believe for a second if somebody else used them to say, for example, that there was an elephant in the back seat of your car. There's an elephant in the back seat of your car, Wayne, but you can't see it because you're not in the right state of consciousness."

He looked at her in surprise. "You're pretty damn smart for a—" He caught himself.

"For a what?"

"Drug addict."

"What about prostitute?" Her voice was steady, hard.

"I refuse to think of you—like that."

"Why?"

"Because I'm in love with you."

"You stupid shit." Her voice was angry, contemptuous, but also suddenly trembling. "You don't remember me on my knees with King's cock in my mouth? You don't want to remember that, do you? You should have seen what he did to me after." The memory seemed to sicken her, and one trembling hand rubbed the back of the other as if trying to wash it. In a minute she pulled herself together, and her voice was low, hard again. "You know what, Wayne? There are these scientists who cut rats' heads open and stick electrodes in the parts of their brains that make them feel pleasure. Then they hook the electrodes up to little bars in the rats' cage. The rats learn that if they push that bar, they feel an intense rush of pleasure. You know what happens? The rats start to push the bar more and more, and pretty soon they push that bar all day and all night, forgetting to eat and sleep, to clean themselves or play with the other rats. They keep on pushing the bar over and over until they die of hunger." She was silent for a minute, the black glasses staring out the windshield. "Whenever you think of me, I want you to think of those rats."

Crabb Lane dead-ended at a rusted chain across what looked like it had once been a dirt road, now choked with brambles and vines, blocked by tree branches.

"Scratch Crabb Lane," Wayne said, backing the car on the narrow blacktop. Her words had made him feel numb, hollow. He wanted to tell her he loved her again, but instead he said: "I talked to your father yesterday."

She turned sharply on him. "Why didn't you tell me?"

"I am telling you. I talked to him for an hour at his office."

"I thought he wouldn't see you."

"When I mentioned you, he saw me."

"And?"

"And he said he wasn't responsible for your problems. Even if he did give you a shot, which he didn't admit, and even if it contained some kind of vaccine, which he also didn't admit, it didn't work, and even if it had, it would just have made you better and stronger."

"That cocksucking bastard," she said savagely, but there was a misery underneath it. "He's going to pay me. He's going to pay me, that bastard." She was silent for a minute, hands knotted. "Are you going to put it in your book?"

"I don't know. One of the most interesting parts of what we talked about was his idea how there really is no other world, and religion is just a figment of a certain kind of brain dysfunction. You and he have a lot in common in some ways."

"Go fuck yourself," she snarled.

"Back to Old Lawrence Road," he announced. "I'm taking a right." The pavement was smoother again, and he speeded up.

"He crippled me and made it impossible for me to live in this world, to have the feelings it takes to live in this world," she yelled hoarsely at Wayne. "I want you to tell people that."

"He says drug addicts always have excuses for—"

There was a terrific blow to the right side of his face. As soon as he could see again he was barreling toward a telephone pole.

He slammed the brakes and the car skidded sideways, squealing, stopping finally half in the ditch, Gail's side less than two feet from the pole.

He jammed it into park, grabbed Gail furiously and slammed her against the passenger door.

Her sunglasses flew off sideways, out the window. The pupils in her green eyes were shrunken, and for a terrible moment they were a child's eyes, confused and terrified. Then she started to cry. Her face contorted and sobs came in silent gasps, shaking her body.

The rage withered in Wayne's chest. He put out his hands, but she shrank away. "Take me home," she whispered.

"Gail—"

"Take me home," she whispered between gasps. "Take me home."

"I should never have—I'm sorry—"

"It's all right." She tried a horrible smile, but only, he knew, because she thought it might get her home quicker. "Take me home," she whispered in agony, arms wrapped around herself.

He squealed the car around on Old Lawrence Road and drove with urgent speed back to the apartment house, as if he were taking her to the Emergency Room. The second they pulled up to the curb in the warm, electric-still overcast, she had her door open and was fumbling her crutches out of the back, hands shaking so she could hardly hold them. She let Wayne help her out of the car, but ignored him as he followed her up the smelly, narrow staircase to her apartment. She burst in, crutched quickly to the bathroom, and slammed the door. He could hear her breath hissing in there, and then the sound of vomiting. Then water running, gargling and spitting. Then the door opened and Gail stood there, body lax, face sleepy and vacant, the green of her eyes eaten by black holes.

"Gail—"

"You still here?" she said dully, sleepily. She pushed his hands away distractedly, crutched out into the living room. She switched on the TV and lowered herself onto the soiled bed pillows.

"Gail, please forgive me."

"It's OK," she said, eyes on the TV. "It doesn't hurt. Go away."

He drove north in the deepening dusk. The storm appeared to be approaching across the Lake with the utmost gravity in the neutrally warm, utterly still air, the sky an ominous dark slate above the water. The distant thump of dance music came from the model-beauties' house as he crossed Bolling's patio in the otherwise complete stillness, the dust his car had made hanging in the air above the dirt road. Out his kitchen window he could see lights flashing in time with the music through the model-beauties' downstairs windows, as if they were having a party. It fit the atmosphere peculiarly well: of course, it made sense that they would unthinkingly react to the weather in just the right way—after all, didn't their beauty signal their utter, unconscious *rightness*, their complete harmony with this world? They were the strong, the blessed; whatever person or process had made the world was their friend, their ally, perhaps even their lover. Could God himself be in love with them? And was it the same God who had twisted and broken Gail? Did that please him too?

He went inside and tried to write, then read, then watch TV, keeping all the time half an eye out the window facing the model-beauties' house. It grew very dark outside, though the storm seemed no nearer than before.

Around nine o'clock the phone rang. It was Ann. Her voice was calm, but ready to be defiant or triumphant. "I picked up your messages. And Lily told me you called her." Lily was her lawyer. "There's no need to get hysterical about this; we just went to the beach and have been busy."

"Can I talk to the kids?"

"They're asleep. No—don't yell at me or I'll hang up. We just got back from the boardwalk and they were exhausted."

He tried to contain his anger. "You take them away without telling me, don't give me your phone number, ignore my calls for a week, and now you call me when they're asleep—!"

"And what about you, running off to the beach without notice? We're just supposed to sit home and wait for you to come back, is that it?"

"Ann, I'm working here. I told you, my new book—"

"Don't give me that. You don't have to spend all summer at the beach to work on your book."

"Well, but—you don't understand." He had always had the fantasy that if he could just make her understand, things would be all right. The old habit was strong. "I'm—I'm on the trail of something out here."

"On the trail of what?"

"Some—strange things. Some experiences, mystical experiences that seem to be associated with a place out here. I can't leave yet, not until I run this down."

"Mystical experiences?"

"Yes."

"Are they the same mystical experiences that made you so abusive when we were married, and that keep you from cleaning your apartment?"

"Ann—"

"Are you ever going to get a clue?" She sounded genuinely upset suddenly, almost as if she would cry. "You don't seem to realize that I know you better than you think. I watched you deteriorate for years, losing your grip, indulging yourself in these fantasies, refusing to come to terms with reality, getting farther and farther out, and kidding yourself that it was OK because you were a science fiction writer. It broke up our marriage, it's made you a pauper, and now you're leaving your children behind chasing something that everybody else knows isn't real."

"Ann—"

"Have you looked at yourself lately? Really looked at yourself, in the mirror? You're turning into one of those tattered old men, almost like a street person, mumbling about 'mystical experiences' and who knows what. This is killing you, and you don't even know it."

He was silent.

"Well, chase it then. It's not my job to take care of you anymore. But if you want to talk to the children, you're going to have to come back to town. Call us when you get back."

She hung up.

To calm himself, and to fight the impulse to go look at himself in the mirror, Wayne took a walk around the house in the black air, barefoot on the cool flagstones and grass. The sky was a black-grey ceiling, the air breathless. The singing of crickets in the yard seemed subdued; the wash of the surf was very quiet, as if the Lake itself was listening; the only other sound was the faint dance music. Finally he went inside and went to bed.

14

His dreams were jumbled and intense, full of Gail and misery, and he woke several times sweating and tangled in his sheets, and each time the heaviness and stillness outside his wide-open windows was unrelieved, and each time there was the faint, tireless thump of music.

Then, toward the middle of the night, he woke again—woke, but he was still dreaming, as he had the night he had woken up in a dream of the Indian; but this time it was even clearer. He was awake and conscious, remembering that he had gone to bed in the front bedroom of Alphonse Bolling's beach house, yet now finding he was in a different place, a place in which he could think and look around and move just as he could in the waking world; but he knew that this place operated under the magical rules of dreams, so that, for instance, if he exerted his will in just the right way he would be able to fly or make someone appear from thin air. The shock and uncanniness and excitement of it—this undeniable

occasion of the interpenetration of dreams and waking—
made adrenaline burn through him, and he felt himself
starting to lift off the ground, as if the adrenaline rush
produced its corresponding physical state of flying. But
then he realized that he would wake up if he freaked out
too much; he tried to calm himself, look around. He was
in a church. Empty, but organ music playing mournfully,
echoing in high stone arches. He was wearing a dark suit
and so was Raymond Hall, whom he now saw standing
next to him. Hall was holding a folded handkerchief
over his mouth, as if he were going to cry or vomit. They
were at a funeral, Wayne realized. They were standing by
an open casket, and Gail lay in the casket, eyes closed,
face still and pale, as if she was asleep but concentrating
on something she was dreaming. Her face looked like
the face of a child, all the anger and hardness and misery
smoothed away. Looking at her, an enormous blob of
anguish rose from his stomach into his chest, and then
through his throat, emerging as a wail.

He struggled, and the feeling of his body lying in bed
in Alphonse Bolling's house tore through the feeling that
he was standing up and wearing a suit, so that by the
time the wail died away he was starting up in the dark
bedroom, sorrow stabbing through his heart like a knife,
and wind was rushing in the trees outside and rushing
through the windows.

He jumped out of bed, heart pounding, sweat cold in
the wind, and shut the windows, then ran through the
house shutting others. When he was done he put on
clothes. It was pitch dark outside, the wind gusting so
hard that he was almost afraid he would be carried off on
his way to the car. He heard the tearing crack of a tree limb
coming off somewhere; he hoped not on the road. Lightning flashed and played over the Lake horizon almost con-
stantly, lighting thrashing trees and huge whitecaps on the

Lake, but there were only a few stray raindrops in the air. The inside of the car felt warm and protected, though it rocked in the wind. It was hard going keeping it in his lane on the county highway, and the high bridge over the St. Clair River was utterly terrifying: twice he thought the car would fly off into the blackness, but he got over, and by the time he pulled up to Gail's building rain was slashing down sparsely in huge, stinging drops.

He barely touched the door of the apartment before she had it open, standing in near darkness on her crutches, face and hair wild, the clothes she had been wearing that afternoon disarranged.

"Where have you been?" she gasped in trembling anguish.

He put his hands on her. Beneath her thin shirt the flesh was soft over strong muscles. She hung back from him, but he was stronger; he pulled her to him, nuzzling her dirty, beautiful hair. He heard her crutches bang to the floor. The door slammed behind him in a gust, and he realized that her windows were wide open; he could feel spray from the savage rain even by the door, and now a vast, boom of thunder shook the apartment. A dim light was coming through the doorway of a small bedroom.

He held her desperate, trembling body, sharp bones of her pelvis pressing against him, her breath sobbing in his ear. He lifted her—she was very heavy—and carried her through the lit doorway. A Mickey Mouse night-light showed a sordid, dirty bedroom. He laid her on the unclean bed. She lay looking up at him, and slowly her arms went back so that her trembling fists were by her head, breasts lifted and taut, small nipples showing through the shirt.

Very gently he put a hand on her stomach, and the muscles jumped. She closed her eyes as if to better feel the hand, but opened them again when he knelt by her and kissed her cold lips. She sobbed suddenly, and he pulled away to look at her. She faced him helplessly, crying. He kissed her tenderly again, and after they had kissed for a few minutes she was gasping and pushing rhythmically, as if they were already having intercourse. He pulled off her shirt, revealing her pale, naked breasts, and she lay back again, putting her hands back by her head, closing her eyes, lips trembling.

He unzipped her jeans, unsheathed her hips. She wore a pair of soiled cotton briefs. He pulled the briefs and jeans off in one yank, and then he saw her legs, one long, shapely, and strong, the other six inches shorter and splayed to the side like a rotten tree branch, bone-thin, gnarled, the knee and ankle joints grotesquely swollen.

She was up on her elbows suddenly, alert, watching his face as he looked at the leg. He put his hands on it, touched the wrinkled crone's skin. He knelt on the bed and looked at it, blocking the rest of her beautiful body out of his vision. It was ugly, vulnerable, like a diseased animal that had gone off by itself to die. He stroked it gently, kissed it. Poor animal.

She was crying hard now, face red, body convulsed, but he couldn't hear her over the rush and moan of the wind, slash of the rain. He pulled off his own clothes, then lay and cradled her. Her skin was cool, but where she pressed against him he felt her deep heat. He kissed her, and slowly she stopped crying. One of her hands went down and caressed his penis, gently kneading his testicles. The horrible memory of her hand on King mingled with an intense column of sweet fire through his body.

He knelt between her bent, widely spread legs, and her body arched in expectation, breathing deeply, rhythmically, her eyes closed. His thumb massaged the swatch of black hair at her crotch, opening the wet, puffy flesh and releasing her fishy, sour smell. As soon as the tip of his penis found her, he moved up and put his hands behind her shoulders.

Gently, very gently, he pushed into her, feeling the slippery warmth cover him. Her face convulsed and she rocked a little to get him all the way in. Then her eyes opened as if in surprise, and he was drawn into their emerald depths. He became aware suddenly that they were both slick with sweat and the rain blowing in at the windows, and there was lightning and thunder around them. They began to move in their own silence, bodies intensely concentrated. She gave a low cry, trembling as if with effort. He was blinded by her eyes. They moved, sometimes gently, sometimes wildly, sometimes cooperating, sometimes fighting. Finally she arched her back and started to jerk gently and convulsively, and a spout of fire started at the base of his spine. Lightning must have hit him then, because he was illuminated from within and at the same time unconscious, straining with his utmost strength and at the same time serene beyond touching, full to bursting both with savage lust and softest tenderness.

He became aware that she was sobbing and gasping, and that he was making some kind of noise too, and slowly the fire ran out of him, and slowly they rocked themselves quiet, and he lay and held her like that. The wind howled and lightning flashed and thunder boomed, and after a while Wayne groped and pulled a sheet over them, and she held him, face buried in his shoulder. Outside the sheet the wind whipped and moaned at the windows, the rain rattled and spattered, but inside they were cozy, warm, still, a hibernating family.

Finally she pulled her head back and pushed the sheet down a little so she could look into his face in the dimness. She studied him evaluatingly, coolly. Her pupils were small. She moved to disengage herself. "I'll be right back."

He grabbed her wrists. "No." It felt strange to talk, as if he could hardly form the word.

She pulled to get loose. He held on.

"You'll tell me to go away," he said.

"I won't take that much," she said gently. "It's OK. I won't take that much. You'll see." She kissed him.

He let go of her and she got out of bed. She was beautiful, strong, despite her awful leg. She went out of the room, leaning on the wall and doorjamb and hopping expertly. He heard the bathroom door shut. Three minutes later she was back, with no smell of vomit, and her pupils hardly bigger than normal size. She was rubbing one of her arms inside the elbow. He took it as she crawled back into bed and looked at a raw needle mark surrounded by pink and a tiny bit of blue, and there were many older marks, ugly purple bruises, scars, and some hard lumps like peas under the skin.

She lay against him under the sheet, abandoned and at rest.

Finally he said, his voice trembling: "Can't you stop taking that stuff?"

"No," she murmured against him. "I'll die."

"You won't die. People get off it all the time."

"Their brains aren't damaged."

"There are a lot of brain-damaged people who don't take that stuff."

"They should."

"But—"

"Look," she said, pulling back from him to look in his face. "You go to your imaginary world, and I'll go to mine. Your brain happens to malfunction in a way that lets you make the stuff you need to live; mine doesn't, so I have to get it from outside. OK? So don't get superior with me about my dope. OK?"

She looked at him another few seconds, then sighed

and put her head back down against his shoulder. With his left hand he massaged her skull through her damp hair, massaged the back of her neck.

"But what if," he said slowly, "what if your brain isn't as damaged as you think, and the dope is covering up some real perceptions or feelings that might make it worthwhile to live. What if the dope is just obscuring a real world that isn't as bad as you think?"

"What if *your* brain malfunction is obscuring the real world? And what if it's *worse* than you think?" she said into his shoulder, breathing in relaxation against his massaging hand.

He massaged thoughtfully.

"What about King?" he asked after a while.

She moved uneasily against him. "You let me take care of him," she said. Then she pulled back and looked at him again. "But you can't be jealous, OK? I use a thousand dollars' worth of stuff a week, and there's no way I could get that without King. You have to understand that, OK?" She looked anxiously into his eyes.

He nodded, looking away from her, but she grabbed him by the hair with both hands and made him look at her. "OK?" she demanded fiercely.

"Just tell me," he said, "that it's not impossible. That you just might quit taking it, and we could move away from here, back to the Mid-Atlantic Region where my kids are, and we could get married and live in some dumb little apartment, and I could get a day job writing Star Wars knockoffs, and you could go back to school, and I could cook for you, and we could fight a lot and get old."

Her doped face softened and she got a faraway look, and a little smile came on her lips.

"It's not impossible," she said.

———

The storm blew and roared and crashed itself out during the night, and when Wayne woke in a tangle of damp, smelly sheets and flesh, the morning was bright and baby-blue, a few puffy, fairy-tale clouds floating in the sky, a light, cheerful breeze rustling the leaves outside Gail's windows. She was asleep, curled up facing away from him, her dead leg bent clumsily in front of her like a rotten log. He sat and wondered at her beauty and ugliness, feeling himself becoming aroused. After a while, as if sensing his gaze, she stirred, opened sticky eyes, and looked sidelong at him. She closed her eyes again.

"Fuck me," she said thickly after a minute, and moved her hips slightly to make herself accessible.

He knelt behind her and put his hard penis into the pink flesh that his fingers opened in the black hair, started to thrust gently. At first it was sticky and impenetrable, but it quickly puffed and got slippery and he went in. Soon she started to cry out softly and sweat beaded on her back. Then her face twisted dizzily and her hands went flat against the bed, as if she was trying to push something open, and it was as if an angel had touched the underside of Wayne's body with celestial fire, and he cried out too.

They lay together afterward spoonwise, he cupping a sweaty, exquisite breast, smelling her musk and sourness, but before long a car door slammed on the street, and there was something about that slam, some quality of proprietary swagger, that made them both sit up and peer out the window.

The drug dealer King was moving along the sidewalk with his soft, arrogant gait.

"You have to get your stuff on and get out of here," Gail said to Wayne, and pushed him urgently. "Go!"

"But if he hurts you—"

"He's not going to hurt me. I can handle him. OK? But you have to get out of here." She grabbed his hair and made him look into her anxious eyes. "You're not going to be jealous, remember? Now go!" She pushed him again.

He got out of the bed and pulled his underpants and pants over his sticky genitals, threw on his T-shirt, stuffed his feet into his still-tied shoes.

"He's going to see me on the stairs," he said, fear grasping at his windpipe, partly for her, partly for himself.

"I don't care if he sees you on the stairs. But you can't hang around outside either." She was stretching herself out on the bed, making no attempt to get up or put on clothes, but pulling a sheet over her crippled leg. "Go look for your Shangri-la today. I want you gone."

Wayne didn't see King on the stairs. He didn't see him until he opened the downstairs door and stepped out onto the porch, and then King had just reached the top of the porch steps. When he saw Wayne he stopped and stared, just stood and stared expressionlessly from his red eyes, as if he was seeing something very grave, something which would call down the wrath of God, but something which he had almost expected. Wayne stood and looked back at him.

Finally King tipped his chin up in a dominant gesture and said: "I thought I told you good-bye, Fredrick."

"My name's not Fredrick."

"Then what is it? And where do you live?" King's voice was suddenly demanding and irritable, threatening.

Wayne said nothing, just stood looking at the sinister little man.

"I asked you a question," said King.

Wayne got up his nerve and stepped past King, started

down the porch steps. "See you later," he said, managing to sound breezy.

"No, you won't see me later," said King to his back, "because you're not going to be back here no more. You got that, Fredrick?"

Wayne kept walking, gave no sign that he had heard.

King said to his back in a regretful, expressive voice: "You're gonna wish you listened to me, Fredrick. You'll really wish you did."

———

Despite Gail's instructions, Wayne stood on the patchy grass just around the corner of the apartment house, a dozen feet from her window. At first there was silence over the cool breeze rustling in the elm trees above him. Then there was the sound of voices, but he couldn't make out the words. This went on for a few minutes, and then Gail began to scream. Wayne had taken two running steps back toward the porch before he realized that they were screams of dominance, delivered in her brassy, lower-class tones.

"Get your hands off me, you bag of shit! You try that shit on me again, you're gonna get nothing!"

Then arguing voices, of which Wayne could catch only a few words. This went on for ten minutes. Then the voices got lower. Then silence.

He walked quickly to his car before he heard noises he didn't want to hear.

He didn't go looking for Shangri-la. He was caked with dried sweat, semen, and vaginal fluids, as well as whatever oily products were on Gail's sheets. He went home and took a shower, went swimming in the sunny, chill metallic blue storm water of the Lake, left a half-angry, half-entreating message on Ann's machine in the

Mid-Atlantic Region, then took his laptop out onto the bluff to work. He was full of a strange mixture of feelings, but, blessedly, he could concentrate, and the book flowed over him like soothing water. It was late morning when he heard the distant sound of a heavy motor wavering on the breeze, and looking over toward the model-beauties' house, saw a truck pulling into the driveway.

Moving out? he wondered with a pang. It came to him suddenly with a complicated feeling, part grief, part yearning, part satisfaction, that his encounter with Gail had driven the silky girl out of his mind, the goddess with the ocean eyes and angel flesh. He had broken his vows, abandoned her, and now she was moving away. But no; his thing with Gail was merely a detour, he told himself, and a necessary one at that, one of many that he would have in the next year or two, so that he could come to the silky girl in the end strong and victorious, and she would know that he had picked her out from among all the women in the world, any of whom he could have had.

A couple of workmen with their bellies sticking out of sleeveless T-shirts got slowly out of the truck in the mild, lazy sunlight, opened the back, and started unloading foam rubber mattresses and carrying them to the house. Wayne watched them attentively. They unloaded maybe fifty mattresses. Then they drove away.

Fifty foam rubber mattresses. Wayne ate lunch, then worked for another hour, until another truck pulled up at the model-beauties' house. A man in a uniform unloaded boxes, what looked like spools of cable, and ungainly black metal struts of the kind you might use for sophisticated lighting.

Some kind of fashion photography shoot, or maybe a porno film, with a set made out of foam rubber mattresses. He watched for any sign of the male stars, the idea of the silky girl in a porno film twisting in his mind, but no one showed up. The early afternoon was left mild and breezy and empty, the vast freshness of the Lake overwhelming and driving off the land airs, so that the bluff seemed just an outpost, an island in a world of fresh water.

At about three in the afternoon he took the five-minute walk up to the county highway to get Bolling's mail and whatever of his own mail had forwarded here. The Lake breeze made all the greenery around him seem alive and young, clean and cheery, waving and fluttering in vegetable gladness. Up on the county highway Bolling's mailbox held a square envelope of heavy, expensive paper, addressed to Mr. Wayne Dolan.

He tore it open. It was an invitation, printed on the same heavy, expensive stock:

PLEASE JOIN US
FOR A NIGHT TO REMEMBER
PARTY AND DANCE
AT
12038 R.R. 31
COLONY, MICHIGAN
AUGUST 5, AT 8:00 P.M.
SPECIAL PRIZES AND SURPRISES!

At first he mistook 12038 R.R. 31 for his own address, and wondered whether it was some practical joke or advertising gimmick—but no, Bolling's house was 12030. A sudden thought struck him, and he walked the hundred yards up the shoulder to the next mailbox. Yes, 12038.

He had been invited to a party at the model-beauties' house.

He stood blankly, wondering. How they had gotten

his address, for one thing? Had they come over when he was out to visit him? But how would they have learned his name? Had they recognized him as the writer Wayne Dolan, maybe from the Science Fiction Writers of America web page? But the web page didn't give his address, and there was no forwarding sticker on this envelope; anyway, given the sales volume on his books, half a dozen young models were about as likely to recognize him as to be struck by meteorites. Unless one of them happened to be an avid science fiction reader, maybe by some enormous coincidence one of his fans. He wondered for a second whether he should just walk down and ask them, but electroshock could not have implanted as strong an aversion to approaching them as his previous experiences; after a few seconds of cold sweat he rejected the idea. He would find out at the party. As he walked back to Bolling's, he fantasized the one he had seen naked cooing up at him worshipfully, while the silky girl looked on full of wordless desire.

It was dark when he finally headed for St. Clair. Gail was fucking the animal King for dope, he reminded himself; yet he remembered last night too, how she had put her trembling hands up by her head, opening herself to him, afraid and vulnerable. And anyway, there wasn't much he could do; he was in love with her.

This time she was neither spurning nor desperate when she opened the door to his knock. The TV was off and all the lights in the apartment were on. She was tidying up, she herself showered and wearing fresh jeans and shirt, and she was in a good mood, her face occluded with drugs but the pupils not too huge. She put her arms around his neck and kissed him like a young, doped wife. She smelled like clean clothes.

A couple of loads of laundry wrapped in sheets lay by the door.

"I want you to take me to the Laundromat, and then let's have dinner," she said, smiling into his eyes.

"What happened with King?"

"Nothing happened with King. I handled King," she said. She kissed him again gloatingly. "You're not going to be jealous, remember?"

"I am jealous."

She pressed herself against him, pouting sexily through her drugged face. "Later I'll persuade you not to be. But first let's go to the Laundromat."

⟋

That night they lay on clean sheets, and after they made love she sat up and rummaged in the drawer of her rickety bed table. "I almost forgot—"

She thrust something into his hand, and when he focused in the streetlight glow from the window he saw that it was money, twelve one-hundred-dollar bills.

"I don't need it anymore," she said. "Though you might have to let me borrow it again sometime."

He held the bills. "What do you mean?"

"I used it to convince King."

"Convince him of what?"

"I told him you were some rich guy I was stroking, and that he better not cut me off or you would sugar me so I could buy the stuff myself. I showed him your wad to convince him. So he's going to keep on giving, and I can keep on seeing you."

She seemed immensely pleased with herself.

"And he can keep on having you too."

She was silent.

"I'm not sure that's what I was looking for," he said. "I'm not sure—"

"Oh, shut up, you self-righteous piece of shit," she
snarled out of the darkness. "Do you have any idea what
I went through for you today?"

"For me?" he said, stung. "Or for you?"

She sat up in the darkness, her beautiful, strong body
taut with anger. "No, not for me. Look, look," she cut
off his protest, "if it was a competition between you and
dope, you know which one would win? Hands down?"

"Yes."

"You're damn right. I have no time for anything but
dope, you understand? You know why? Because my father, that bastard you admire so much, damaged me so I
can't make the chemicals inside my head other people
use to go on living. I see things cold and clear, so cold and
clear that if you saw things the way I do, you'd want to
die. No, don't give me your bullshit about Shangri-la.
You'd want to die." Her voice was harsh and shrill. "So
dope is all there is for me, and I'll do whatever it takes to
get enough to live. Do we understand each other?"

"I guess we do," said Wayne, his voice shaking, and
he pushed himself up and out of bed.

"No!" she shrieked as if he had burned her with a red-
hot iron. "No!" She leapt at him and her hands closed on
his arm, but she lost her grip and her bad leg couldn't
hold her. She fell off the bed and heavily to the floor with
a cry.

She had grabbed the hand holding the hundred-dollar
bills. Thinking that was what she wanted, he threw them
at her on the floor. They fluttered around her in the dark.

"No!!" she shrieked even more desperately, and tried
to crawl after him. "No!!"

Her shrieks and crying had an insane sound, and they
tore his heart. The image flashed on him of a child abandoned, left alone in an empty house. He knelt and pulled
her up so he could hold her, hold her hysterically sob-

bing body kneeling on the floor. He was sobbing himself, he realized.

"But why?" he said finally. "This only complicates your life. It would be much simpler without me. All you want is dope. You just said so."

"Because," she said, still gasping hysterically, and he could feel the supreme effort she had to make to talk, to save herself, "you're the sunshine. You come from outside. You love me."

He picked her up. She was very heavy. He laid her on the bed and held her.

—

"It's all very codependent," she said the next morning, a bright replica of the day before, but without the breeze. They were driving along White Rock Road, which ran through woods and head-high cornfields. Wayne didn't remember any such landscape on his way to the cottage, but it was one of the roads beyond the transmission wires, so they were running it down.

"You want to rescue the poor little crippled addict-girl because it makes you feel needed and strong. You don't have a lot of self-esteem, so you think only someone weak and defective can want you. You think if you rescue the little addict-girl, you'll earn her love. And the little addict-girl herself is so needy that it sounds like a terrific offer to her.

"So what happens? Pretty soon the little addict-girl starts to resent the rescuer because she's so dependent on him. On the other side, the rescuer starts to resent the little addict-girl because she's a burden and not even grateful for being rescued. A pattern of criticism and rage builds up, but they can't let each other go because the rescuer still needs to feel strong, and the little addict-girl is still so needy. So they get locked into a cycle of mutual hate and recrimination, suffocating each other in some shabby Mid-Atlantic apartment. Partly because of the stress, and partly because she knows it hurts the rescuer, the little addict-girl goes back to using, and gets tied into the local drug community. Pretty soon she starts sleeping with sleazy dealers for drugs."

"Right on Boggs Lane," said Wayne, taking the right, his stomach churning.

She marked the map with the red pen. "Finally either the apartment gets busted or the little addict-girl leaves the rescuer for one of the big strong drug dealers who is helping her with her itch, or physical abuse starts up, or, if the rescuer can get enough of his mental health together, he leaves her."

"That's very nice. No wonder you take heroin."

"I told you," she laughed, and a pretty flush came on her pale cheeks. "You were probably thinking of sunsets and wedding dresses and long evenings spent gazing into each other's eyes. See, your brain makes the chemicals you need to cover up reality. Mine doesn't."

"Like father, like daughter."

Her voice got dangerous. "You want to get hit upside the head again?"

"No," he said humbly. Then after a pause: "But let me ask you two things. Three things. Where did you learn this shit about codependence and all that?"

"Read it in a book. Just because someone is a whore and a drug addict doesn't mean she's stupid."

"Hm. And second—I mean, let's say, just hypothetically, that I was imagining a future where you get off drugs and we both go to therapy, and we make an effort to get better and treat each other decently, and maybe even write a book together, say about how good sex is between neurotic, low-self-esteem, unsuccessful writers and drug-addicted prostitutes—I mean, maybe the likelihood is lower than the scenario you mentioned, but it's *possible*. And if you make up your mind in advance that things could never work out any better than you described, how could they have any chance to? You know?"

She was smiling, though he couldn't see her eyes behind her black sunglasses. "What's the third question?"

"Well—if you believe everything you said, what do we do? I mean, if there's no point to it, what do we do now?"

Boggs Lane ended at two faded whitewashed boulders beyond which stretched halls of green roofed by branches in which birds sang, penetrated here and there by shafts of crystalline sunlight.

"We hold on as long as we can. Until it gets dark," she said. "Why not? It's better than nothing. Something is better than nothing."

It was still early afternoon when Gail suddenly announced that she had to go home. He couldn't tell if she was itchy for a shot or had to meet King, but by now he was used to her moods, so he turned the car around on a hopeful-looking hilly road running through some woods and—making sure she marked the map—headed back to town. He helped her out of the car and walked upstairs slowly behind her, and when she had opened her apartment door she turned and took off her sunglasses. Her pupils were a little narrow but not too bad.

She kissed him lightly, like any girlfriend might kiss her boyfriend, and smiled at him. "Go away now," she said. "And don't hang around."

A slight flush highlighted her acne, and she looked happy for once, and very beautiful. He put his arms around her and held her warm, strong, precious body.

She kissed him again. "Go on," she murmured, and pushed him gently. "Go."

He pulled away from her, reluctantly let go of her hand, and went. At the top of the stairs he looked around at her watching after him. She blew him a kiss.

———

Back at Bolling's house there was something about the sunlight that made you think of years long past; perhaps it was just a touch of lengthening yellowness that suggested that summer was coming to an end like all the summers before it, that even the celestial brightness and clarity of these days over the Lake would age, yellow, and turn to dust. A little breeze ruffled the uncut grass of the lawn, the lazy sound of surf came up from the beach, and there was a feeling, at once melancholy and exalted, that everything was fleeting, but that something lasted forever too, or at least came around again, and that there was more to this life than met the eye, than existed in the minds of the scientists and their equations, their proofs and experiments. Somewhere—the image sprang unbidden to Wayne's mind—somewhere a beautiful girl stood on a cliff above the ocean and looked out at the water, and didn't that refute all their theories? Somewhere was that village in Ontario he had hitchhiked through one summer decades ago, the air soft and completely still under a pale afternoon overcast that was almost sunlight and almost mist, so that it made the air soft and neutral and motionless, and the village seemed deserted, silent in the afternoon, though cars were parked along the streets under the huge, arching trees, and to get into town the road passed over a canal, its waters completely still and clear in the pearly afternoon, like a mirror, and Wayne had looked down into it leaning on the rail, and had seen his reflection young and wondering in the still, green water, and didn't that refute their theories? And the model-beauty with her ocean eyes and face full of unconscious pale loveliness, didn't she refute their theories? In every square centimeter of this world were depths, everything was full of implication, nothing was simply itself. He had walked down a steep, winding road one chilly autumn morning when the leaves were falling, and had seen a white horse grazing in a field, so he knew this was true.

The clear blue sky tinted with the ripe yellowness of high summer had not been made by a person or process that wanted you to die and for darkness and cold and emptiness to be after all. Its color framing the bright green and dark green of trees, their leaves stirring in the breeze told him that, just as a painting by Picasso told you that he had not been cruel, not in the end. Wayne knew this other artist from within too, knew he could not be cruel, not in the end. And what about the dream he had once had, of sitting in his car in a gravel parking lot near a railroad bridge across a murky, narrow river, its banks grown with pine trees and birch, in the clear, still blue of evening, and in the front seat next to him was Her, dark and silent, but knowing everything that passed inside him, and he full of silence, knowing Her also, and knowing he would never die, and knowing that in the end he would not be denied, could not be.

A breeze from the Lake fluttered the leaves of the bluff trees, and fluttered leaves over vast miles and miles of bluff and forest baking in the sun which glittered on the Lake's waves as far as the eye could see. And what was to say that She wasn't hidden in this world somewhere, illuminating it all from within? And what was to prevent him from living forever?

A sound from the model-beauties' house jerked him out of his vision, standing on the bluff lawn: the ringing whine of a power saw. As he watched, a workman came out onto their deck and leaned down attentively, measuring something. Construction going on over there. Preparing for the party? A sudden rush of warmth for Gail came over him as he realized that he could go to the party and meet the silky girl and Gail wouldn't prevent him, that she wasn't his jailor. And perhaps that was why she had been smiling at him so this afternoon: because she knew she could have both him and the other things she needed, and he wouldn't prevent her.

15

The next morning was bright and breezy, high clouds floating through a vault of blue, the Lake sparkling with small, blue waves tipped with foam. It was all cheerful, innocent, and young, and the ripe yellowness of yesterday seemed just a figment of imagination; today it was easy to believe that summer would last forever; there seemed a promise on the fresh, electric breeze of days like this stretching in breathtaking perspective as far as the eye could see, like the Lake. A perfect day to hunt for lost mystical cottages in the countryside. Wayne, feeling young, swam, showered, ate his two bowls of cornflakes, and before his hair was quite dry headed into town.

The grey apartment house looked almost picturesque in the mild white sunlight, elm leaves fluttering around it against blue sky. The breeze seemed even to have penetrated the stairway at the back of the building: as Wayne climbed and knocked at Gail's door the sour smells of old cooking and old wood were almost gone. There was no answer, so he knocked again. There was no sound inside the apartment. Maybe she had stayed overnight with King and hadn't gotten back yet, he thought with a stab of jealousy. He turned the knob, opened the door. The little living room was full of daylight and fresh air from open windows. The two pillows on the sofa had clean covers on them and were plumped up, as if no one had sat on them yet, but the TV was on with the sound muted; a blonde woman with a dazzling smile pointed to blue swimming pools.

The bathroom door was shut. Gail only shut it when she was shooting up, as far as he knew. He listened at it. Silence. Was there a faint bad smell, like something wafting through the cracks around the door?

A sudden fear took him. He tapped at the door. "Gail?" He tapped again, then opened it.

He knew right away that she was dead. Her arms and head hung down nervelessly, though she hadn't fallen off the toilet seat where she had sat to give herself the shot. The syringe still hung from her left arm, which was bloated and grey as cardboard. She had vomited, and brown, stinking slop made a track down her shirt and the crotch of her jeans, had run down the toilet in a dozen rivulets and pooled on the floor at her feet. Her hair covered her face. Some of the vomit had gotten in her hair.

He stood holding the doorjamb with one hand. He seemed only to be able to take tiny breaths. A small but dreadful trembling had started in his stomach. He wondered if he should touch her, just to say good-bye, but he didn't. She didn't look like herself anymore, except, strangely, her hard, shapely hips splayed on the toilet seat still looked alive, casual. He backed away from the bathroom door, trying to get enough breath. He felt dizzy.

He had never seen a telephone in her apartment. He closed the door behind him very quietly and went downstairs. He guessed the neighbors had phones, but the idea of telling them this sickened him. He went out to his car. He couldn't think what to do. Finally, he drove ten blocks to the nearest grocery store and used a public phone in the parking lot.

—

The St. Clair Police Department was in a narrow, high brick building like an old fire station, a spiral metal stair between floors taking the place of the traditional brass pole. It was a warren of small rooms, dim and crowded with metal desks and filing cabinets. A large, middle-aged Detective Sergeant Stanzik questioned Wayne as he sat numbly in a folding metal chair. He looked at Wayne's arms for needle marks, and Wayne consented to a urine test and pissed in a plastic bottle in the old-fashioned yellow-tiled bathroom. Stanzik wrote up a statement with painful slowness on a yellow legal pad, and Wayne signed it.

When Stanzik seemed done with him, the question that had been burning in his mind came blurting out of his mouth. "Did she—was it suicide?"

Stanzik shook his greying head. "Probably accidental. They shoot too much and go to sleep, choke on their own vomit. You see the grey color of her skin? That means the oxygen all went out of her blood before she died. She suffocated to death while she was sitting there asleep." He looked suddenly tired and sad, a worn-out middle-aged man with wrinkles around his eyes. "We'll be able to say for sure when the lab report comes in."

They let Wayne go, asking him to inform them if his address changed. By the time he stepped out into the breezy white-and-blue afternoon he was so numb that it occurred to him to wonder if he had really cared for Gail at all.

—

But that night he dreamed of her. They were in a garden, half landscaped and half wild, which bordered on a forest and also on a cliff over the ocean. It was dawn, the pale, bluish twilight before the sun comes up, cool, damp, and still. Gail wore a suit of figured golden silk and her eyes were laughing. She walked gracefully without crutches, and he saw that her crippled leg was healed and that her eyes were normal, and she smiled at him. He woke up crying.

—

He swam all the next afternoon, swam out so far that the bluff looked like a tiny model of his former life shrouded in haze, far out in the rocking swells turning grey as the sun sank, and under which he touched a layer of icy water if he stretched his feet down, out so far that his thoughts of Gail and death and his children seemed after a while remote and unimportant, as if they belonged to a past that was gone now, and then he thought he would swim to the horizon where the sun was approaching the water in a haze of grey and gold, swim out as he had done in his dreams many times, toward the far continent. But instead he turned and swam back to shore, finally slogging exhaustedly up onto the beach where yellow and blue shadows were stretching across the sand.

—

Next day he sat at the top of the bluff, hands slack on his laptop, gazing out toward the source of the wind on the blue, choppy Lake horizon, when the phone rang. He answered it in the kitchen. It was Detective Sergeant Stanzik.

"We got the lab report. Naw, it wasn't suicide. The stuff was just stronger than she thought. Fifty percent pure, the way it comes across the border. She took her normal dose, but it was five times stronger. Shut her down so she couldn't wake up when she was choking. Happens all the time. Whoever sold it to her made a mistake."

But as the afternoon wore on, Wayne began to wonder whether there had been a mistake.

King.

Wayne sat at the top of the bluff hanging on to his laptop for dear life, swaying between rage and sorrow and guilt and numbness. Had King ambushed her, killed her like a misbehaving animal? Should he call Stanzik back and tell him? But he had no evidence except the things King had done to Gail, and the kind of person King was, and if he called Stanzik back with the story he would have to admit that he knew more about Gail than perhaps he had let on before. And maybe after all it had just been her recklessness and hunger for the drug that had betrayed her. And anyway what did it matter now? She was dead, and neither that nor anything else would bring her back.

So he swayed at the top of an awful precipice looking down upon the earth far below, an earth where on a beautiful breezy summer day Gail Hall had died, and where another beautiful breezy summer day was going by, going by to who knew where. He hung on to his laptop for dear life.

⁓

The funeral was two days later. Wayne learned about it from a small obituary in the *St. Clair Post-Dispatch*:

Hall, Gail Amanda, 27, daughter of Dr. Raymond J.
Hall and Mrs. Evelyn M. Hall; July 30, 1999, in
St. Clair. Survived by Dr. Hall. Services St. Mark's
Church Thursday 9:00 A.M.

That morning Wayne took out of its plastic hanger
bag his dark blue suit, which he had bought long ago for
the infrequent firm dinner parties he went to with Ann,
and which he had brought to St. Clair against the unhappy possibility that appropriate attire would ever be
required. He had also brought two ties; he chose the
dark blue one, and after several attempts managed to
knot it.

When he was done he looked at himself in the closet
mirror. The suit was slightly too small and the tie hung
short. *I'm sorry Gail,* he thought. Strange: this poorly
dressed, confused-looking man who had known her for
a week would come to her funeral, and then she would
be gone.

And as he pulled into the church parking lot at 8:50
on a cool late-summer morning with high, filmy clouds
against a light blue sky, birds singing and sunlight dappling through the leaves of the little town, it seemed indeed that he was almost the only mourner. The parking
lot was an empty expanse of quiet grey asphalt, only a
hearse and a black Mercedes parked near the church.
Wayne put his beat-up little Honda next to the Mercedes. He hadn't been to a funeral since his mother's, he
realized. A glimpse of her came again into his mind, standing on the porch in the summer evening.

He pulled open the heavy door, smelling the faint,
sweet odor that churches absorb after years of worship and incense. The kind of organ music you expect at
a funeral was playing heavily. It was a medium-sized
church, but it looked huge empty. There was a casket at

the front with flowers at its head and foot, and in the front pew a single large, dark-suited figure. Hall. Wayne walked softly up and sat in the pew just behind, at the opposite end.

Hall turned and looked at him. It seemed to take him a minute to recognize Wayne. He looked ill. His large back was bent and his face was creased into a perplexed frown, eyes red and suffering, as if he had a flu. His big hands were clasped tightly and somehow helplessly in his lap. When the priest in his white robes came and leaned over to say something in his ear, Hall looked up uncomprehendingly so that that priest had to say it again. This time Hall shook his head, glancing at Wayne. The priest straightened and raised his hands in an automatic gesture so that his wide sleeves fell back, like a surgeon taking his scrub. He nodded to the organist, who gracefully brought the formless, solemn music to an appropriate denouement, then sat with respectful, professional absence at his big keyboard.

In the resonant silence the priest went behind his lectern and raised his hands again, signaling Wayne and Dr. Hall to rise. "Dear friends." He paused impressively, as if the church were full to bursting with dignitaries. "We are gathered together today to say farewell to our dear sister Gail Amanda Hall, beloved daughter of Raymond Joseph Hall and Evelyn Margaret Hall . . ."

His rich, solemn voice echoed from the PA system in empty stone vaults, against high arched windows luminous with blue and red and green glass, and outside the cool bright day was all blue and white and green, stretching away into gulfs of sky which somewhere held storms, vast and dark, towering with lightning over fields and mountains, oceans, cities.

". . . we know that all flesh must in the end return to You . . ."

Wayne glanced at Hall standing obliviously with his head down. He could probably have filled the church with colleagues, employees, and hangers-on if he had let it be known that his daughter had died. But he had preferred to keep it quiet, perhaps to avoid questions about how she had died, and other questions those might lead to. Resentment for the man swelled in Wayne's chest.

". . . a young woman of great beauty and intellectual gifts who struggled against a crippling disability and difficult life problems . . ."

But looking at Hall again, Wayne's anger shriveled. Hall looked lost, helpless, ill, even unbalanced, a far cry from the great doctor of philosophy who had enthralled the multitude with his unflinching theories at the Deriwelle Convocation Hall. Now he clasped his hands and hunched his shoulders with a haunted look.

". . . tragedy reminds us of our own mortality . . ."

At least he had arranged a funeral instead of having her shoveled into the ground quietly somewhere. Or maybe, Wayne's cynicism spoke up again, he was doing the respectable thing to deflect any possible questions about how he had treated his daughter when she was alive.

". . . in Jesus Christ . . ."

Wayne's eyes registered the coffin with a sudden shock, as if he had only just realized what this was about, that Gail was in that box. He couldn't see into it from where he stood, only that it was shiny pale wood lined with white lace and plush like the bed of a princess.

". . . for our dear sister Gail, we ask Your blessing, that through the miracle of Your blood she may be raised up to eternal life . . ."

And this was the best they could do for her, the best they knew how to do, a primitive ritual in a superstitious scapegoating religion, a highly rationalized form of the shaman transferring the tribe's sins to the sacrificial goat and then hurling it off a cliff so tomorrow's hunt would go better. This was the best they could do, when she had been a breathing, anguished woman with beautiful, drugged green eyes.

"... we ask in Christ's name. Amen."

"Amen," Wayne mumbled desperately, though he didn't believe a word of it.

The organ music started again, and when Wayne raised his eyes he saw the priest looking expectantly at him and Hall. Hall was still staring blindly at the floor. The priest gestured to Wayne, toward the coffin.

Wayne steeled himself and came forward.

He had wondered whether when he looked at her he would say to himself that it was not Gail in there in the white, lacy gown like a bride, hair combed onto her shoulders and makeup caked on like plaster to cover the grey skin, that her spirit had flown, leaving only an empty shell behind. But now when he peered down at her the realization came to him that it *was* Gail, but a Gail to whom something terrible had happened, a Gail whose face was swollen, the mouth set wrong, two deep creases running from the nose to the corners of the mouth, hands crossed too tightly over the mound of her breasts, as if in the end she had decided to become some kind of school-girl saint. It was a Gail to whom something had happened that could never be repaired, and Wayne could not escape the feeling that the woman herself lay there in the box, that no spirit had gone out of the flesh, but rather that it had fallen in on itself and died as she sat asleep and suffocating on the toilet in her apartment.

He caught a movement beside him. Hall stood there. He held a handkerchief over his mouth, his eyes above it wide behind the large glasses, as if he were going to throw up or cry. And with an irresistible pull of déjà vu, Wayne found himself back in the dream he had had the

night of the storm, with Gail in her coffin and Hall holding a handkerchief over his mouth, and the feel of the
dream was all around him, the blare of adrenaline as
he realized that he had woken up in it, the feeling that he
was about to lift off the ground and fly, the conviction
that he could make things or people appear if he thought
about them. It struck him suddenly that if he wanted
Gail to be alive again all he had to do was to concentrate
and at the same time relax and let go, and she would rise
up out of the coffin, her death mask of exhaustion and
misfortune and makeup falling away—

"Excuse me, sir," a voice said next to him. "Sir?"

A tall young man in a black suit was standing there.

"The interment will be held in half an hour at West
Colony Cemetery. Mr. Hall has asked that we close the
coffin now. I'm sorry."

Another young man in an identical suit was standing
on the other side of the coffin with a shiny, contoured
wooden lid and a large screwdriver.

Wayne stepped back in horror. The young man with
the lid swung it up and fitted it over the open part of the
coffin, a shadow falling over Gail's face. The last thing
Wayne saw of her were her crossed arms in their ruffled
sleeves. The lid clicked down flush. Wayne turned and almost ran from the church, out into the cool blue and
white day that towered around it.

Just outside the door he came face-to-face with Raymond Hall. Even in grief or illness the man was overwhelming, the sensation of some strong current of thought
coming out of his large, solid body making Wayne feel
small and vulnerable.

Hall reared back slightly from Wayne as if with repug-
nance. The two of them stood there for a second.

Wayne tried to find his voice. "Dr. Hall, I'm terribly—"

Hall's large face puckered as if he were going to cry or

shout or vomit. "So," he said, and his voice was vibrating with emotion. "What do you see in this? Some underlying pattern? Some higher meaning? What is it? Will you tell me that? What is it?"

⸻

The hearse glided with dignified slowness through the morning streets of St. Clair, the priest's respectable dark blue Oldsmobile following it, Hall's Mercedes behind that, and Wayne's dented Honda rattling at the back. They took the bridge above the brown, mud-smelling river and headed north on the county highway. The air was clear and soft, the sunlight gentle, and Wayne thought he had never seen such a beautiful day. It occurred to him that if Gail had waited another week to die she could have seen it too.

They drove to the cemetery in the woods where Wayne had seen Dr. Carvery. Four sturdy, handsome young men in black suits climbed out of the hearse, opened the back, slid the coffin out on some kind of rollered extension, and waited respectfully. The priest got out of his Oldsmobile with a book and started through the cemetery gates with a practiced air. The four young men followed him carrying the coffin, and Hall and Wayne brought up the rear. They didn't speak or look at each other. The grave wasn't far. It was a deep, sharp-edged rectangle cut into the patchy grass a little distance from some other headstones. Two older men in overalls leaned on shovels behind a mound of reddish dirt.

The four young men set the coffin down gently on the grass. Birds were singing in the trees, and there was the cool smell of greenery, through which sunlight dappled down. The priest had a book open and was reading prayers from it in a low voice, and after every few words he wrung holy water from a silver sprinkler into the grave and onto the coffin. At his nod the four young men lifted the coffin and maneuvered themselves onto opposite sides of the hole so that the coffin was suspended over it. Wayne, standing next to Hall, felt an almost unbearable suspense, as if everything hadn't already happened. Then the coffin began to descend slowly with a slight hissing of cords. It went down into the hole, and the cords went slack. The young men loosened them and pulled them out. Then, as the priest read and wrung holy water, the two men with shovels stepped forward and each took a shovelful of dirt and threw it into the hole. The dirt thumped hollowly on the coffin.

Birds sang and a little breeze stirred cool under the trees, and soon the dirt fell quietly onto dirt, and after a while the reddish-brown color of it brimmed to the top. Wayne noticed that the four young men were gone, and that the priest had taken Hall aside and was talking to him, Hall shaking his head dully. Finally the priest put his hand gently on Hall's arm, nodded to Wayne, and walked slowly toward the cemetery gate, wrapping his silver sprinkler in a white cloth.

—

On Shaman's Mound everything was as Wayne remembered it in the bright air. The Lake was a dreamy dark blue tipped with white chop, fading to a haze on the horizon that seemed to mimic the high, filmy clouds. The breeze was the freshest, clearest air Wayne thought he had ever breathed, full of the cool maritime smell of the Lake with its memories of long days of sunlight glittering on waves, squeals of children and seabirds, the rocking, cool water, the vast blue-grey horizon holding always a hint of storm, a hint of fine weather.

If Gail had waited another week to die—Or a month, or a year, or six decades. He had only known her a week, he reminded himself. He had only slept with her twice, kissed her maybe a hundred times, only held her in his arms a couple of dozen times, had only exchanged a few thousand words with her. He could turn away from this unscathed, look away as he did from the memory of his mother on the back porch that night long ago. But someday it would be his turn, he knew. Someday that weird mole would be cancer, or that chest pain would be a heart attack, or that buzzing in his ears a stroke. Some bright morning of the world like this one would be the last; then they would come for him and put him in a box and bury him in the ground. So if he turned away now, it would only be for a little while.

He sat on the rough rock seat, looking out over the Lake. The squeals of children and seabirds echoed in his mind. Summers from his childhood that had seemed unending, as if he had been transported to a different world, bright and breezy and sea-smelling, with never any school and never any reason to go to bed unless you were tired, and the ever-present ocean to play in, build sand castles at the edge of, walk along, hunt for shells on the beach, your skin browning to a rich healthy tan and your body straightening and strengthening—as if you had been transported to a celestial world of strong hungers and robust fulfillments, sunlight and sometimes storm, when the breeze would stiffen and the sea horizon would fill with grey and thunder, the grey surf would run far up the beach and pull at your ankles like an animal that wanted to pull you down and out to sea, to roll you in the tremendous grey swells, roll you deep and quiet, deep, forever—

He walked on a beach, the sunlight bright and hot in a hazy pale blue sky that faded to a remote grey at the horizon, as if there were a storm brewing somewhere at the ends of the world. The beach was deserted, only sea-gulls swooping and mewing in the brisk noon air. The water near the shore was blue and gentle, rocking with swells, the sound of the surf soothing, but farther out toward the horizon the water was dark blue and cold-looking. The tide was going out, leaving pools and drift-wood and clots of sea wrack behind on the sand and rocks, and in one of these clots of sea wrack Wayne thought he saw two small, grey feet. Heart pounding, he knelt and pulled the seaweed aside, and it was a little boy, the body of a little boy, and as Wayne gathered the limp, breathless body into his arms, he saw with an intense shock that it was his son.

He stood up, holding the child, his body throbbing with shock and sorrow, and now he saw that the storm the horizon had hinted at had formed in a black and roiling wall of cloud torn with lightnings, and it was rushing toward him, still far off but terrifying, the water rising in a great wall of waves, impossible to measure at that distance.

—

He woke up crying. Afternoon was lengthening, the bright sun over the Lake glittering past noon on the waves, the long sound of surf coming distantly from below the trees. Crying, he went back down to his car. If that was all the Indian could give him—but probably there had never been a real Indian—probably it had all been a figment of his imagination.

—

For the next two days Wayne slept little. He lay in his bed watching for dawn to come creeping in blues and greys and purples and gold across the sky, and when he saw it he got up and showered, went to his car, and headed for

St. Clair, and through St. Clair, and out onto the little country roads beyond. The map lay on the seat where Gail had left it with the red pen, and as the day brightened and the air warmed, long, dewy shadows shortening and dust coming up on the roads and lanes behind his tires, he drove, marking the map, talking in his mind to Gail, sometimes perhaps talking to her out loud, telling her the names on the road signs, and whether he thought he had gone too far in some direction, and whether he thought he recognized the road. Then by afternoon, hot and exhausted, he would drive back to Bolling's and take the celestial narcotic of the Lake, and when he was far out in the grey-green swells, the bluff small and misty behind him, the urge would come over him again to find the far continent, and he would turn to that horizon. But every time he remembered the terrible storm and wall of waves from his dream, and a panic would come over him far out in the drowning waters and he would swim back desperately to shore, exhausting himself.

He saw no sign of the model-beauties all that time. But the thought of the one with the ocean eyes was growing on his mind again, as if only the silky girl could help him now, as if only she could compensate the sorrows of this world, as he had thought in the weeks after his separation. When he lay awake in the dark, exhausted from thoughts of Gail, the face of the silky girl would come, and he would lie there in an agony of desire, hope, and sorrow.

16

The third evening after the funeral was still and warm, and Wayne sat on the bluff in deepening blue dusk tinged for a while with a faint lavender among the motionless leaves, an unearthly beauty like second sight. The air was so still that he could hear the gurgle of the swells behind the sleepy hush of surf, and the scents of grass and the orange day lilies that grew on the bluff came to him like medicine. So much swimming and so little sleep had worn him out; as dusk deepened he fell into a peaceful drowsiness. He was almost asleep when a sound came over the whir of crickets in the still air.

The thump of dance music.

His heart moved in his chest, and he sat up blinking.

Deep red light throbbed in the downstairs windows of the model-beauties' house.

He counted in his head. Yes; August 5. Their party; he had forgotten all about it. He rested his head back against the lawn chair, trying to recapture the blissfully comfortable position from which he had been jerked awake, closing his eyes. But he was wide awake now. The music thumping through the celestially quiet night brought an involuntary tingling, and into his mind came the face and eyes of the silky girl, her long braid, her pale body in its bikini.

—

He showered, shaved, and walked down the beach, carrying his shoes and socks, the cuffs of his freshly washed jeans rolled up. Cool sand squeaked under his feet and surf hushed placidly to his left. There was no moon yet, and the lights of Bolling's and the model-beauties' houses blanked out all but the brightest stars, so that night hung like a smoky curtain to his left, blotting out the Lake; to his right the humid pale sand and clay of the bluff rose to dark trees.

Lanterns had been put up at the corners of the model-beauties' deck, and warm yellow light leaked down onto the wooden beach steps. Halfway up, Wayne dusted off his feet and put on his shoes and socks. At the top, more lanterns lit a grass-choked flagstone walk that led to the front door. Music was loud through the open windows, but the only neighbor within half a mile was himself, so it didn't matter. It occurred to him belatedly that maybe they had only invited him to preempt complaints. Swallowing this thought, he walked to the front door and rang the bell.

It opened almost immediately on loud music, thick air, and the clamor of conversation. The black-haired girl stood there, this time with clothes on—a very short, becoming silver dress. Her hair was braided and beaded like Cleopatra's, and the dark eyes in her beautiful, wide-browed face were clear and flashing. She showed perfect teeth in a delighted smile.

"Oh, hi!" she said excitedly, putting her hand on his arm. But then a half recognition came into her face. She tapped her chin and wrinkled her forehead in a show of thinking.

"The other morning, when you all were dancing," Wayne helped her out. "I had a bottle of wine."

A flash of memory and calculation came into her eyes, quickly covered by a delighted laugh. "Oh, yes, yes! Oh, God, then you're the one who saw me—" She covered herself with her arms in a pretty show of embarrassment. "I'm sorry—we were so—" She gestured at her head and rolled her eyes. "You're the man who lives next door. They've told me all about you." She was excited again. She took him by the hand and led him down three steps into a sunken living room full of smoke and thump, crowded with people and tables with food and drink. "I'm Candy," she said in his ear. "We'll be dancing again later on, and then who knows *what* will happen." She gave his hand a squeeze and smiled.

The doorbell rang.

"Oh, excuse me," she said, and headed back toward it.

He puzzled for a couple of seconds after her beautiful backside, then turned around to see if he could get some food.

Samir Farris was before his face.

"Dolan, man!" said Farris above the music in a voice as pleased and friendly as Candy's, and they shook hands. Farris was holding a glass of something that looked like punch. Farris wasn't the first person Wayne had expected to see at a party given by apparent floozies, and indeed, Farris seemed to be of the same mind: he glanced around guiltily. "How are you, man?"

It felt strange making small talk after not talking to anyone for three days. "Looks like a wild party. Who's giving it?"

"I was going to ask you," said Farris. "You live near here, don't you?"

"Next door. But I have no idea—" At that moment over Farris's head he caught sight of Brad Tollaksen and Maureen Allison. "Look at this," he said to Farris.

A woman was talking to Brad. She was standing slightly closer to him than customary conversational distance, but maybe it was just to be heard over the music. She was tall and slim, had auburn hair bobbed at her chin, and wore a flimsy dress of some purple silk stuff. Wayne had seen her on the beach in a bikini. She stood very straight on high heels, holding a drink, her chin tilted up to look into Brad's face, talking self-confidently. Even from where he stood Wayne could see her nipples through the dress. Brad looked as if he was having a hard time following what she was saying. Maureen stood to one side watching doubtfully.

"Gentlemen," came a voice. They turned to see Eric Drensler in one of his expensive brown suits, his tie off and collar button open to reflect the informality of the occasion. He looked a little drunk, his muddy brown eyes glazed, and he grinned widely, showing crooked, brownish teeth. "Wonderful party."

"Eric, man," said Farris. "Who's giving it? It's full of Institute people, but I've never heard of the Institute giving a party like this."

"I heard it's one of the scientific supply companies," said Drensler. "The girls will probably haul out their latest gene sequencer later in the evening and pose naked on it or something. The things these people think of." He sipped his punch and rolled his eyes. "Samir, I want to introduce you to someone. Excuse me," he said to Wayne.

Sure enough, the party *did* look like mostly Institute people, many pale, out-of-shape males looking around curiously as if unused to such delicious decadence. To his surprise, Wayne saw Edmund Carvery with a sandwich and a glass of punch, talking to a statuesque, dignified woman who was some senior researcher at the Institute. Carvery looked wrinkled and tired, but better than when Wayne had seen him in his office, like a man recovering after an illness.

"He's on antidepressants," said a voice at his elbow. "His people finally persuaded him. They were afraid if he went crazy his work would lose whatever credibility it has."

Ray Daniels stood there with a glass of punch.

Wayne filled a plate with hors d'oeuvres and got some punch. The hors d'oeuvres were salty and the punch was delicious.

"Who's giving this party?"

Daniels shrugged. "Are these the girls you met on the beach? They don't seem too unfriendly."

"Not tonight. Drensler thinks it's a sales party given by some equipment supplier."

Daniels shook his head. "If it was, the Administration would be here. They're the ones who buy equipment. And have you seen upstairs? Go look. I'll catch up with you. I have to find Farris."

Wayne drank a second glass of punch. In the next room the music was deafening and two of the model-beauties danced unselfconsciously in thick pulsing light with half a dozen men who seemed to be gyrating a bit wildly for scientists. The air smelled of perfume and sweat, and the flimsy blue dress of one of the model-beauties was plastered to her so that it was possible to detect that she was wearing nothing underneath. On the far side of the room double doors opened to the lantern-lit deck.

Wayne jostled back out through the living room just in time to see Maureen Allison, a chastened Brad in front of her, slamming the front door and ignoring Candy, who was saying something. A long, tanned, and freckled model-beauty with curly blonde hair was leading a paunchy, drunk-looking man up the front staircase, talking earnestly over her shoulder. Wayne tried to catch up to them, guessing this was the house tour, but when he reached the top a door in the hall was just closing. He hesitated for a moment, then tried the knob. It was locked.

Four other doors opened off the hall; two of them were open. Wayne put his head in curiously at one, a dim purple-lit cave. There was no furniture, but the floor and walls had been upholstered. It looked like foam rubber mattresses covered with purple satin, and big satin pillows scattered around.

Just then one of the doors behind him opened. He turned to see a man come out. It was Adam Burschevsky. His long grey ponytail was a little disarranged, his patrician face flushed and happy, eyes glazed and intoxicated. He didn't see Wayne standing in the shadow of the doorway. He went downstairs toward the noise and light of the party.

Burschevsky had left his door ajar, and behind it Wayne could see a dim red glow. Then the door opened all the way and someone stood there.

The silky girl.

She was wearing short jean cutoffs and a denim halter top, but on her they were like a queen's ermine. She stood haloed by the decadent red light and looked at Wayne as if she saw nothing, one hand on the thick silver-gold braid that snaked over her shoulder, stroking it almost autistically, as if anesthetized to everything else. The ocean-blue of her eyes looked almost black in the light, and her skin the skin of an angel, pale, untouchable, her face pure, unconscious, like the face of someone unborn, or a soul released from its earthly prison. Her small, high-arched feet were in clogs. One of her long, beautiful hands went to the jamb of the door.

Wayne felt sick. He bowed his head before the apparition and felt that he would vomit. The hallway, the house tilted around him. He held on to the wall, light going dark before his eyes, the blood seeming to leave his head.

In a second it passed, and he could see again, thought he could walk. He didn't look at the girl again. He swayed to the stairs and went down jerkily, holding on to the banister. At the bottom he headed toward the front door.

"You're not *leaving*, are you?" came an amazed voice. "It's so *early*."

Candy had her hand on his arm and was looking up into his face with her wide black eyes.

"I'm not feeling good," said Wayne. "Got to go home."

"Oh, I'm so sorry," said Candy without much depth of feeling. Then a thought seemed to occur to her: "Would you like to lie down upstairs for a little? I'm sure I could make you comfortable." She looked up at him with a strange look, appealing and innocent yet full of an ancient knowledge, as if they understood each other perfectly.

He shook his head, feeling sick again. He got his hand on the doorknob.

"Well, maybe you can come back later if you feel better," Candy suggested brightly.

<hr />

There had been something in the food, he realized after he had sat in his garden chair for half an hour listening to the crickets and the surf and the distant thump from the model-beauties' house and trying to figure out the dizziness, slight distortion of his senses, and the swollen feeling in his body. He had thought at first that he was catching something, but then he had caught the druggy, euphoric edge of it—not unlike the effects of some of his college recreations—and realized that he had been slipped a mickey. Something in the food—or better yet, in the punch. There had been nothing to drink but punch, he remembered thickly, and they had made sure to get people dancing, sweating, thirsty, and the hors d'oeuvres had been salty. He had started to think of Gail, of course, as soon as he had climbed down to the beach, but soon he could think only of her body, the animal pressure and heat of her, her musky, dirty smell, her thick hair and breasts, strong sides and stomach, and his skin had started to itch at the touch of his own clothes.

But who would anonymously give a party with six high-class prostitutes and aphrodisiac punch? And invite a good number of the senior scientists from the Deriwelle Institute for the Technological Study of Religion? He was too fuzzy to figure it out. He sat at the top of the bluff, and the half moon had come out limpid above the Lake, making a yellow, scribbled trail on the black-grey water, and Gail was gone, and the silky girl was probably just an expensive prostitute, and his children were growing up without him, and someday he would die. That was as complicated as he could make it in his muddled head, and he started to cry silently, tears running down his face and dripping off his jaw.

There was a sound. He turned his head, listened. It seemed to have come from the bluff, like someone climbing the flagstone steps in the dark. Yes, there it was again, and then a soft breath.

Then a gleam of gold rising out of the darkness down the bluff.

He stared, frozen. The silky girl stood looking at him from the top of the bluff steps three yards away, her chest rising and falling from the climb.

Her face was half in shadow, half in moonlight. Moonlight through the trees streaked one of her arms, her side.

The sound of the waves washing gently, rhythmically came up from the beach. The pebbles at the edge of the flagstone walk glimmered like silver coins. The air was warm, very still.

The girl took two slow steps forward, a panther-angel streaked by moonlight. Then, watching him steadily, blindly, she untied her halter, unzipped her cutoffs, and writhed out of them gently. She stepped out of her clogs. She was naked.

She stood looking at him blindly. She was as beautiful as the oceans, the galaxies. So beautiful and so vulnerable was she, offering herself to him in her bone and muscle and skin that it would have been sacrilege to let her stand so and not to take her, prostitute though she might be. Wayne stood up, feeling clumsy and thick and strong, stood in front of her. Her skin as she stood on tiptoe and put her arms around his neck was cool, ivory-smooth, soft.

Suddenly, with a cool, euphoric shock they were kissing, her lips cool and soft, her tongue hot and hard, and she pressed against him, helping him as with trembling hands he unbuttoned and unzipped himself, dragging the clothes off his body, and then the oceans and galaxies pressed against him naked until he trembled and gasped with the pure intensity.

He felt the chill grass on his back, soft and damp and alive, and she straddled him, taking his hard penis in her fingers. Then her expert wet flesh went down on him and she rode him, expertly and tenderly and blindly, and he clutched at her arms, and she let him take her arms, and he pulled her down so he could feel her delicate, perfect breasts, and she let him kiss her, even kissing him back and even putting her hands in his hair, but mostly she was intent on riding him, their flesh rubbing and rubbing and rubbing, and she was in no hurry, but even stopped and cocked her delicate, muscular pelvis up and off him twice when it seemed he would come, and then rode him again slowly, patiently, rubbing, rubbing, the wet of her dripping down his testicles.

But finally, looking down at him almost maternally as if she thought he had had enough, she started to go a little faster and to sigh in her high, sweet voice, and she slipped one hand down between his legs and pressed the place just behind his testicles, and with a great burn, thrusting up into her and holding her delicate hips like one insane, he came, crying out and weeping. It took him a long time, and she rode with him, patiently, even tenderly, watching him, as if gauging him.

Finally he was done. He lay still and she sat atop him. She seemed in no hurry. Her graceful finger traced patterns in the wet of his stomach as if she had forgotten where she was. Then she absently stroked her long golden braid as if it was the only thing real in the world, as if she were anesthetized to everything else.

He sat up, still holding her on him, and kissed her. She was blind, like a soul unborn, or one released from its earthly prison. He held her sadly in his arms.

At last she stirred. She pulled away from him. She dressed, not looking away from him, but not at him either, as if nothing in this world was real. The distant dance music from the party thumped on bright and eager. She let him kiss her one more time, and kiss her hand. Then she went.

He woke next morning to the ringing of a telephone strangely thin and distant, and he was cold. He stirred, opened his eyes. He lay naked on the dewy grass of the bluff in grey dawn, and the telephone was ringing in the kitchen. The answering machine caught it after the sixth ring, but after 30 seconds it started again.

He thought suddenly of his children. He leapt up and ran clumsily inside, realizing as he did that he had a splitting headache.

He got the phone on its fifth ring.

"Wayne?" It was Maureen Allison. She sounded excited. "Sorry to call so early. Were you at that horrible party last night? I know it was somewhere up by you. Brad and I left early, we hated it so much."

Wayne mumbled something polite, trying to wake up all the way.

"But I thought you should know, for your book and all: Ray Hall is dead."

"Say what? Slow down, Maureen, I just woke up. Ray Hall? You mean his daughter?"

"I didn't know he had a daughter. No, I mean Ray Hall, Dr. Raymond Hall. Suicide. They found him late last night. He hanged himself. A couple of days ago, they're saying. Apparently it was quite a mess; there were flies, the whole thing. He hadn't been to the lab, and then he was supposed to meet someone last night to go to a party, but when they got to his house his car was there but he wouldn't answer the door, so they called the police. He had tied a rope around his neck and jumped off his upstairs landing."

Wayne and Maureen exchanged expostulations. Maureen didn't have any more details, but she was continuing to get calls from Institute friends and would certainly tell him everything. Wayne promised to drop by. Then he took two aspirin and a hot shower, trying out this news on his befuddled brain alongside his as-yet-unprocessed memories from last night. He was coming downstairs, toweling off, when the phone rang again.

It was Detective Sergeant Stanzik of the St. Clair Police Department. He wanted to know whether Dr. Raymond Hall had appeared distraught at his daughter's funeral, which he somehow knew Wayne had attended. He was annoyed when Wayne knew that Hall had killed himself. "Seems you been in a lot of trouble since you came to our town," he groused, and he wouldn't answer any of Wayne's questions.

The phone rang one more time before Wayne got in his car. It was Ray Daniels.

His breathy voice was hard to read. "How are you feeling this morning, Dolan?"

"Moderate. Got a headache. Why?"

"That was a strange party last night."

"Yeah," said Wayne, wondering what Ray was getting at, and whether he should spill his story about the silky girl. "Did you ever figure out who gave it?"

"Not exactly," said Ray. "But I have an idea. So you're feeling OK?"

"Yeah. Just a headache."

"Anything else?" asked Ray. "Aches, pains, fever?"

"No," said Wayne slowly. On the chance that Ray hadn't fallen for the prostitutes, Wayne decided he didn't want to admit that he had; at least not yet. He changed the subject. "You heard about Raymond Hall?"

"What about him?"

Wayne told him. When he was done, there was a silence on the phone. "Ray? You there?"

"I'll call you back," said Ray distantly. "I need to check on something."

Wayne spent most of the day at Maureen and Brad's, brunch, midafternoon pizza, coffee, excited conversation and phone calls, and Institute people popping in and out. Adam Burschevsky was one of them. He seemed tired and his skin was greyish. Wayne could hardly bring himself to look at the man, but Burschevsky didn't stay long, and was uncharacteristically subdued.

It seemed, based on all the intelligence Maureen could gather, that Hall had been in good spirits up until a few days before his death, when he had gotten ill. His researchers had urged him to stay home, but he had come into the lab and locked himself in his office, staying until late at night, apparently working. It was only after the police had found him dead that his researchers had heard about his daughter. Putting two and two together, it appeared that he had been distraught over her death, killing himself as the result of a "Brief Reactive Psychosis." As the afternoon went on and this dismal story was repeated in different variations over and over, Wayne's memories of Gail seemed to accumulate like ghosts in the corners of Maureen and Brad's well-appointed living room until finally, at about four in the afternoon, he realized that he wasn't feeling well.

"Probably just tired," he said as they saw him to the door, wishing he would stay, and the phone ringing undoubtedly some new piece of Hall news from yet another Institute friend. "I've been swimming a lot, and there was that party last night."

"Oh, wasn't that awful!" said Maureen, her eyes widening. "And those *girls*. One of them practically humped Brad right in front of me." Wayne didn't tell them about his own humping.

So he drove home, now seriously feeling ill, and got there just in time to throw up in the toilet, tomato sauce and partly digested cheese and pizza crust. It made him think of Gail in her bathroom. Afterward he felt cold despite the heat of the afternoon, and very tired. He decided to wrap up in a blanket and lie down on his bed for a little while.

The phone ringing woke him at twilight. He fumbled for it confusedly.

It was Daniels. He sounded sick himself, congested, tired, his voice cracking. "How you feeling, Dolan?"

"Terrible. You too? You think it was whatever they put in the food at the party? Or the punch? I threw up about ten gallons of pizza this afternoon."

"You talked to Hall, right? For your book?"

"Yeah."

"Did he ever tell you— Did he ever ask if he could try to convince you that religion was an illusion or something like that?"

Wayne thought about it, rubbing his aching head. He tried to sit up in bed, and kind of half succeeded. "Yes. Yes, he did. When I interviewed him at his office. Why?"

"And did you say yes?"

"Yes, I did, as I remember. What's going on, Ray? Do you think I made him kill himself or something?"

"No, nothing like that. I'll have to call you back."

After he had fumbled the phone back onto its cradle, Wayne realized that he was ragingly thirsty. But he was so tired and cold that the idea of going to the bathroom sink seemed almost impossible. He fell asleep again trying to decide what to do.

—and woke up twelve hours later with the phone ringing again. It seemed like an hour's hard work to become conscious and roll over and fumble for it, peel open his parched mouth to croak: " 'Lo?"

"Dolan?" It was Daniels, sounding like an old man. "Dolan, how are you?"

Wayne let out a gust of breath that even he could smell

was bad. Sweat seemed to have come out and dried on him all night, and his skin was greasy and hypersensitive. His head was hot and throbbing.

"Listen to me, Dolan. You'll want to come down here. There's something important."

"I can't even stand up."

"Listen to me. You need to drink about a gallon of water and take four aspirin. You have some saltine crackers? Chew a few with the aspirin. Lie down for half an hour, then take a hot shower. Then wrap up good and drive down here. I'll expect you at 9:30."

"Ray, what is it? Why are you—?"

"I think maybe Ray Hall infected us," said Daniels, and hung up.

17

Daniels's prescription of water, aspirin, and a shower worked as well as anything could be expected to, and at 9:45, wearing jeans, a sweatshirt, a baseball cap (not the wired one), and wrapped in his raincoat against the breezy, grey, damp weather, Wayne shuffled out to his car. He drove slowly to Columbia Road hunched over the steering wheel, wishing he could lie down. When he got to Building B he was surprised to see only half a dozen cars in the lot; then he remembered it was Sunday.

Daniels' lab door was open, and the white fluorescent light dazzled Wayne. There were four people in the lab and three of them looked sick. A sixty-year-old version of Ray Daniels sat hunched on a lab stool wearing a raincoat and an old hat; his nose was red, his face lined, eyes rheumy. Wayne saw with a start that Edmund Carvery was there too, sitting on another stool. He looked as much worse than Ray as he had when they were both healthy, which made him an imitation of death: skeletal face and bald head a color of grey Wayne had seen once before; on Gail, he realized with a churn of his stomach. Carvery's raincoat was as wrinkled as his face, and the hands that held it shut were skeletal and purplish, blue veins standing out. He seemed to be trembling slightly with fever.

In an armchair by the TV Samir Farris sat wearing a heavy sweater and black jeans, hands clutched between his knees. His smooth brown complexion was greyish and his eyes were red, his face drawn into an expression of exhausted anxiety.

The only healthy-looking person in the lab was Ray's assistant Tom, leaning against a workbench in his lab coat, eyes wide with dismay. It came to Wayne then that he hadn't seen Tom at the model-beauties' party.

"Dolan," croaked Ray. "I wondered if you were going to show up. We were about to leave without you."

Wayne slumped down in the armchair next to Farris. "Leave for where? What's it all about, Ray?"

"Raymond Hall."

"You think he gave us his monkey virus?"

"A lot of the human transfection vectors are sexually transmitted. And as far as I know, only people who had sex with the girls at the party are sick." He looked at Wayne levelly.

Wayne held his gaze for a few seconds, then closed his eyes and leaned his head back against the chair. "Hall gave the party?"

"I found the realtor who rented him the house."

"This is the wages of sin," said Farris, his voice trembling, whether from fever or fear Wayne couldn't tell. "I knew it was wrong when I did it. I wish I had listened to that feeling instead of—"

"There wasn't much you could do when they put

an aphrodisiac in the punch," said Daniels. "Tom, get the car."

Tom ducked out of the lab.

"Who else is sick?" Wayne opened his eyes to ask.

"Drensler, for one. And he has this triumphalist attitude all of a sudden. Even more than usual."

"What about Burschevsky? I saw him come out of a room with—" The memory of it, the silky girl's pure, otherworldly face burned in him again.

Daniels looked at him for a moment, then turned to a phone on the worktable. He dialed a number. "Hello, Adam?" he said after a moment. "Sorry, is Dr. Burschevsky there? Ray Daniels. Uh-huh. What's the matter with him? No, that's all right, I'll try him later." He hung up and turned back to the others. "Has the flu," he said.

There was silence for a minute. The death's-head Carvery sat sunken into himself, his glazed eyes abstracted, a million miles away.

Tom's head appeared in the doorway.

The air outside was damp and fresh; a brisk breeze carried the smell of the Lake, and the grey overcast had lowered. Tom had pulled up by the Building B door an old but immaculate Galaxy 500, with enough room for twice the five people who now got into it, four of them slowly and unsteadily. Wayne sat in back next to Carvery. He had the faint smell of something that had been left in the refrigerator too long.

"Where are we going?" he asked as Daniels got in front next to Tom.

"Building A," said Daniels.

Tom turned the big car in the parking lot and coasted down the immaculate asphalt.

"You think those girls would let themselves be infected with something like that?" Wayne wondered anxiously to Daniels. "Even for money?"

"He could have made them carriers without causing the brain effects."

"Can't we take something? Antiviral medicine?" asked Wayne, panic flaring in him. He remembered Gail on her knees in front of King. But the serum hadn't worked on her, Hall had said—"We need to get some antiviral medicine right away."

"Against what virus? Even if we knew, it can take years to develop a drug."

As they glided into Building A's large, empty lot, it began to sprinkle. Tom pulled up close to the door, and the four old men got out. Ray pressed the door buzzer.

Three burly ex-police security professionals were alert and ready for commando action as they watched the four men come in through the metal detector. One of them, brush-cut, his neck as thick as his head, hands blunt and ready, stood up behind the counter and said: "Yes, sir. Can I help you?" in a warning tone.

Daniels headed for the door that opened into the labs.

"I said, can I help you?" said the security man, putting his hands on the counter and leaning toward Daniels, shoulder muscles bunching. The two other guards stood up behind him. When Daniels still ignored him, he burst through the gate in the guard station, one hand unsnapping the holster of a large gun on his belt.

Daniels' hand went up, holding an ID badge in front of the guard's face. The guard's hand stopped an inch from Daniels' arm and he read the badge.

"You're cleared for entry under normal conditions, Dr. Daniels," he said. "But this building has been secured by order of the St. Clair police."

"The St. Clair police don't have jurisdiction here. This is Colony."

"Well, I'm sure they're working together on this."

"Has anyone from the Colony force contacted you?"

"Dr. Daniels, I'm going to ask you to take your hand off that doorknob."

"The St. Clair police force has no jurisdiction in Colony, so if you touch me you're committing an assault against an Institute scientist cleared for entry into this facility and his designees, and obstructing an investigation into possible manufacture of germ-warfare substances used against U.S. civilians, which may mean treason, conspiracy, and construction of a weapon of mass destruction."

The guard hesitated.

Daniels flicked his card into the slot next to the door and turned the knob.

———

Raymond Hall's office was empty—empty as Gail's apartment, the thought struck Wayne—and silent except for the whisper of windblown raindrops on the windows. Daniels flicked a wall switch and lights came on silently.

"Is the Institute really in Colony?" asked Carvery shakily in an old man's voice. "I thought it was St. Clair."

"Who knows?" mumbled Daniels. "But lock the door in case they try to get at us. I only need a few minutes."

Tom snapped a dead bolt.

"We shouldn't be in here, eh," said Farris anxiously, sitting tiredly in one of the visitor's chairs. "The police—"

"Come over here," Daniels said to him, going behind Hall's desk. "I'll need help on the password." He switched on Hall's computer. There was a small, rising whir and the chatter of disk drives. "Yeah, it's passworded. Farris, come over here."

Farris got up tiredly.

In a few minutes a siren wailed in the distance, melancholy in the rain.

Daniels and Farris were leaning over the computer and talking in low voices, pecking at the keyboard and watching the screen. Carvery sat sunken in a visitor's chair with his eyes closed. The siren was definitely coming in their direction, and soon it was shockingly loud even through the closed windows, and then it died slowly, like a bagpipe deflating.

"We have to go, eh," said Farris urgently.

"OK," said Daniels, and swayed, grabbing at Farris for support.

All of them crowded out into the hall. The second Tom had Hall's door shut behind them the door at the end of the hall burst open and a commotion of hard voices and bustling bodies came through. Detective Sergeant Stanzik was in the lead, with the security man who had accosted Daniels half a step behind, and half a dozen policemen and guards following. Wayne saw Alan Rilfsbane in the rear, his face white and shocked.

"Stand where you are!" snarled Stanzik. "Put your hands in the air."

Frightened into motionlessness, Wayne started to raise his hands, but seeing that Daniels kept his down, he did likewise.

"I said put your hands in the air!" yelled Stanzik. He pulled a pistol from a shoulder holster and held it pointing at the ground.

"What is this all about?" asked Daniels. "Rilfsbane, what is this all about?"

"We'll explain it down at the station," said Stanzik angrily, and catching sight of Wayne: "What are you doing here?"

"He's with me," said Daniels. "And if you're arresting us, I want to know why. Rilfsbane, you're a witness. What's the charge, Officer?"

"Breaking and entering," snapped Stanzik. "Interfering with a police investigation."

"You're mistaken," said Daniels. He held up his Institute badge ID. "I'm cleared to enter this facility."

"Not today you're not. The guard told you this facility was secured by order of the police, and you pushed right past him. There's an ongoing investigation into the death of a scientist working on top-secret technology, as at least one of you well knows." He glared at Wayne. "Come on, let's go."

"The guard didn't say anything like that," said Daniels. "I showed him my badge and he let us in."

"That's a lie," snarled the bull-like guard, his shoulder muscles bunching.

"Rilfsbane, I object to your allowing Institute researchers to be subject to this kind of abuse," said Daniels. "I intend to hold the Institute responsible. And I guess Dr. Carvery will leave the Institute if you let him be treated this way."

Carvery nodded his death's-head, looking like a starved vulture.

"Officer, I believe there has been some misunderstanding," said Rilfsbane, pushing to the front of the straining law-enforcement professionals and wiping his face with a monogrammed handkerchief. "Dr. Daniels is cleared for entry to the facility, as he has said, and has the right to invite others to enter. He says he was not warned that the building was closed—"

"Which is a lie," the bull-like security man said again, his two colleagues nodding vigorously behind him. "I told him very clearly—"

"I don't believe I've seen you before, young man," said Rilfsbane coolly. "How long have you been employed with us?" The security man looked unhappy. Rilfsbane paused, then went on. "Could Dr. Daniels perhaps have misunderstood your warning?"

"Well—" the guard choked out finally. The two other security men were stone-faced.

"You see," said Rilfsbane to Stanzik. "I believe there has simply been a mistake. I can certainly vouch for each one of these gentlemen." He wiped his face again.

Stanzik looked from Rilfsbane to the guard in disgust, then back at Daniels narrow-eyed. "What were you doing in here?"

"We came to check on an experiment. But the laboratory door is locked."

"You didn't get into the lab?"

"No."

"Will you agree to a body search?"

Daniels shrugged.

The uniform cops patted down Wayne and each of the others, and examined their house keys, kleenex, and penknives. Finally, Stanzik said angrily. "OK, you can go." He turned on the bulky security man. "I'll want a word with *you*."

Back in the Galaxy 500 heading for Building B, Wayne asked shakily: "What now?"

"We read Hall's hard drive," said Daniels. "I transmitted it to my lab over the Institute LAN."

There was a horrible rasping, gurgling sound. It was Carvery laughing.

—

Back at Daniels' lab, Wayne found that he was cold and shaking. He lowered himself into an armchair. "Anybody got aspirin?" he asked with chattering teeth. Tom got him four and a glass of water, then joined the others clustered around Daniels' computer. Wayne listened to their sporadic talk and the click of the keyboard, and even called out a few questions, but after a while exhaustion came over him and he wrapped his raincoat tightly around himself, closed his eyes, and leaned his head against the high, soft back of the chair.

⸺

Someone shook him awake by the shoulder. He focused his bleary eyes up at Daniels in the fluorescent lights.

"We found it," said Daniels. "We're reading it now."

He looked exhausted, skin grey, cheeks hollow, dark bags under the eyes. And was there something in his face Wayne had never seen before? Fear?

Wayne blinked in sudden panic and his heart pounded. "Is it—? What does it say?"

"Come see," said Daniels, and turned away.

Wayne struggled out of his chair. The clothes next to his skin were damp with sweat, and standing up made his ears ring. His mouth was dry and his stomach unsteady. He shuffled trembling after Daniels, who pushed a stool his way. Tom's and Farris' eyes were wide and tense on the computer screen. Only Carvery seemed no more deathlike than before, sunken, skeletal, patient. Wayne sat behind them, focusing blearily on the screen between their backs.

It was covered with text. A date and time were printed at the top: "July 30, 1999, 9 P.M."

"The earlier entries are mostly technical, but they talk about renting the house and hiring the girls," Daniels told Wayne, and then Wayne started to read where a sentence carried over from a previous screen.

". . . appropriate way to be initiated into the wonders of Truth! The part of me that still craves ritual has been satisfied; c.f. the temple prostitutes of ancient religions. Jung identifies the door to the soul

as being symbolized in the unconscious by a beautiful member of the opposite sex. How fitting and
somehow touching that entry to the new world of
clarity and objectivity should be facilitated by such
a perfect ritual, the last we will ever need. I was
also glad to see that the girls followed my directions exactly. They are very skillful, as one would
hope. It is a bare 24 hours since our contact, and already I am beginning to feel fluish; the reproductive vector seems even higher than I had thought. I
am afraid, of course, as I suppose any explorer is
afraid, but more than anything my spirit is flying
with the anticipation of meeting my new brain.
And no less of welcoming my colleagues on this
voyage with me. I only hope I won't be too sick to
go to my party!

Daniels clicked to the next screen, dated July 31.

The news about Gail struck me harder than I could
have thought possible. Perhaps it's because of the
primary infection, which appears to have the physical and emotional effects of influenza. On the way
downtown to identify her body, I could not keep
out of my head the image of her beautiful face on
that day when she was seven years old, but when I
went into the morgue and saw her lying on a pallet,
the reality was hideously different. It shocked me
in a way I can't describe, and the shock is still with
me. Strange that it should have happened on the
very day I was contracting the infection. Perhaps it
is just as well that she died, given how she had
lived. All the same, it has filled me with anguish
and a strange kind of dread. Perhaps I shall see it all

more clearly in a few days, and then I shall understand. Yes, I'll wait for the clarity and objectivity to
come, and then I shall understand.

The next screen was undated.

it is unspeakable. could the test have been wrong?
It is emptiness, darkness. nothing. devouring

Daniels clicked the screen again several times, but
there was nothing else.

There was a pause, filled by the flat white and faint
buzz of the fluorescent lights. Finally, Daniels stirred.

"Well, that's it," he said.

Farris spoke with trembling voice: "How long from
infection did it take him to get to—that point?"

"At least three days. And at most five. He killed himself on August second."

"We're on the second day," said Farris.

"Isn't there anything we can do?" Wayne asked, and
he realized his voice was croaking, cracked, dry. "Antiviral drugs . . ."

"Not against HR-17," said Daniels. "Which is what
this is. It reproduces too fast. And brain changes of the
kind he's talking about are usually irreversible. Though
in time other brain areas may take over the functions of
the ablated tissue."

"I don't think so," mumbled Wayne. "In this case."
He didn't elaborate; he didn't want to talk about Gail.
No one seemed to have heard him anyway.

"Well, that's it," said Daniels again. "I have to go
home. I'm not feeling well."

There was a rustle in the silence as they all got up.
Daniels turned off the computer.

"If anyone needs a ride—" said Tom, his voice vibrating with emotion. His eyes were wide behind his thick glasses.

They shuffled out silently, and out on the sidewalk by the parking lot they all shook hands, even Carvery. His hand was cool, skeletal, fragile.

"If anybody needs anything, call me at home," said Daniels gruffly.

"See you guys later," was all Wayne could think of to say. "After—"

Then they were all walking to their cars, heads bowed, each sunk in his own thoughts. The sky was low, grey, and looked like more rain, and it was getting dark.

———

He woke sometime in the dim morning with a headache and an awful feeling, for a moment not remembering why. The sky was grey and low, rain blew against the windows, and it was chilly and damp. Then he remembered. Infected with the virus. Gail gone. The silky girl a prostitute. Cold dread took him, and he closed his eyes, huddled in the covers, trembling with fever. *Should I kill myself?* he wondered. It was the third day.

Finally he pushed back the covers. A thought had come to him, an urge. He chewed four aspirin and a few crackers that he had on the night table, then struggled up and hobbled into the bathroom and drank three glasses of bad-tasting water, turned on the shower very hot.

An hour later the grey wind hissed through the trees at the top of the model-beauties' bluff, making deep green shadows move and flutter where before there had been shades of emerald brightness. The house looked empty; there were no lights on, and no vehicles in the driveway. Wayne stumped along the overgrown flagstone walk and rang the doorbell several times. There was no answer. He tried the door. It was unlocked. He went in.

The house was vacant and dim, lit dull grey through the windows and skylights. The sunken living room was devoid of the elegant furniture, potted trees, and throw rugs he had seen at the party. A couple of lakeward windows were open, and the wind hissed and even whistled a little in the screens, and a distant roar of surf came into the house. "Hello," Wayne called a couple of times without expecting an answer.

He walked through the house. A nearly empty bottle of Jim Beam stood on the kitchen counter next to a couple of paper cups. A lipstick and a cheap plastic compact had been forgotten in the upstairs bathroom. A tiny blue silk camisole was wadded up in one of the bedroom closets. Wayne held it up in the light from the window, through which the grey lake could be seen rolling with whitecaps out to the grey horizon. He threw it back into the closet with a sudden revulsion.

18

It is unspeakable. The words came to Wayne as he lay in his bed in a pitch-black night, exhausted and sick but unable to sleep. He lay and waited for it to come, the unspeakable, and he almost thought he could feel it eating his brain, eating away at the same time the world around him, leaving nothing but a black void. *Nothing.* A monotonous wind was blowing across the Lake, and the surf was a monotonous roaring outside his closed windows, like white noise, or rather black noise filling the blackness. He tried to relax, but noticed a few minutes later that his body was tensed and sweating.

What would life be like without higher meaning? He thought with terror for the hundredth time of Gail on her knees with King's thick penis in her mouth, sucking him eagerly for the drug that would let her escape this world. Her father had said the serum hadn't worked on her, Wayne remembered hopefully, also for the hundredth time. But maybe that had been wishful thinking, or a lie to protect himself from her lawsuits, or to protect his twisted mind from doubt.

Had he been insane? The great Raymond Hall, Nobel laureate and professor at the world's great universities? If so, maybe he hadn't killed himself because of the virus; or maybe it really had been a "Brief Reactive Psychosis" resulting from the loss of a loved one. Except that he hadn't loved Gail. Had he? Wayne shuddered in his cold sweat, trying to imagine what it would be like to lose a child.

He *would* lose them, and they him, it came to him, though he should have known it all the time. A knowing seemed to be creeping upon him, hard and clear, sweeping away illusions and fantasies, to leave—what? Tremblingly, he looked into it as into an evil sorcerer's crystal ball. And as he looked, he knew things. His life passed before his eyes, transfigured in the new hard, clear light.

Because he had been going to be a famous writer while still in his twenties. He had intended to live quietly in a house on a cliff over the ocean or in an old farmhouse on a country road, and he had been going to have a study with a rolltop desk and a leather sofa, a big tree outside the window. He would write every morning, and in the afternoons wander the countryside at the edge of the ocean, waiting patiently for the visions that come to those who watch and listen. On one of these wanderings, on a country road, or a cliff above the ocean, he would meet a girl who carried the depths of the world in her eyes, as if she were the very essence of the beauty he hunted, which was this world transfigured. They would know each other practically without speaking. They would marry, and would have horses and country Christmases with deep snow and beautiful children, and he would continue to penetrate into the soul of the world, and to gain praise in the great cities he would visit occasionally to receive writing awards and money and adulation.

For a while it had even seemed that he was making progress toward these dreams: he had started to sell stories in his mid-twenties, and then met Ann, who, while not the silky goddess/lover of his fantasies, was pretty and smart and admiring. They married and had Alice, whom he loved violently and unexpectedly, reinforcing his fantasy that life held even more than he had dared hope. He sold a novel, and then his second nearly took off and he got a big advance on the third and quit his day job, and Ann made partner at the firm, and they moved to a house in the suburbs. He was thirty-six, and blissfully unaware that he was right then and there at the pinnacle of his success and happiness.

Because from there the youthful strength and optimism and willful blindness that had seemed to build things up so high started to ebb, and with it everything else unraveled. His third novel flopped about the same time Danny was born. It took him three years of writer's block and rejection slips to sell another, for a minuscule advance. During that time his temper turned ugly, and he and Ann had screaming fights. Ann got lines in her face and grey in her hair, and more and more she was angry and resentful. His fourth book did poorly, but he limped along with another. Ann had been making 90 percent of the household income for years, and one night they had a fight and she called him a leech, and he knew he had to leave. He moved out the following month, Alice hiding in her room and Danny watching him and crying desperately and uncomprehendingly. He looked in his mirror the first morning he woke up to the silence and dead smell of his new apartment and saw a man with enlarged pores and greying hair, getting a stoop, teeth yellowing, and he made up his mind to start using facial cream and whitening toothpaste and working out again, but deep in the back of his mind he knew it was useless: while there were places to go besides down, in the end it was the gravitational pull of that direction that would win.

His fantasies of the silky girl had flared up again then, fresh from his adolescence, as if with one last panicked squirt of his glands before they dried out, but watching himself in the mirror he began to doubt that she would want him even if he ever did find her. In a lapse of time equal to that from his college graduation to his divorce— a blurred flash of memory—he would be an old man. And between now and then he would live in dingy apartments, see his children less and less, watch TV more and more, and finally one bright morning of the world would be his last; his children would walk behind his coffin and cry, and after that he would be gone, forgotten, at first quickly as to most things, and then gradually in the last two minds that contained traces of him, until finally they too were stilled.

And what did it all mean? He racked his brain, because this was the test of Hall's serum. What *could* it mean? Could a higher meaning really have escaped the detection of five hundred years of scientific study? Could it have survived five hundred years of systematic retreat by religion from one stronghold to another, while science proved that everything that had once been thought numenal was only the outworking of dead, mechanical laws? And of greatest importance in all this retreat, had there been even one single objective fact left standing that argued in favor of an afterlife?

And once you conceded that it was unlikely there was anything after, where did that leave you? What could life mean then? What good was it to grow up full of fantasy and yearning, as his children were doing now, to work

and desire and love and strive if in the end there was
nothing but end, nothing?

The silky girl—her beauty and intelligence, the depths
of her eyes, her voice like incense, the smooth, white fire of
her body: perhaps she was what it meant—perhaps she
could reconcile him to go on that journey, holding tightly
to her, growing old together and then diving off into that
cold with bittersweet love held tightly in their hearts.

But the silky girl was an illusion, a fantasy constructed of bits of movie stars and his adolescent daydreams and religious yearnings. He had met the silky
girl, had possessed her, he thought bitterly, and she was a
prostitute suffering from some kind of dissociative disorder, and the gift she had given him was Hall's virus. No,
the scientists had long ago figured out fantasies like his
silky girl: evolutionary tricks, mirages planted by natural
selection to make sure the male animal pursued the fittest
females and mated with them, all chemicals and circuitry
and physical laws, their grinning death's-heads hovering
over the nuptial beds.

His children, then, were what it meant. His love for
them at least was real. But now they were gone from him
and there was no way back. He had let go of them, let go
of everything, and at his age the tissues were dry and cau-
terized themselves when they were cut, and it was as if he
had let go of a hold he had somehow gotten on a steep
slope when he was younger and everything moved more
slowly, so that now he was sliding down it faster and
faster, and every day went by faster, and every day it was
harder to grab on to something to stop his fall. It was
all going by so fast now; by the time he finished thinking even this long thought he would look in the mirror
and his hair would be white, his face wrinkled, and
they would be adults, twisted and confused, remote
from him, too hurt and traumatized to ever see him as

anything but a figure in a dream, tormenting, puzzling, best forgotten.

A memory rose up in his mind. A sunny spring afternoon only a few months before when Ann had come to pick up the baby from staying with him for the day, and for once they had been civil to each other and she wasn't angry, and he had ridden down with them in the dingy elevator, Ann wearing an old-style pink dress and holding the baby by the hand, and as they had walked away through the crisp air and the bright light and shade of the cheap apartment complex trees, she had turned and smiled and waved, and told the baby to wave, and the baby had looked back and waved, and then they had both turned around, hand in hand, she walking and he shambling with his thoughtful baby steps, away from him, and a sorrow had gripped him, a steely, final sorrow that couldn't be argued with, they borne away on the currents of time, which would never return, and he would always have that image in his brain, of the bright sunlight and the woman and the little boy walking away from him, he left behind, stranded.

Because even if he could have cried out, run to them, begged and been forgiven, and gone home with them, returned to his life as husband and father, saving himself in the nick of time before it was too late, and even if by some miracle the strange, bitter entropy that had eaten the heart out of their marriage had disappeared and he had by some miracle been able to return and live a long, happy life, still that bitter day would come when time, after hiding for so long that one had almost forgotten him, stepped forward suddenly with his death's head and sickle and swept everything away. That day would come to him, Wayne Dolan, he knew now for a certainty; it had burned its foreknowledge into him. Perhaps not for decades, but what difference did that make? It would just put the goodbyes and the incomprehensible pain off for those few years, less than a flash in the face of eternity.

Jesus, he prayed—not to Jesus, but using the name because he didn't know any other—what could it mean? What could such a thing mean? And the answer was, it means nothing. It means nothing. Gail and the silky girl and himself and Alice and Danny and Ann and his mother and father. Nothing.

He tried to cry, managed to squeeze out a few small, stinging tears; but it was something beyond crying about. He lay and held on to his bed for dear life, as if the spinning of the galaxy might cast him off into the darkness between the stars.

Finally, exhausted, he fell asleep.

———

That night he dreamed that the weather changed. The clouds blew away, peeled back like a layer of mold. Dawn came clear and bright with a breeze off the Lake, late-summer branches waving serenely, and the lilies nodding their orange heads on the bluff. A touch of autumn dew quickly dried in the yellow sunlight, leaving the world quiet and thoughtful, waiting for him to wake up.

In his dream he did wake up, got dressed, and drove up the dirt road to the highway, and down the highway to St. Clair, and through St. Clair, out through the winding country roads beyond, remembering the way perfectly this time, until he pulled up under the willow trees that leaned over the road in the sunlight. From there he walked, the road running through woods and between fields, until he came to the white cottage at the top of the rise, shaded by willows and surrounded by its white picket fence. A warm breeze stirred the willows and the geraniums and pansies in the window boxes. Wayne stood looking up at the cottage, and a gladness he couldn't stop seemed to take root and bloom in the cold and dry of his chest, the knowledge finally that everything was going to be all right, better than all right. The sunlight that fell around him was ancient and full of a retiring wakefulness, as if someone walked there reflecting everything in his eyes, the whole world. It was very quiet except for the breeze stirring the trees and flowers and even the grass, as if everything was alive; alive and serene, resting in the bright yellowish sunlight that lit a time that would never end.

Finally, trembling, Wayne moved. He had turned away from this gate once, left it and lost it, and he knew now that he couldn't afford to do that again. He walked over the long, soft crabgrass, opened the gate with tingling hands. As he did, someone came around the corner of the cottage.

For a second he thought it was the old man who lived there with the old woman, but it wasn't. It was the Indian in the jacket and string tie and cowboy boots whom Wayne had met in the blue-green office. He moved slowly, face calm, almost sleepy, as if enjoying the sunlight. Wayne stood just inside the gate, hands still on it. A few bees hovered over the jewel-bright flower beds.

The Indian walked down the sloping lawn and stopped in front of him, studying him with his grave black eyes.

"I told you we were directing the most important research at your Institute," he said finally. "Now you are ready to see the other side."

He held his hand out gravely to Wayne. It was an odd gesture from one grown man to another, but Wayne took the hand, and the Indian turned and led him like a little boy up the lawn. The Indian's hand was gentle, but hard and sandpapery, like the rock on Shaman's Mound.

The Indian led him not toward the door, but toward the corner of the cottage. When they reached it, under

one of the big willows, Wayne saw that the cottage stood
on the very top of the rise. About thirty feet from him
across the long, lush grass another set of flagstones led to
another gate in the white picket fence, the yard running
downward on this side, and beyond the fence was not a
road but an orchard running down a gentle hill. Beyond
that was another orchard, sloping even more steeply, and
the descents and vales of a vast mountain fell away beyond them, steeper and steeper in orchard slopes until
the haze of summer distance hid its cliffs. On this side of
the cottage the breeze was fresher, with a maritime smell,
as if it came from the ocean, and as Wayne raised his eyes
from the cliffs falling away below, he thought he caught
a gleam of water in the distance haze, and rising beyond
that, far and vast, like a dream on the very edge of sight,
another land rising out of the mist.

A yearning took him. He turned to the Indian's grave
eyes. The Indian let go of his hand and nodded. Wayne
walked down through the warm summer grass to the
gate. He looked back once at the Indian, incongruous in
his Southwestern getup against the cottage and its flowers, and then he turned and opened the gate.

He walked a long time down the orchard slopes in the
soft, aromatic air between the quiet trees, the ground always a little steeper as he went. Long after he had lost
sight of the cottage above him, he came to the edge of a
steep bank, almost a cliff, upon which stunted fruit trees
clung precariously, and he looked out over vast space
and saw that another continent did indeed rise in the distance. He could scarcely see it in the haze, but he could
smell it because the breeze that ruffled the crabgrass and
swayed the branches came from there, and it had a smell
of the vast waters it crossed, but too there was a sweet-
ness, as of the grass and flowers and trees of another
land, a strange but almost familiar land.

Wayne sat at the foot of a tree at the edge of the cliff and gazed out through the summer distance. As he had walked—for hours it seemed—a feeling of anticipation had grown in him, even in the breezy, quiet solitude of the orchards. And now, as he gazed out across the gulf, he seemed in his dream to go into a trance or a doze in which his eyesight became preternaturally keen, and brought faraway things close, like a telescope or an eagle's vision. Far across the gulf he looked, to the other continent, and he saw that that continent fell down in vast orchard slopes on its side too, and that the breeze stirred the grass and trees there too. And as he looked, he saw two figures walking. They were hurrying down the slopes hand in hand, and as he looked closer he saw that they were a woman and a child, their faces intent and lit with an inner eagerness and expectation. The child was a tiny girl, no more than two years old; she stumbled frequently and would have fallen in the haste of their walking if the woman hadn't held her firmly by the hand. Her face was smiling and eager, and her dark baby hair was in pigtails. The woman had green eyes and black hair, and her body was strong and round-breasted and graceful, and both her legs were strong and whole.

—

The weather *had* changed in the night just as he had dreamed, and when Wayne woke in the bright morning, shafts of late-summer sunlight sparkling on a touch of autumn dew, the air smelling like the morning of a sea-journey, he wondered whether he had really been asleep or whether he had been half-awake all night, watching the wind blow the clouds away and the sun come up. Or perhaps he was still asleep and dreaming; had he really woken up? He was used to the transition between sleep and waking being abrupt and clear; one world fled away

and the other replaced it. But this was different somehow; he felt that he had been as conscious in his dream as
he was now, and while he was sure he was awake now,
the day he had woken to seemed exactly like the one he
had dreamed, and the feeling of the dream seemed still
around him, a feeling that seemed to come back through
long years of memory, though from where he didn't
know. His chest felt bursting with warm excitement, like
youth and hope and the knowledge that everything was
possible. His life was going to start over again. He knew
it somehow. He had seen the far continent.

He sat up. He had sat for a few minutes before he noticed with surprise that he wasn't sick anymore. In fact,
he felt better than he had in years, though how many
years he wasn't sure. It was as if the sickness had cleaned
him out, as if the smelly, oily residue on his sheets and
skin was the soul-eating poison he had sweated out, and
which could no longer give him nightmares.

But, the thought came as he got all the way awake—
and suddenly memory flooded back: he infected with the
virus, Gail gone, the silky girl a prostitute. A familiar
chill began to creep into his chest—

But—

But here he was on this beautiful morning, with this
feeling welling up in him. And he had *seen* the far continent, the other world, though in a dream. He had *seen* it.
And as for the virus, he wasn't sick anymore, and he felt
good. And he could feel somehow his life just beginning,
and the soft sound of the surf, the breeze fluttering the
leaves of the trees, the late-summer-morning sunlight on
this day which had finally come. And everything was beginning, the whole world on this newborn day with its
ancient sunlight full of a retiring consciousness, the trees
fluttering as if alive in the living breeze.

He tried again to steady himself, out of habit and out

of his fear of losing control and his fear of disillusionment. Better test this feeling against reality, test on it all the antidotes for bliss that he knew so well to make sure it was real—the scientists' proofs that there was no higher meaning, his divorce, the certainty of death—but somehow all those things seemed beside the point. He had *seen* it, seen it himself, though in a dream, and he could see with his waking eyes the sunlight, hear the breeze and water—

He looked around, trying again to make sure he was really awake. The feeling of the dream seemed still soaking everything with its sinuous, numinous feeling, making the stillness of the sunlight and the movement of the breeze seem conscious, alive, making his own story seem part of something vast and important, giving him a certainty that he would never die.

The interpenetration of dreams and waking.

It was the virus, the revelation came to him. The virus had eaten something out of his brain, but it was a something that had obscured something else, he was sure now as he went downstairs. What had the Indian said? "I told you we were directing the most important research at your Institute." Hall's research? He knew what he had to do now. But first, what had happened to the others? He went into the library. There were two messages on the phone machine.

The first was from Daniels, an hour old. His voice sounded excited. "Dolan? Dolan, are you there? How are you feeling? I think Helios was right. The dopamine striping, the whole brain inputs—the 'God module' is an *inhibitory* complex. It integrates inputs from all over the brain that add up to religious perceptions, but shuts them down when they get too strong, to allow us to concentrate on survival tasks. Without it, we see—well— Do you feel . . . ?"

Wayne skipped to the second message. It was from Far-ris. "Hey, Dolan, man, how are you?" He laughed. "You know what I think? I think Hall was right after all. The 'God module' *was* a source of illusions. He killed him-self too soon, while he was still suffering the emotional ef-fects of the primary infection, and with the tragedy of his daughter—"

Wayne skipped the rest of the message.

After all, there was something he had to do. He went out through the breezy summer morning, smelling the geraniums and the Lake, to the cool vinyl upholstery of his car. The map, marked in red, lay on the passenger seat as if Gail had just put it down. He started the car and headed up to the county highway, to turn right and drive through St. Clair to the little roads and woods and fields on the other side. He would find the cottage. He knew he would. He would find it again.

ABOUT THE AUTHOR

JAMIL NASIR was born in Chicago, Illinois, of a Palestinian refugee father and the American daughter of the inventor of the fork-lift truck. He spent much of his childhood in the Middle East, where he survived two major wars, hiding in cellars and storerooms with his family. He returned to the United States and started college at age 14, studying hard sciences, philosophy of science, English literature, psychology, and Chinese literature and philosophy, finally graduating from the University of Michigan in Ann Arbor with a Bachelor of General Studies.

Between college stints he hitchhiked extensively over much of North America, working as a carpenter, assistant gardener on an estate, shop clerk, warehouseman, apple-picker, and paralegal, among other things. He finally found himself back in Ann Arbor, where he got a law degree in 1983. Since then he has been employed part-time at a major Washington, D.C., law firm.

He has sold science fiction stories to *Asimov's*, *Universe* (vols. 1, 2, and 3), *Interzone*, *Aboriginal SF*, and a number of other magazines and anthologies, including Steve Pasechnick's 1990 best-of-the-year anthology *Best of the Rest*, and Dozois' and Dann's *Angels!*, a reprint anthology. He won a First Prize in the 1988 Writers of the Future competition.

Mr. Nasir meditates three hours a day, likes to cook, listen to music, play computer games, read, and walk. He lives in the Maryland suburbs of Washington. His first novel, *Quasar*, was published in 1995, and his second, *The Higher Space*, in 1996.